Indian Hollow Road

Books in the Thomas Night Crime Novel Series

Indian Hollow Road

A Thomas Night Crime Novel

Book IV

Paul Casper Scherer

Soul Attitude Press

Indian Hollow Road

Published by Soul Attitude Press
Pinellas Park, Florida
www.soulattitudepress.com

ISBN 978-1-946338-52-5

Printed in the United States of America

Table of Contents

Introduction

The criminal legal system is the most ineffective when it has to deal with a monster, particularly if the monster is one of the system's own creation.

List of Characters

Francis Aloysius Barnes

"The Senator"- retired State Senator-his family owned Plantation #7 in North Ormond, Florida. The Senator, a widower, organized a company called CCC that owned timberland, saw mills and semi-trucks that delivered lumber to the Northeast US, used to construct housing after WWII.

Francis Aloysius Barnes II

"Frank" –the Senator's son- married to Beatrice "Bea" O'Brien-Barnes. Frank headed CCC, creating the largest privately owned timberland and saw mill operation in the Southeast USA. Frank was the natural father of Jimmy and the adoptive father of Robert, Albert and Jenny Johnson-Barnes. He and Bea lived at the Homestead which was in Holly Hill. Frank's best friend and attorney is Thomas "Tom" Night. They attended school together at Stetson University in Deland, Florida and they created CCC. Ultimately CCC was sold to JRD Corporation and Frank and Bea formed Homestead Creamery.

Beatrice "Bea" O'Brien Barnes

Bea married Frank when she was 15 and Frank was 17. They had a child, Jimmy, who was born breach. His spine was injured by forceps used in delivery and he suffered severe cerebral palsy as a result of oxygen deprivation during birth. Bea devoted her life to Jimmy and her adopted children, Bob, Little Al/Albert and Jenny. Bea also operated the dairy on the Homestead and developed the dairy into a large milk and cream processing facility that shipped dairy products by rail throughout the USA. Bea sold the dairy and she and her husband started Homestead Creamery.

Thomas Night, Esquire

"Tom" was orphaned as a teen. Father, Mother and brother died from pneumonia as a complication of influenza in St. Petersburg, Florida. Tom was raised by two aunts who were professors at Stetson University. Tom met Frank at Stetson. Tom studied law and his first clients were the Barnes Family and their businesses. He began his practice in Daytona Beach and then moved back to St. Petersburg and established a law firm specializing in business law and criminal law. Tom is an alcoholic.

Marlene James

"Marla" grew up in St. Petersburg. She took business and secretarial courses in high school. Her first job was as Tom's legal secretary. Marla was trusted by Tom and Frank and the Senator and she helped Tom and Frank's family and the businesses. For years she was Tom's girlfriend, then Bob Barnes' girlfriend. Ultimately she married James M. Reynolds the president of JRD Corporation.

The adopted children

Robert (Bob), Albert (Little Al) and Jenny were born to Mary and Albert Johnson Senior (Big Al). Mary was schizophrenic. Big Al was an alcoholic. Bea convinced Mary to let her take Bob into her home to help her care for Jimmy then later after Mary became mentally ill and neither parent could care for the children, Frank and Bea adopted their children. The children all worked in the Barnes Family business

Roger Adams

Partner in Night, Adams and Street, P.A. (Deceased)

Alphonse Alesse

Partner in Night, Adams and Street, P.A.

Smiley Brown

Wife of Robert "Bob" Barnes and mother of Robert Brown

Robert Brown

Son of Smiley Brown and stepson of Bob Barnes

Anthony Stewart

Investigator for Night, Adams and Street, P.A. (Deceased)

James DeMarco

Partner in Night, Adams and Street, P.A.

Judge Waters

On call judge

Jim Faircloth

Former police officer – St. Petersburg Police Department, investigator for Night, Adams and Street. Faircloth replaced Anthony Stewart.

Darlene Street

Partner in Night, Adams and Street, P.A., married to Thomas Night

Thomas N. Thompson

General partner of Thompson Timber Fund, a hedge fund. The fund loaned money to Belize Resources and Barnes Lime Rock.

Mark Luke John Person

An accused

Henry T. Logan

An accused

Clemenso Me Bondi

An accused

Rick Ibn

Airplane pilot-husband of Anna Hernando M.D.

Andrew Prince

Former Solicitor General-chief legal officer in the County of Belize City

Anna Hernando, M.D.

Doctor in Belize City, wife of Rick Ibn

John Hale

State Attorney in Florida

Part I

Predation

Chapter 1
Predator

The police in Summer County had been on alert for a predator who over seven years had kidnapped and killed five young girls. The young girls were last seen walking to middle school or waiting for a school bus and then they disappeared.

The police were targeting a white male, 25 to 50 years of age because that's who the FBI criminal psychologists believed committed the crimes. They were also looking for a red, rusty truck because that vaguely described vehicle was seen at or near the scene of all of the kidnappings.

There had never been a witness who came forward who saw a kidnapping or who knew the perpetrator of the crime. So there was no description of the criminal other than the educated guess of the FBI profilers. There was no hard evidence as to the identity of a suspect.

The Summer County Police were on guard this day because there was another girl missing on the way to school. She only had to walk two blocks to the bus stop from her home but she never arrived.

***

It is foggy near to and inland of the west coast of Florida in the spring. A ground fog hangs over the surface of the land and burns off at about mid-morning.

The children at the bus stop on Indian Hollow Road, all in middle school, reported that the fog was thick the morning that Becky Sue Painter went missing. The classmates reported the fact that Becky was not at the bus stop to the bus driver. The driver was late and said she explained to the girls that she would tell the principal when she finished her route. Becky was probably sick, thought the driver. Summer County was rural and it was in the middle of a Black Jack Oak forest and the oak pollen was thick with the new growth of leaves. The school kids were susceptible to allergy attacks from the oak pollen and the day Becky went missing the driver noted at least five students absent due to sickness, although those student's parents had provided a note for the absence.

The principal's secretary called the Summer Sheriff's office with the report that Becky Sue Painter was not at school and the school had not received word from her grandmother that she was ill. The grandmother had no phone.

Since the children in Summer County had begun to go missing, the Sheriff had assigned a deputy to investigate reports of missing children. Parents, guardians and schools were encouraged to report their children missing to the Sheriff's office as soon as the fact was discovered.

The FBI said one or two detectives should be assigned to this duty and they would be required to remain current on any report of a missing child in the region. There were now five girls that were lost to the predator. Three bodies had been found. Those three were buried in shallow graves and had been dug up by animals, probably coyotes, and then the remains were discovered by humans. All three children were found in rural fields. Most of the fields were just off the interstate (I-75) and the fields were progressively farther away from Summer County and closer to Gainesville, to the north of the place where the children were kidnapped.

Two other children, young girls, (in addition to the bodies of the three children found) were missing and the only explanation for their disappearance was that they were kidnapped and had been murdered.

Over the years the gap of time between when each child was last seen and then reported missing had shortened considerably.

Becky was reported to the detective by the principal's secretary to be suspiciously absent from school within two hours of when her grandmother sent her out the door of the trailer where they lived.

This was the first missing child report of the day. Detective Joseph Rainey was on duty and he immediately went to Becky's home. She lived in a double wide trailer at the end of a short, dead end, limited access road that was just off Indian Hollow Road, in the country outside (east and north) of the city limits of New Retirement City.

Det. Rainey interviewed the grandmother, Alma Lee and discovered the following:

Becky was not angry or upset when she left out the door. She loved school. She had done her homework. There was no reason she wouldn't want to go to school that day. She never skipped school. If she was sick she stayed at home in bed. She was not sick that day and she did not suffer an allergic reaction from the oak pollen.

She had friends on the bus. No one bullied her. She got along with everyone.

She was an average student and she got average grades.

Her parents were gone. They never saw her. Alma Lee said, "Her father, my son, is still in prison. Her mother is out west in Sturgis, at least that's the last I know. She never visits or calls."

The State awarded the grandmother custody because Becky's mother and father failed to care for the child. The mother had other children who she birthed and spread over the country who were living in foster care." Five children, I think," said Ms. Lee.

"My son never had anything to do with Becky. He never writes her, or calls either. He was a drug dealer. He doesn't care about anything but drugs."

The grandmother had not seen anything suspicious that morning. There was no vehicle or stranger hanging about. Maybe she saw an old red truck up the street yesterday or maybe last week but she was not sure. "There are a lot of red trucks around," she commented.

Det. Rainey broke off the interview and went to his car and called the Sheriff.

"This could be another abduction. There is a report of a missing female child and the sighting of a red truck the day before," said the detective.

The Sheriff called the Retirement City Riding Club and the bloodhound handlers from the state prison to aid in the search.

Rainey continued the interview. Becky did not drink or use drugs ...

***

The bloodhounds were on the scene in 25 minutes. Alma Lee retrieved a pair of dirty shorts belonging to Becky to give the hounds a scent. The dogs picked up the trail easily and followed it up the dirt access road to a large wax myrtle bush. There was a field of tall grass behind (east) of the wax myrtle.

There was a trail into the grass.

"Do not disturb the trail," ordered the detective.

"We'll loop around and see if the trail comes out of the grass up on Indian Hollow Road," said the dog handler.

Det. Rainey followed the trail but did not disturb the path. He stayed out to the side of the path and came to an area where the grass was beaten down as though someone had been rolling in the grass. It was trampled, maybe the scene of a struggle. Rainey saw a white rag in the area.

"We found a trail out of the grass," yelled the dog handler. "There are tire tracks at that spot."

"Get those dogs out of that area. Go down the road and see if you can pick up the scent anywhere else." Rainey walked back to the wax myrtle bush and then up the access road to Indian Hollow Road and he found the trail out of the tall grass. It looked like the trail had only been made by a single individual who was coming out of the grass to the spot where the tire tracts were located.

"How much did Becky weigh?" Rainey asked Alma Lee when he got back to his car.

"She was pretty good size ... maybe 95 pounds. She is five feet tall," said the grandmother.

The dog handler returned. "The dogs couldn't find anything more. We went a 100 yards up and down the road. Did you see the blood near the tracks?" asked the handler.

"Damn. No I did not." Rainey had not walked in the right of way. He avoided the tire tracks and the footprints where the trail emerged from the tall grass.

Rainey got on the radio. The Sheriff picked up immediately.

"I need forensics ... blood ... footprints ... tire tracks. Mostly, I need a cherry picker so we don't contaminate this scene.

The sheriff called the electric power company and commandeered one of their trucks with a cherry picker (a long mechanical arm with a bucket to hold a man) and the men to operate it. The electric company wanted to know who was going to pay.

"You get that equipment out to Indian Hollow Road now, or someone is going to be arrested." The sheriff was very dramatic and not well-liked by the civilians who dealt with him.

The sheriff got back on the radio to Rainey. "What are we looking for?"

"An old red truck on or near Indian Hollow Road near or on Interstate 75. You need to contact the Highway Patrol as well as all the local authorities. The truck has at least a two hour head start. I need the riding club to search along the other access roads off of Indian Hollow Road to see if they can find anything. The girl may have been thrown in the woods alongside the road if the perpetrator got spooked."

"Ok … done … I will be there in 15 minutes. What was the child wearing?"

"The grandmother reported she had a pink cotton dress with a red sweater, buttoned up to the neck. She had on cowboy boots. She always wore them. She has a pink backpack with horses printed on the pack."

The power company truck arrived. The driver beeped the truck's horn. The truck had been just a couple of miles away when they were ordered to go to the scene.

Detective Rainey ran up the access road from the double wide to Indian Hollow Road where the bucket truck with the cherry picker was located. Once the arm of the cherry picker was extended, the machine would reach 75 feet in the air. With stabilizer pads in place the machine would extend horizontally out over the long grass so Rainey could see what was in the field from the basket at the end of the arm extended above the grass.

As the men stabilized the machine, Rainey got in the bucket and waited to take it up in the air. One of the men from the power company jumped in to operate the bucket.

"I'm looking for the path through that grass."

The operator swung the bucket over the grass and then maneuvered upward so they got a good view. There were drag marks from the access road near the large wax myrtle bush to the trampled down area in the center of the grass and there was a single foot path out of the grass to Indian Hollow Road.

The operator pointed to the location of two objects – a backpack and a red sweater – that looked like they were thrown into the grass away from the area where the grass had been trampled like someone had rolled around in a tussle.

Forensics arrived.

"I need you to get photos," yelled Rainey to the technician over the noise of the utility vehicle. Traffic was backing up on the road. The deputy called in for traffic control assistance.

Rainey had the operator maneuver over to the gravel road and he drew a map showing the drag trail and the trampled area and the footpath out of the grass and the general location of the backpack and sweater and the white rag.

Rainey gave the map to forensics and said, "Make sure you also get photos of these items with a Polaroid in case we have a screw up with the 35 mm camera."

Rainey's mind conjured what happened. The criminal parked on the side of Indian Hollow Road. He walked into the tall grass to the bush by the access road from the double wide and hid by the wax myrtle. As Becky walked by the wax myrtle, the criminal grabbed her and dragged her into the grass. There was a struggle and Becky was rendered unconscious. He took off her sweater and the backpack and threw them into the grass. He picked her up and carried her to the red truck in his arms and put her in the truck somewhere, either the front seat or in the back. He drove off, probably east to the interstate.

Rainey took the crime scene technicians to the south side right of way of Indian Hollow Road where the tracker stood. The dogs were in their cage. The handler pointed out the location of the foot path track coming out of the grass, and the location of the blood, and the vehicle tracks where a vehicle drove off the road onto the right of way and parked off the road.

The two technicians took photos of the tracks and footprints and blood on the grass. The blood technician said it was a lot of blood, probably from a facial wound. The tech took samples of the blood. The print technician said that he saw only one track in and one track out. The footprint was made by the same shoe, probably a man's shoe, a boot maybe, from the shape of the imprint of the heel in the soil.

"It is probably a cowboy boot and the man is heavy." said the tech. "The boot really sunk in the dirt. There is a distinct, fresh imprint ... good evidence."

Rainey yelled at the operator to try to follow the track out of the grass to the gravel road. "Look for child-size cowboy boots."

If she was unconscious and she was carried out, the boots could have slipped off her feet, Rainey thought.

"There, in the path," said the photographer. "The boots are just inside the area where the grass is trampled."

"Get Polaroids of the boots where they lay," said Rainey.

***

The Sheriff arrived and he was at the double wide consoling Alma Lee. With this criminal on the loose, any mother or grandmother was concerned if they had a middle school aged girl living in Summer County. Some parents had left the area. They simply moved away from Summer County. They worried their child would be kidnapped. They had no faith the sheriff would find the perpetrator and protect their child. The odds of the return of a child who went missing were remote. Five girls were lost and none returned alive over the last seven years.

The sheriff had won the election on the promise he would find the perpetrator of these awful crimes. It's time for me to put up or shut up, thought the Sheriff. Two of the five children had been lost on his watch. Now the number taken was six. The Sheriff thought about where he might find a job in the private sector if he didn't make an arrest for this crime.

"Do you suspect anyone who might have done this, Ms. Lee?" asked the Sheriff.

"No," said Alma Lee.

"Have you noticed anyone in the neighborhood who might have had an unhealthy interest in Becky?"

"Unhealthy?" Alma Lee stared blankly at the sheriff. She was in her 60's, dull and worn out. The word "unhealthy" was foreign to her when used in this context.

"A pervert, ma'am."

"Oh no, no one like that. We stay to ourselves. We don't go to parties or socialize. Becky has friends but they are all girls and I don't think she knows about the birds and the bees yet. I haven't told her. I hoped they would teach her in school. She knows she has private parts and no one but the doctor is to touch her there."

"What does she enjoy?"

"She wants a horse. She thinks she's a cowgirl. Let me show you." Alma Lee took the Sheriff into Becky's bedroom. There were horses everywhere. There were posters on the wall and stuffed horses on the bed and a rocking horse with a real horse hair tail.

"I see," said the Sheriff. He began to tear up. His youngest daughter loved horses. Jesus, he thought. "Where is that son of a bitch?" he mumbled.

"What?" said Alma Lee.

"Do you have anyone to be with you? Friends ... church ... family ..."

"No, just Becky."

"Come with me." The Sheriff went to the car and called in to headquarters and made arrangements for a female deputy to stay with Ms. Lee until they knew what was what. It was too horrible to even think what they could find, if they found anything of Becky. More likely than not, Becky would become another ghost.

***

The Sheriff stayed by Alma's side until the female deputy arrived. "Do you like coffee?" he asked.

"I do."

"This is Martha, a special deputy. She will help you. Show her where the coffee is and she will help you make it," said the Sheriff as he walked up the access road to the power truck.

The technicians were still working. The Sheriff pulled Rainey aside. He asked for an update.

Rainey told the Sheriff what they had found and what he conjectured from the facts on the ground.

"Where do you think Becky is right now?"

"She is in the red truck or she has been dumped on the side of the road between here and the Gainesville exit on I-75. My guess is she is somewhere in Paynes Prairie."

"Is that what your gut says or do you have hard evidence?"

"We found the last body near Wilder. I figured the next likely spot to bury a body with easy access from Interstate 75 is the large preserve at Paynes Prairie."

"Then trust your gut. Go to Paynes Prairie," said the Sheriff. "This is all technician crap here where she was snatched. We need to find the girl. She'll be dead soon if she's not dead already."

"Can you get me the chopper?"

"Hell, yes, it's on the way," said the Sheriff. "They will meet you up the road near the interstate."

Rainey got in his car and drove to the interstate three miles to the east with another deputy. Rainey got out of the car and the deputy stopped traffic and laid out some flares in the road to make an area for a landing pad for the helicopter.

The chopper landed and Rainey boarded. The pilot took off and headed north. Thirty minutes later they were at the Micanopy exit just before Paynes Prairie.

Rainey directed the pilot to follow the fence line along the interstate. When they found nothing, not even tracks where a vehicle had driven on the right of way into the grass, Rainey directed the pilot out over the prairie. The prairie was nothing more than a swamp with about 21,000 acres of sedge brush and wax myrtle and understory tree growth – bay, tupelo and wild apricot trees.

They found no red truck but they were utterly amazed. In a rutted road they saw the body of a female child dressed in a red print cotton dress. She was shoeless and moving.

They called in the location requesting an ambulance and investigators.

The crime scene had matriculated from Indian Hollow Road to a spot in Paynes Prairie 40 miles north.

The chopper landed. Rainey told the pilot to stay with the aircraft and fly about 100 feet above the ground so the cavalry could find them. Then Rainey jumped from the chopper.

The chopper then rose to an altitude of 100 feet above the girl.

Rainey ran down the rutted dirt road to Becky. She was alive and sobbing.

Rainey held Becky in his arms. He looked up to see if he saw anything that was large and red, but he saw nothing, just a bunch of green vegetation. Rainey knew the criminal was close. They had to be patient to catch him.

Rainey was just happy they saved the child.

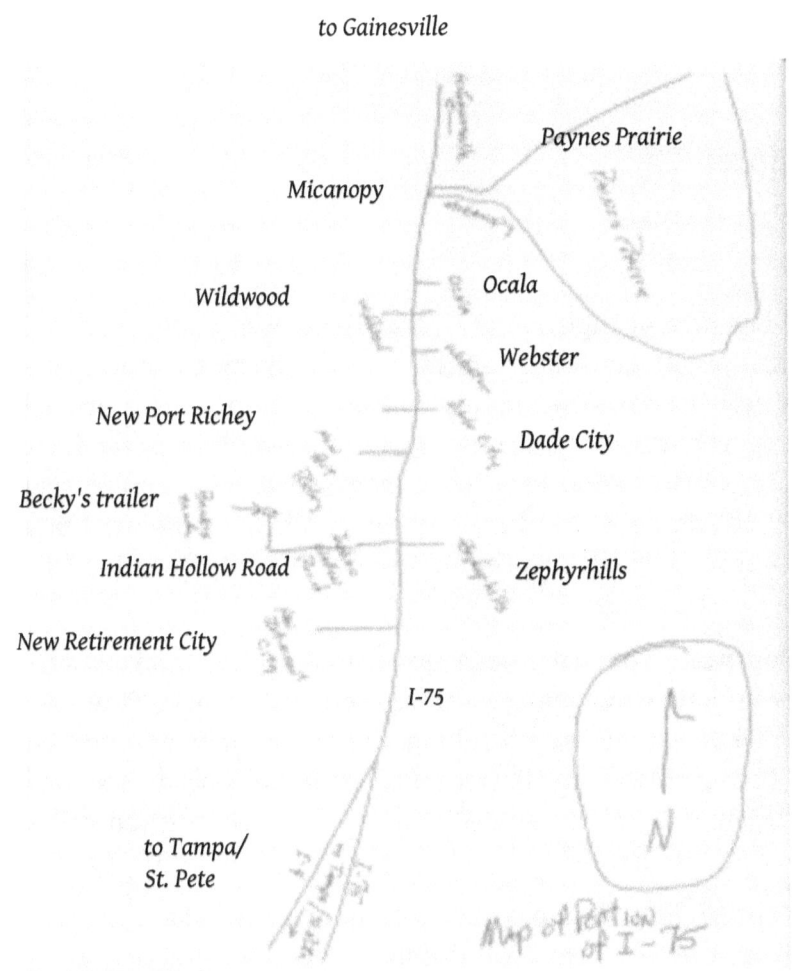

Hand-drawn map of crime scene from Indian Hollow Road to
Paynes Prairie

(written legend typed for clarity)

Chapter 2
Pro Bono

The law firm of Night, Adams, and Street was established by Tom Night. He got his start representing the Barnes Family when he first left school. This family presented him with a myriad of problems over the years from huge multi-million dollar financial transactions to adoptions. Tom then added criminal cases to the practice and he enlisted Roger Adams to help as the firm expanded. Roger began to represent insurance companies in personal injury cases.

Roger and Tom were both alcoholics but they worked hard and were effective lawyers in spite of their bad habits. Tom married Darlene Street and quit drinking. Roger was unable to quit before the booze killed him. Darlene had come on board before Roger died. James DeMarco and Alphonse Alesse were hired following Roger Adams' death.

Tom Night and James DeMarco handled all the criminal trial work at the law firm. The criminal appellate practice was handled by Tom's wife Darlene Street. The firm's civil practice was managed by Alphonse Alesse. Alesse took over Roger Adams's cases after his death. Most of Alphonse's work was insurance defense, fighting over nickels and dimes, trying to save money for the insurance industry. Tom still handled all the work that came to the firm from the Barnes Family and he handled most defendants charged with homicides that were committed in St. Petersburg, Florida. Tom did the work of three attorneys.

Night, Adams and Street had a good reputation which had been established by the hard work of Tom, Roger and Darlene and then bolstered by DeMarco and Alesse. Alesse was considered a wizard in civil practice, Alphonse was quiet but he did not have to advertise for clients. The insurance companies knew he was super smart and they sought him out when it looked like they were going to have to pay a large judgment. All Alphonse had to worry about was money. His clients did not go to jail. There were no philosophical considerations to his work. James and Tom had to be concerned with their clients going to jail and in some cases meeting death at the hands of the state in the electric chair. In most cases Darlene's clients were in jail. They had gone to trial, lost their case and they were arguing the state had committed some error in the trial and they should be retried.

James DeMarco saw the criminal practice as a calling. He saw the profession as existing for a higher purpose than producing a paycheck. He never became frustrated by the legal process because the fact that the process existed was its purpose. It was self-evident. His job as a defense attorney was required for the process to exist. He felt the practice of criminal law was a duty. Innocence was not a prerequisite for a defendant to receive due process. Denial of Liberty, imprisonment by the state, was constitutional but only after a suspect was proved guilty beyond a reasonable doubt at a trial by jury following the rules of procedure. That was the standard of justice.

Sometimes DeMarco got carried away and Tom Night would have to remind him of reality. There were innocent victims who were also to be protected by the system. They deserved justice too.

Unlike James DeMarco, there were times that Tom Night became totally frustrated with the system. The case he and DeMarco were handling on a motion hearing in court on the day Becky Sue Painter was lost and then found was an example.

Tom and James were representing the driver of an auto charged with vehicular homicide. The facts of the case were that a two vehicle collision had occurred on a street in St. Petersburg. It was 1:00 a.m. Both drivers had just left separate taverns and there was a collision at an intersection. The right front of the victim's vehicle collided with the left front of the client's vehicle. Both drivers were blind to the existence of the other's vehicle before the crash because a large building obstructed their view until the moment the collision occurred. The drivers cannot even see each other's headlights because the street lighting is so bright in the area. There is a traffic control device but no one witnessed the accident except the drivers of the two vehicles. Tom's client says he had the green light and he was going the speed limit and otherwise obeying all traffic laws. There is no evidence to prove otherwise because the victim was killed in the collision and there were no witnesses.

Interestingly, both of the drivers were legally intoxicated.

Neither driver took any evasive action to avoid the collision.

Should Tom's client to be held criminally at fault for the death merely because he happened to be legally intoxicated? The other drunk driver caused the accident by failing to obey the traffic light and stop his vehicle.

James felt the court should dismiss the case on the motion to dismiss. There was no need for a jury trial in this case.

The State Attorney agreed that the facts as pled in the Motion to Dismiss were correct. However, the State Attorney believed the judge should let a jury determine whether Tom's client was at fault for the death. The State Attorney argued that the negligence of the victim running a red light is not a defense to the defendant being under the influence. The fact the victim contributed to his own death was irrelevant. All the law required was direct proof that a death occurred, that death resulted from the operation of a vehicle, and that the defendant was intoxicated at the time he operated the vehicle.

The State Attorney correctly stated the law as it existed in 1979 and the judge denied the motion to dismiss. James DeMarco felt the law needed to be repealed.

James' solution to the perceived inequity in the law was to suffer through the procedure and lose at trial and hope to win on appeal. The likelihood a jury would find his client not guilty was remote after they heard evidence that the defendant's blood alcohol level was over the legal limit.

Tom's approach in this situation was to negotiate a plea bargain using the fact of the victim's intoxication and violation of the traffic laws to get a reduced sentence with little or no jail time for his client.

***

James still brought indigent cases to the firm. Some were cases where the defendant was charged with a crime that was unconstitutional, yet still prosecuted (adultery, homosexual conduct, cohabitation of a man and a woman without benefit of marriage, fornication, etc.), and he would handle the case through an appeal, trying to convince the court to nullify the law. If the trial judge would not find the law unconstitutional, DeMarco would file an appeal. Darlene Street participated in the defense of these cases when the appeal was filed.

Tom was not involved in these cases.

Tom objected to the firm taking these cases because the firm was not paid a fee, the cases were never ending, and no other law firms in town provided free representation. Every year since James had become a member of the firm in the early 70s their office had been awarded the Pro Bono Award for providing free legal service to the poor. The award was little reward in Tom's way of thinking.

At firm meetings, which were mandatory, to be attended by all employees (clerks, secretaries, attorneys and accounting staff), there was a period set aside to allow any gripe to be aired. Everyone knew Tom would address the firm's staff members and Tom always told the firm that they were going to drive him out of the practice of law if they continued to represent clients pro bono. Tom would always start his diatribe by apologizing to Alphonse Alesse, Esquire. Alphonse had been wrongfully charged with Aggravated Battery and the firm, then consisting of Tom, Darlene and Roger Adams, handled Alphonse's case for free because he was innocent and his innocence was evident.

"But now," Tom emphasized with his hands waving as he talked, "there are always poor people on the west coast of Florida who are wrongfully charged and it seems like our firm is the only one handling these cases. We don't have the ability to serve all of these people competently and also serve the people who pay the salaries and overhead for the firm.

"Further," Tom continued on his soap box, "it is much harder to represent someone who is innocent, or convicted of a law that is unconstitutional. The entire legal community has to step up to the plate and offer the services that are needed by the poor."

There was an Office of Public Attorney, but it was just getting started. The County was contributing the salary for the Public Attorney and providing office space and the courts were providing costs for the defense of cases but their office was overwhelmed with cases, particularly since the Supreme Court had ruled the courts had to provide an attorney for any indigent defendant who could be sentenced to jail.

Darlene would normally intervene at this point in Tom's speech and say that the Night law firm had been lucky. The country had experienced two serious recessions but the law firm had weathered these economic storms.

"We have an obligation to the community and a duty to provide service to the indigent and to protect the helpless. Unfortunately, we see many more of these cases now than in the past. We also see individuals who take advantage of the system and our good graces. We have to weed out those cases and help the truly disadvantaged. I don't think Tom would ever turn away a case where the defendant was innocent but unable to pay for an attorney. The office of the Public Attorney will eventually handle all of these cases. We just have to be patient."

But Darlene knew the firm was going to have to establish guidelines for the indigent criminal defendants the firm would agree to take. A long drawn out pro bono case could bankrupt the firm. Darlene asked Tom and James if they would agree to establish proposed guidelines to determine which defendants the firm would represent without charge and present the guidelines at the next meeting. They said they would.

Tom had philosophical differences with the concept of the Public Attorney. Tom objected to the County establishing the Office. Tom's belief was that the Public Attorney created another bureaucracy within the judicial system. Tom felt it would be better if the court decided which of the defendants were unable to pay an attorney and the court would issue a voucher that the defendant could take to any attorney and hire the attorney to represent him. The court would set the amount of the fee. The question was whether an attorney would undertake the representation for the amount the judge felt was a fair price for the services. Tom felt that if the court failed to provide sufficient funds in the voucher that the attorney could contact the court and ask for additional funds at a hearing. The County would be given notice since the County was ultimately responsible for payment of the fee and the County could object if they thought the attorney was asking for too large a fee to represent the particular defendant.

If there was a voucher system, all of the work involving indigents would be spread among the attorneys who wanted and who would accept the work. These attorneys would take the case into their office and handle the defendant like any other client. If the attorney did not feel he could take the case for the amount set in the voucher, the attorney could refuse the case or take it and petition the court for additional funds.

Tom felt indigent defendants would have less mistrust of the system if they could choose their own attorney. Tom knew that defendants, particularly minority defendants, did not feel they obtained fair representation from the Public Attorney. The Public Attorney was a young white male, while the defendants were poor, unemployed Negro males.

Chapter 3
Mark Luke John Person

Paynes Prairie was in Alachua County. Alachua County was best known as the home of the University of Florida (UF). The predator terrorizing children in Summer County lived in Alachua County in the city of Archer, and worked as a carpet cleaner in the surrounds of the city of Gainesville.

The man's name was Mark Luke John Person. He fit the FBI profile. He was white and 31 years old. He went by the single name "Person", ignoring the religious trappings his mother gave him by naming him after three of the Apostles.

Person was abandoned by his natural mother to his aunt when he was an infant. His mother said he was too much trouble to take care of. This fact, abandonment as an infant, was an important stressor that psychiatrists would point to when they tried to determine what made Person who he was—a child killer.

Person was born in the heart of Connecticut. His family worked for a factory making jet engines for military aircraft and the Person Family had done manufacturing work of one kind or another in central Connecticut for over a century. The factory had been unionized and the workers made good wages. Person was not hired by the aircraft industry where his family had been employed because (although he was not convicted of a felony) he had been to prison for five years as a "youthful offender". If he had not been in prison he could have worked at the factory in Meriden, Connecticut. He would have made double and triple the amount he earned as an hourly worker in Florida. Person always complained about what he was paid to clean carpets. He told everyone who would listen that he was worth more than what he was paid.

After Person was released from prison as a youthful offender at age 22, he came to Florida, following his aunt to the state in the wave of humanity retiring to Florida with their second or third or fourth husband or wife. These parents were paid a severance package to take early retirement as the manufacturers retooled and de-unionized and integrated their work force and paid markedly lower wages. White kids (Caucasians) no longer wanted to work in the factory with the new lower non-union wages. The work was monotonous and difficult and dirty and the white kids would have to take much lower pay than their parents had made and so they declined the factory work and piddled along aimlessly as cashiers or service workers and relied on their parents for room and board. When the white kid's parents retired to Florida, their children begged to come along, and the parents reluctantly agreed to let their kids follow them to the Sunshine State.

Normally the people Person spoke to about what he was worth were other Caucasians who were sitting on a bar stool in the XYZ Lounge in Archer, Florida. Person inhabited the stool in the bar as soon as he was done with his last cleaning job of the day. The XYZ was his home.

As he walked in the door of the XYZ the bartender would see him coming and put a lite beer on the bar and Person would exhale and say, "SSSHHHIIITTT. What a day." He would swallow the entire contents of the bottle seemingly in one gulp and then go on to describe the raunchy people he dealt with. The apartments were crummy and the people were stupid and their kids were rats and they were "niggers ... heebes ... spics" and on and on.

Person was better than all this. And the people in the bar, mostly men in their late twenties and early thirties, agreed. They were all better than what they had or were doing. They were all working at a dead end job or not working – waiting for the next dead end job. They were in the XYZ and grabbing a beer and griping, griping, griping.

Besides the booze, the patrons of the XYZ snuck in the john for some smoke and shared a toke with a comrade to smooth out the rigors of the day by getting high on weed. The weather was hot and humid most of the time and the heat aggravated their mood. They tried to cool down with a beer and some smoke and then went in the air conditioned lounge to the video game machines with a roll of quarters and played video games (Missile Commander, Pac-Man, et cetera) until late at night in the air cooled, smoke filled cave called the XYZ Lounge.

Normally Person could occupy a video game for 15 to 30 minutes for 25 cents before the missiles destroyed his position, so he needed about $2.50 in quarters to get him through the night. Then he looked around to see what little tidbit was available to satisfy his cravings.

He liked to go to the girl's digs. If he went home, he had to sneak the girl in the garage apartment at his aunt's third husband's home where he slept. That was embarrassing. He felt like he had to explain to the girl why he was 31 and still living with his folks, and that made him really angry. Really, he was angry a lot and to compensate he had begun to smoke more and more reefer to mellow out.

If there were no easy pickings at the bar, Person went into the address book in his head. He thought about who would feed him and "SSSSSSCCCCCCRRRRRREEEEEWWW" him and not complain too much.

He decided on the fat girl most nights because she was always home alone. Person had trouble remembering her name. But when he came knocking on the door he magically remembered her name.

"Doris, let me in."

And she would let him in, eventually.

Sometimes he had to talk to her through the door while she remained inside her apartment at the door listening to Person beg.

"Honey, open up, I'm real hungry."

That was normally enough to get him in the door and into the shower and into bed and he SSSCCCRRREEEWWWEEEDDD her and then he had a liverwurst sandwich (Doris worked in a deli). And after he ate the sandwich with hot mustard and mayo he told her he would see her again sometime and he left.

He never said thanks. SSSCCCRRREEEWWWIIINNNGG the fat girl was animal behavior. It was not love-making. It was like what was done to him the first day in prison in the shower with everyone watching and hooting.

***

There was a crowd the time Person lost his cherry. He never forgot it. The faces swirled around when he dreamed of it, laughing at his pain.

***

Person was almost 18 when he went to prison. He was small and skinny and weak, and the older, bigger prisoners took advantage of him sexually. He tried to play along, to just take the abuse, but he was violently raped regularly and dehumanized. He was not a willing partner to these attacks. He did what he could to avoid an encounter. But if the man wanted it he got it. There was no one to complain to.

Person graduated from high school in his third year at the youth facility. He thought he was very smart. More accurately, he was street wise. In particular he knew what everyone had that he did not. Freedom. He had been denied freedom. And he knew that was not his fault. If you asked him if he was angry he would tell you that he was generally angry about the fact he had been sent to prison.

"Sure I did the crime but do I deserve prison on a first offence when I am only 17?"

That's what he asked the judge the day the judge sentenced him to five years in a youth facility (prison by any other name).

"I shouldn't have gotten more than one year." But it was for his own good. The judge said he sentenced Person to a youth facility for up to five years so that he would have the advantages of high school and college classes or he could learn a trade.

Person's judge had carefully read the pre-sentence recommendation that was written by the parole and probation department. The report stated that at the scene of his crime Person was found in a broom closet with a four-year-old female. There was confusion among the witnesses as to what exactly Person's intent was for the child. Some thought he was fondling the girl. The girl was screaming. Person appeared to be oblivious to her screams even when the door was opened revealing him smothering the girl and continuing to fondle her. He was found to have ejaculated copious amounts of seminal fluid. He was drooling. He remained in a daze, continuing to strangle the girl, until he was struck in the ear repeatedly by his teacher and he yowled in pain.

The aunt felt the appointed attorney had tricked her nephew into pleading guilty and denied him his right to a jury trial. The aunt believed her nephew's intent in restraining the four-year-old girl was to quiet her because she was having medical issues that caused her to scream incessantly. The aunt argued that Person could not stand the hollering and tried to silence her but she screamed even more.

The judge thought the argument was specious. Why was Person drooling and why had he ejaculated and why did it appear to at least one witness that Person was fondling the child? The judge felt the appointed attorney had done a good job confusing the facts and he had convinced the State Attorney to reduce the charge from a felony (assault with intent to commit rape) to a misdemeanor (simple battery). Person pled guilty to the reduced charge and the case was set for sentencing after a pre-sentence review by the parole and probation department.

The probation officer said in the report that he did not believe Person could be rehabilitated and he should be sentenced to life imprisonment: "Mark Luke John Person is a sick individual. He will hurt women (perhaps female children) in the future. This deviant sexual activity for which he was arrested was not an isolated incident but has probably occurred on numerous prior occasions." The probation officer had investigated rumors that Person had an over active sex life and that he was manic, but he could not pin down the facts of other crimes committed by Mr. Person due to interference from the aunt.

If the judge had his way he would have done what had been recommended by the probation officer and sent him away for life. He looked at Person and listened to his Aunt speak on his behalf. The aunt blamed everyone for her nephew's legal predicament, particularly the court-appointed lawyer who represented Person without charging a fee. Although the aunt was wealthy, because Person, then an unemployed 17 year old, personally had no funds to hire an attorney, the county paid the legal fee. The aunt said her nephew was not a bad kid and it was all her sister's fault for leaving him as an infant.

The judge saw Person in a different light. The judge knew this young man before him at sentencing was a dangerous kid, but the judge was restricted by the plea bargain. Person had no prior record and the State Attorney had allowed him to plead to a Battery charge which carried a maximum sentence of only one year in the County Jail. This negotiation restricted the court.

To maximize his incarceration, the judge was allowed to sentence Person as a Youthful Offender because Person was under 20 years old and the crime charged carried a sentence of 15 years or less. Under that law Person remained under the jurisdiction of the court until he was 22 years old, but housed with other youths. The judge intended to sentence Person as a youth in order to keep Person incarcerated as long as he could legally in the special facility for youthful offenders. When the judge issued this sentence in open court the Aunt erupted, complaining loudly that they had been promised that her son would be incarcerated for no more than one year.

"Now he's looking at five years. That's not fair, Judge. You know that's not fair," the Aunt yelled at the judge.

For the record, the judge stated the sentence was indeterminate. Person could be incarcerated for a day, a month, or until he was 22 years old. It was up to Person how long he was in the facility. Further, the judge stated over and over for the record, Person was not in prison, he was being housed in a youthful offender rehabilitation facility.

Later, when Person's aunt visited, her observation was that the place was a "gulag".

The judge ignored the harping woman and left the bench and the bailiffs struggled with the Aunt and Person, who were locked in an embrace. They would not let go until a guard slapped Person in the ear. The judge issued a special order that allowed the warden at the youth facility to preclude visitation between the aunt and her nephew during his incarceration if the visits caused any further disruptions.

Every time Person's sentence came up for review, the judge recommended the "youth" remain in the facility for the full five year term.

***

When Person got out of jail when he turned 22 years old he was 6' 2" tall, and 200 pounds of muscle. Before he left the rehabilitation facility Person had crushed both elbows of the man that got his cherry in the shower in front of a jeering crowd of prisoners the first day Person was in the youth prison. Breaking the man's arms was satisfying.

Once Person became strong physically he was the person who popped the cherry of the new boys who were sentenced to the school. His fellow inmates applauded his ability to physically control the victim in the shower. Attacking and subduing a weaker opponent and the violence of the act of rape satisfied Person's rage temporarily while he was in prison.

***

Person was like two people. When he was in the XYZ bar he was not the big, mean brute he was in prison. Although he was tall, over six feet, two inches, he wore cowboy boots to give himself additional height because he felt inferior. When he was outside of the bar at work he had a nice manner and his boss got good reviews from his customers for his winning personality. He was pleasant looking and could have moved into a management position, but he had no ambition to move up in the company. Person tried to be part of the landscape – anonymous.

But after he was out of jail, the rage returned. He still had a rage that he could not satisfy. It was like the rage he had with a new boy in the shower. Once he was free he experimented. He tried men and boys on the outside, but they did not satisfy. Then, seven years later, he discovered the middle school girls in Summer County.

After he raped and murdered each of those five children he was satisfied for about a year and then when he could no longer stand it he went hunting again.

In his heart, Person did not think he would be caught, particularly as time went on and he found it was so easy to get the girls into the bright, cherry red carpet cleaning truck. They were so easy to control. Just a little bit of chloroform that he used in his work as a solvent to clean stains in upholstery and the girls were knocked out and in his control. Each time he took the victim to a large farm under a canopy of trees. Each time he came closer to home. Each time it was easier.

***

Victim number six, however, was not a charm.

Person had had the headache that came with the rage for a couple of weeks. He had tried to satisfy the urge with the fat girl and more reefer, but he was suffering and he had begun to find himself driving down lonesome roads in west Summer County. The roads had exits off the interstate. It was spring and it was foggy in the morning. Indian Hollow Road was one of the roads that fit his criterion – a lonesome road with isolated homes with bus stops and young female children.

Person knew the police were looking. He had been stopped more than once for a random check of his vehicle. Lucky for him, by completing the Youthful Offender Program, Person had no criminal record, so when the officer checked headquarters by radio he was told Person was clean. That fact, that he had no record, had also helped him get a job which allowed him to enter customers' homes. If his employer knew of his criminal background for assault of a child Person would never have been hired. If the carpet cleaning company had been aware of his past and if he had assaulted a customer or their child, the company would have been liable for compensatory and punitive damages. But Person had no criminal record. He was a youthful offender. He was clean as the driven snow.

And since there was no record of an adult conviction there was no public knowledge of his past and Person was able to enter customers' homes with impunity. He used the cover of his work cleaning carpets to look for potential victims.

The most recent stop by the Highway Patrol was educational. Person had been sent out to job orders in Summer County and he had been stopped. Person showed the deputy his work order and let the deputy look in his vehicle and they joked around. Person even admitted he had been stopped three times before. "Why was that?" he asked the deputy.

The deputy did not answer. All officers were sworn to secrecy about the plan to capture the predator.

The Sheriff was serious about catching "the animal", as they called him. The police had held a conference to make sure every officer knew that young girls were at risk, that if it was spring and it was foggy, and if a child was missing, and if there was a red truck, that they were to stop the vehicle to check the driver's license and try to search the vehicle.

***

So here, early in the morning of the day Becky was to go missing, Person was pulled over for a fourth time on Indian Hollow Road by a Highway Patrol Deputy.

"What luck," Person said out loud.

There was no report of a missing child, but the red carpet cleaner's truck met the criteria. The deputy added in the fact that it was time for pick-up of school children by school buses and it was spring and it was foggy. The deputy made the stop. He was a smart cop. The deputy had a premonition.

Person could see the patrolman intended to stop him. He saw the patrolman pass him on the left and then whip around and follow him. Person took his time before he pulled over, and he stopped just where he wanted to be on Indian Hollow Road near the access road to Becky Sue's trailer. The deputy got out and approached the red truck and checked Person's license and insurance.

"It's foggy out here in the county. You seemed to be driving a little fast for the conditions, don't you think?"

"No sir," said Person. "I'm out here a lot and am used to it. I thought I was driving the correct speed. I'm not trying to argue with you, though." Person smiled. He felt so confident.

The officer took the license and insurance card back to his vehicle. He sat there for 15 minutes trying to see if the driver would spook and drive off and give him a chance to arrest him.

Finally the patrolman came back to the truck. "You are from Gainesville. Why are you out here on Indian Hollow Road?"

"I have a job down in New Retirement City. I came off the interstate on this exit and I'm heading to US 19 and will head south to the job."

"Do you have a work order?"

"Sure," said Person as he handed over the clip board with his work orders for the day.

The officer looked through all the work orders and then went around to the passenger side of the truck. He inspected the passenger side of the little red truck and asked if Person would mind removing the tarp from the rear of the bed of the truck. The bed contained the cleaning hose and the vacuum pump used to suction the water and cleaning solution from the customer's carpet.

Person exited the vehicle. "No problem," said Person, and he opened the tarp from the bed.

"Ok, thank you." The deputy had poked around but seemed satisfied and he returned Person's license and insurance card. The patrolman drove away. By happenstance the patrolman used the access road to Alma Lee's trailer to turn around.

Person remained at the rear of the truck and re-wrapped the hose and began re-snapping the tarp. Person waved at the cop as he drove by back to the interstate.

The fog was still very thick. After the patrol car traveled 50 feet it was enveloped in the fog and disappeared.

Person smiled. He felt invincible and in total control. It was karma. He decided to let the latest traffic stop act as his excuse for being near the bus stop while he waited for Becky to board the bus. The time was 7:50 a.m.

He had staked out Becky's activities on the road three times before. He knew the bus was due at the access road and Indian Hollow Road at 8:00 a.m. This information was freely given by the Summer County School Board. All Person had to do to obtain the ETA of Becky's bus was to call the school board and identify himself as a parent and they would tell him the time the bus made its pickup at the access road.

In the past he sat out on the right of way in his red truck pretending to study a map on days he was headed to New Retirement City, and he watched the kids come to the bus stop. No parents waited with the kids. The kids were well behaved and spoke in groups of two or three. Person noticed that Becky was always the last one on the bus.

***

After the first crime, when he had no plan, Person had carefully prepared for each subsequent kidnapping. He identified a victim and developed a plan for the snatch. The first time he had just been lucky. A small, young girl had missed the bus and was walking back home. He was able to coax her into the truck by promising to take her to school if she would tell him where he had to go. They got lost but were laughing and having a good time until Person drove down a dirt road to a field. The girl panicked and Person struck her in the head. He did not know what happened next except she was dead and he was in rapture. He took her into the field and buried her. When he got back to the truck he found her panties and he saved them.

Person paid close attention to the news reports each time a girl he kidnapped disappeared. It was like he was not involved. In fact, he dwelled on the crimes to the point where his boss told him his interest didn't seem healthy. From that conversation Person learned to keep his mouth shut about the crimes and confine himself to following developments about the cases in the news.

For a while after each crime Person would feel guilty, but then he would forget what happened. Then to remember, he would have to go back through each crime in his mind, reviewing the facts with the aid of the souvenir he saved from each kidnapping and murder. Person was able to compartmentalize the attacks in some recess of his brain and continue with his life, spending time after work in the bar and smoking the dope and working cleaning carpets, but then about a year on, the rage and the desire became too much and he couldn't control his passion for the violence.

***

By the time Person was prepared to do Becky he had stalked her three times. He had also driven down the access road to

Becky's double wide at the end of the road in the afternoon to see what was there. There were two other trailers on the road but he satisfied himself that they were abandoned by knocking on the doors and pretending to be looking for a customer. He had been confronted by Becky's Grandmother, who explained the trailers were vacant. She insisted she did not order her carpets to be cleaned. Person thanked her. He saw the large wax myrtle bush he could hide behind with the rag soaked with chloroform. He saw the tall grass he could pull her into and then drag her to the truck that would be on the right of way waiting for the human cargo.

The next time he came down Indian Hollow Road would be Becky's turn.

The fact that the highway patrol officer stopped Person on Indian Hollow Road near the limited access road leading to Becky's trailer proved to Person that Becky's fate was ordained by a higher order and Person was merely the instrument to fulfill her destiny.

It was at this time in the process of the act leading to a kidnapping and murder that Person felt he was like Cain and he had the mark of Cain in that he could not be touched or caught by the authorities. He was immune, but he was cursed by the Biblical blood. He shared the stain of that first of all homicides. He was a born murderer. He learned this in Bible study in prison.

Chapter 4
Joseph Rainey

Joseph Rainey was one of the new breed of police officer. His father and grandfather had not been a member of a police force. Rainey had not been in the military police. He was not even a veteran of the armed forces. He learned the basics of law enforcement in college at Florida Technological University (FTU) located in Orlando, Florida. He was an outstanding student. His weakness was his size. He barely made the cut for the height requirement of the police academy. He needed to be 5'8" and he normally measured in at that height, but sometimes if he had jogged a long distance he was a little shorter than the required height to be an officer. His intellect was impressive and he was passed through by his superiors, regardless of the fact he barely made the physical requirements. Other than his height, he was a bit underweight but he was wiry and could wrestle and had competed and lettered in the sport while in high school.

Rainey had never been married and he had no children or any family in Florida. He had come to Daytona Beach as a tourist when he was 18 and liked the beach. He was from New Jersey, near New York City, but the area was blighted (Newark) and he was advised by his parents that there was nothing for him there and he would probably do better if he moved south.

Rainey told his family he chose Orlando. FTU was a state school, relatively new, and Rainey's dad agreed it offered a good yet inexpensive education. The parents were more familiar with the fact that there were a number of tourist attractions being built in the Orlando area. Most people up north were unaware the state of

Florida was going through a growth spurt, expanding the number of colleges and universities. His parents said that once Rainey was established they would visit.

Rainey went to college straight through without a break. He had a job in the college library that paid his room and board and his father sprung for the tuition, books and fees.

Rainey didn't know why he wanted to be a police officer. One of his teachers, a retired cop from Miami, had written a doctoral thesis which proposed there was no difference psychologically between a cop and a crook except one enjoyed chasing a criminal and the other desired the thrill of the escape. Rainey thought that the idea was baloney – any evidence that existed as a basis for the professor's theory was purely anecdotal.

Rainey was a practical man. Well before he finished college he began looking for work. It was the middle of a recession. Florida was growing in spite of the US economy. He interviewed every place he heard might have an opening. One of his professors suggested he try the West Coast of Florida. There were many little communities with small police forces where he could get a start and grow with the State. The advice was sound. After he graduated from college Rainey entered and completed the Summer County Police Academy.

Rainey was hired in Summer County as a deputy sheriff. Once the sheriff realized he had a basic grasp of police work and he could communicate intelligently with lawyers and doctors and he didn't get lost in the court system he was promoted to the rank of detective. County sheriffs are Constitutional Officers. They are elected for a term of years and they have control of a budget. Rainey wanted nothing to do with the politics of the job. A few of the sheriff's men were political operatives but the majority were involved in law enforcement.

In Summer County, the deputies were under extreme pressure to arrest the animal who was roaming the back woods of the county.

The failure to catch the child killer was a political issue but by rights he had to be caught or society would suffer. There were arguments for vigilante action and the Sheriff was aware groups of men had quietly taken up arms and watched and waited to protect their children. If the government could not perform its proper function, society would.

When Rainey was hired the race for election of sheriff was on. The competence of the candidates had become an issue with one of the three candidates alleging the other two were not up for the job of rooting out this criminal. The race for the job became nasty. All of the candidates began to investigate the backgrounds of their opponents. Before it was over all three were shown to have lied and exaggerated about their qualifications for office. As usual, the candidate who was elected was not the person the voters wanted but was the lesser of the evils. At least he promised to improve the department and capture and kill the child killer.

After the election the new sheriff asked Lieutenant McBride, who had headed the search for the child killer, if he needed some help, and he said he did. The Sheriff asked who he wanted and McBride was impressed with Rainey's intelligence and he asked for him. Rainey was promoted to sergeant and he was made the junior member of the team that was chasing the killer. The work trying to capture the animal was frustrating. The case would go hot and cold. There would be hope and then another child would go missing.

By the time Rainey had five years of police work under his belt two children were lost. Jim McBride, the senior member of the team, had been working the child killer case for seven years and all five children attributed lost to the animal were gone and he was all but burned out.

McBride tried to bring method to the search once Rainey was on the team. Rainey's first task was to appropriate a room and organize all of the information that had been collected on the three girls whose bodies were discovered and the other two girls who were missing and who fit the profile of being a victim of the killer.

After putting each document, report, note or paper in the appropriate file, and reading each piece of paper and making notes, Rainey and McBride and the Sheriff sat down and Rainey told them what he believed they could do to thwart or catch the killer. First, the evidence room was locked to keep out other officers who were curious about the case and were reading the file and spreading rumors about who might be a suspect.

Second, Rainey's plan was to meet with the middle school principals and their secretaries and establish a "hot line" that they could use to report a missing child, particularly a child missing from a bus without an appropriate excuse from a parent. Either McBride or Rainey would interview the parent and determine whether the child was actually missing and a potential victim or if the child was playing hooky. They met with the heads of all the police forces in Summer County so that the city police forces would be aware of who they were tracking.

McBride and Rainey worked as partners for two years. But in spite of two years' worth of work, McBride and Rainey had been unsuccessful in arresting a suspect or preventing a crime. For the previous two years there had been two abductions of middle school girls on their way to school and now two years after the last crime there was another case. This one was on Indian Hollow Road.

***

Although Luke Mark John Person had a burning anger that had to be extinguished, he had a plan. He knew he needed to follow through on his plan in order to abduct Becky successfully. He just didn't realize the plan would unravel as quickly as it did.

The fog laid out perfectly to mask his activity after he was stopped by the deputy on the right of way of Indian Hollow Road. After the deputy left and drove west, Person went to the bed of the truck and unsnapped half of the buttons that held the tarp over the vacuum motor and the hose used to deep clean carpet.

He removed the hose and put it in the cab of the truck behind the seat. Once the hose was removed there was a cavity large enough for a child in the truck bed under the tarp. He walked through the tall grass toward the wax myrtle bush and waited with the rag and the small bottle of chloroform. He heard the screen door slam. He heard Becky and Ms. Lee saying good bye. The fog slid up the access road.

Person could hear the cowboy boots scraping along the ground with each step Becky took. Person poured the solution from the bottle to the rag and then slipped the chloroform bottle into his pocket. Then he heard Becky singing softly and she was next to him. But she backed away. She felt his presence and smelled the acetone odor of the fluid in the rag.

Person reached forward as Becky turned to go back to the safety of her grandmother. He got the rag over her face with his left hand but she struggled loose and he had to grab her with his large right hand to control her. He dragged her behind the wax myrtle and into the center of the field. She tried to yell but she couldn't get a sound out of her mouth for her fear. She tripped Person and they tangled up on the ground.

Becky continued to struggle and Person lost the rag. He hit Becky in the mouth and knocked her unconscious. The blow opened a large cut on her lips and bruised her cheek. Person looked for the rag with no success. He took off her backpack so she would fit in the bed of the truck. Her sweater became tangled in his hand. In frustration he threw the backpack and the sweater into the grass. It was not his intent to leave anything in the grass.

He lifted Becky and carried her to the truck. He saw her boots slip off. He dropped her at the side of the truck then lifted her dead weight and threw her into the bed of the truck in the space where he had removed the hose.

Person heard the sound of a large engine and he looked up to see the yellow lights of the school bus blinking through the fog. He abandoned the boots and the rag, the sweater and the backpack. When he lifted Becky she was limp and made no sound. He thought she may be dead.

The school bus passed his truck and stopped thirty feet to the east. He could hear children screaming and he nearly passed out from panic. The children were very close. He quickly snapped the tarp in place and opened the door of the truck and took a minute to collect his wits. He reminded himself that he had to head east on Indian Hollow Road and he was parked in the right of way heading west. He waited for the bus to move and then made a U-turn to head back toward the interstate. He turned onto the entrance ramp of the interstate overpass at Indian Hollow Road. He was on the interstate. The fog was so thick that traffic barely moved on I-75. The limited sight conditions had caused accidents on both sides of the road.

***

The highway patrol will stay busy, thought Person. They won't be looking for me. He felt more in control as he proceeded north slowly with the other traffic; at most he was moving 5 miles per hour.

At the Wildwood exit there was a huge pile-up, maybe 20 cars were involved in a chain reaction crash in the northbound lanes. The police were at the scene. One officer was directing traffic but all vehicles northbound, including Person's red truck, came to a full stop. The crash blocked the exit at Wildwood, so Person's truck was forced to wait in the middle of the road.

Person was stuck in the same spot for two hours. During that time Person fought panic. He believed he was caught. He had no control. He considered going over to the patrolman directing traffic. He would confess that he had abducted a child and she was dead and hidden in the bed of his truck under the tarp.

Person and the patrolman glanced at each other. The patrolman remembered him from earlier in the day when the officer had stopped him on Indian Hollow Road. He seemed awfully nervous, thought the deputy. But considering the circumstances he decided maybe he was just anxious to get to the restroom up near Ocala. The deputy went back to his work and forgot about Person for the moment.

Person began to hyperventilate. He grabbed a bag that had held a donut and he exhaled into the bag and then inhaled the carbon dioxide. He was able to breathe.

Finally the crash was cleared and traffic started to move. The officer was gone. It had wasted two hours.

Micanopy was the last exit north before the three Gainesville exits on the interstate. The road through Micanopy leads to a back road into Paynes Prairie. Person turned into the forest preserve and drove aimlessly and then he was lost in the 20,000 acre park. He drove faster and the red truck, which had a short wheel base began to jump and bounce over the ruts in the road. Person tried to bring the truck to a full stop but instead it fell into a ditch.

He backed slowly using the clutch to rock the vehicle back and forth. He was able to back out to turn around. He became so frustrated and anxious that he would be caught with the girl in the truck that he stopped the vehicle; unsnapped the cover from the truck bed, and threw Becky out of the bed of the truck. She felt cold and stiff.

She's dead, he thought.

***

Person returned to his driver's seat. He lit a joint and inhaled deeply. He put his hand on the steering wheel. He was steady. He calmly drove out the same way he came into the preserve. He got back on the interstate and drove north back to the carpet cleaning shop in the town of Archer. He pulled the truck into the building and began to clean it. There were big chunks of mud in the wheel wells.

"What's with my truck?" groused the boss.

"There was a terrible accident near Wildwood."

"How did it get so muddy?"

"I had to drive through a ditch to get past the accident. The truck needs new tires. There's no tread left. The tires just spun in the mud – no traction."

"Did you make any of your stops?" The boss knew the answer to that question. He had been taking calls all morning from customers who wanted to know why their carpet wasn't being cleaned.

"Jeez, boss have you looked outside? Its noon and the fog is so thick you can't see your hand in front of your face."

The boss chuckled. Then he noticed Person's back. There was blood on his right flank. The boss lifted his shirt and there was a deep scratch three inches long on Person's upper buttocks. It was seeping blood.

"You need to have that looked at. It may be a deep cut." They both looked in the truck. There was blood on the seat but they couldn't see what caused the injury.

"I fell down in Wildwood in the mud."

"Go to the restroom and clean up and see if you need first aid. Go to the hospital if you think you need to."

In the restroom Person found that the bottle containing the chloroform had broken and he was cut by a jagged piece of glass. He changed his clothes and threw the shirt and the pants into the large community laundry hamper.

After cleaning up Person told the boss he didn't feel too good and he was going to head home. He offered to take the red truck home with him and he would wash it.

"That would be good. It looks pretty ugly. How does it run?"

"It runs fine, but it needs new tires," Person repeated.

Person covered the seat with a piece of plastic then he started the vehicle and he pulled out of the shop and headed down Archer Road to University Boulevard. There was a self-service car wash on the corner.

He dug into the glove compartment and pulled out a roll of quarters he saved for video games. He had to feed ten dollars in quarters into the machine, cleaning, scrubbing and blasting the truck inside and out. He took particular care spraying the bed of the truck, then he re-rolled the hose in its compartment.

Person drove the truck to his garage apartment behind his aunt's house and found some upholstery soap and scrubbed the blood stain the best he could. He was able to clean most of it. He spritzed the interior of the cab and the truck bed with Clorox bleach and wiped down all the surface areas that Becky may have touched on the outside and in the bed of the truck.

It took Person hours before Person felt confident he had eliminated all evidence that he had had Becky Sue in his truck. While he was cleaning the vehicle his aunt and her husband came home. Person and the husband did not say a word to each other. They did not get along.

During the afternoon, Person heard an unusually frequent blast of sirens and the bells of fire engines and the sound of a helicopter flying a pattern across the south of Alachua County.

Chapter 5
Shands Hospital

Shands Hospital is the closest hospital with a trauma center near Paynes Prairie and the town of Micanopy. As soon as the first responders felt assured Becky Sue Painter was stable they placed her on a stretcher and drove carefully out of the swamp and headed to the interstate and then to Gainesville and the hospital.

During her rescue the fire department was not cautious to preserve the scene of the crime, but rather to save a life.

Three large ambulances and a ladder truck from the fire department entered the swamp by the road that Person's truck had traveled and in the process obliterated any trace evidence that had been deposited in the road in the park or at the scene of the rescue. There were no foot prints or tire tracks left after the ladder truck with its 36 inch tires rode over the scene. Nor was there any way to distinguish Person's footprints from the firemen's boot prints as they rushed about trying to save Becky.

***

Detective Rainey had left the scene as soon as the paramedics arrived. He was back in the helicopter and he directed the pilot to fly west to the interstate and then fly north and then to fly east over each of the next three exits off the interstate in an attempt to locate a red truck. Although the sighting of a red truck was not a hard clue there were sightings of a red truck in prior kidnappings, so Rainey felt it was at least circumstantial evidence of the whereabouts of the killer. The red truck was the only clue he had and he had to do something.

Rainey felt he was very, very close to the killer. Closer than they had ever been.

In fact, Rainey was close. When the chopper flew down Archer Road they flew over the warehouse that housed the carpet cleaning service. The red truck was in the building and Person and his boss were discussing the condition of the vehicle. By the time the helicopter had flown over each of the exits the truck was at the car wash in a cleaning bay being washed and rinsed of all dirt and grime that was associated with the abduction.

And by the time Person was at his garage apartment giving the truck a once over with water, soap and Clorox, cleaning the vinyl surfaces, the mats, seats and dash, Rainey and the helicopter made a few passes and then he was back at the preserve trying to see if he could salvage any evidence. Rainey was frustrated because the scene had been abandoned by the police.

Rainey had to call the Sheriff and ask that a team come back so they could conduct a neighborhood search to see if the truck was in a garage in Micanopy or at a farm house east of the interstate in Cross Creek. Rainey was upset with the lack of follow through. The girl was saved, but that was only half of the job.

We have to capture this man, thought Rainey. We will probably be out here again next week. He isn't going to stop killing just because we saved one child.

***

Once the police were reassembled on the main street in Micanopy, Rainey sent the copter back to New Retirement City and he borrowed a car and drove to Shands Hospital.

The press was there at the ER. Print news. They asked what all the police activity was to the south of town.

Why were there three ambulances and a ladder truck from the New Retirement City's Fire Department in the emergency parking lot of the hospital? This wasn't their jurisdiction.

Someone from the sports department of The Gainesville Sun heard a rumor that Alabama Head Football Coach Bear Bryant had a heart attack. "Is that true?" the reporter asked Rainey.

Rainey got the reporters into a scrum and explained that this was a police investigation. "The investigation is still active. While it remains active you will need to contact the Sheriff in Summer County for comment. To the best of my knowledge, Coach Bryant is in Tuscaloosa, Alabama."

Rainey decided to stay put and see if Becky could be interviewed. When he felt her body on the road in the preserve and held her, she felt so cold, like she was near death. But the RN said she was stable. She needs to see her grandmother, thought Rainey as he sat in a vinyl chair and tried to catch his breath.

Rainey took out a small pad and began to make notes to recount the day's events.

***

The Sheriff of Summer County was easy to listen to. He had gathered a crowd for the news conference and he gave a short statement advising that there had been an abduction, but his office had been able to find the victim, whose name was being withheld due to her age.

"She is alive and well," said the sheriff in response to the first question.

The sheriff was asked about the suspect and if the police had anyone in custody.

He said, "We're on the trail."

"Where are you looking?" he was asked.

"In Alachua County."

"Can you give us the name of the suspect?"

"Not at this point in the investigation."

Rainey was listening to the news conference on the local radio. The station had broken into its regular broadcast with a bulletin and the newscast.

"Who or what are you looking for?" asked a reporter.

"A man in a red truck."

Why is he saying this, thought Rainey? Don't give up what little we have.

Soon, the sheriff ran out of facts for the press, and he began to talk about his feelings and how he was heartbroken about the loss of the two girls since he took office. Reporters are a skeptical bunch and the news conference ended for them when there were no more facts and the sheriff began what sounded like his pitch for re-election. The press began to shuffle their feet and walk away.

Finally a newscaster said, "So, to wrap this up, there was an attempted abduction of a young girl. She is safe and well and you are looking for a man in a red truck."

"Well, yes," said the sheriff. "Thank you for coming."

One reporter observed to another that there were probably only 20,000 red trucks in Gainesville, Alachua County and its suburbs and outlying farms.

***

The man in the window of the house in front of Person's garage apartment had been watching Person wash and re-wash his red work truck as he listened to the special broadcast.

That night he commented to his wife.

"Your nephew was home early from work today."

"Yes, what of it?"

"He was washing that red truck from work again using our water."

"Yeah?"

"Well, I don't want us to be charged with aiding and abetting him."

"What are you saying?"

"There was another abduction in Summer County. He's using our water to wash the truck. They say they are looking for a red truck. He has a red truck."

"He's not involved," said the aunt. "He's our son."

"We can't keep ignoring this," said the husband. "He is sick. How many children will he kill? I do not understand how the police can be so incompetent. Why can't they catch him?"

"You are to keep your mouth shut," said the aunt. "He is family."

He's an animal, thought the stepfather, agreeing with the police.

***

The psychiatrist explained to Rainey that Becky had suffered a mental and emotional shock. Everyone needs to let her come around to talking about the incident in her own good time. It could take a long time. You can't rely on her providing you with any information to help you solve the case or identify the assailant.

Rainey called McBride and updated him with what they had in Gainesville. "It's a big goose egg up here. Every time I get on the highway I see another red truck. We need a break to solve this – just a little luck."

"I will spell you," said McBride. "Go home and get some sleep."

"Tell the sheriff the girl probably won't be able to help us" said Rainey. "See if he will let the deputy stay with the grandmother for a while. Alma Lee is plenty spooked. When she heard the sheriff say Becky was well, she was afraid the killer would come after Becky to eliminate her as a witness."

"That would be pretty grim."

"Actually, the old lady is being very realistic about what could happen. They need protection for a while."

Chapter 6
Jenny Barnes

Plantation #7 was incorporated in the state of Florida and it practically ran itself. It was a small company that was diversified. It was a manufacturer of jams and jellies produced from its own orchard of fruit and citrus trees. It had a wholesale operation, selling to large department stores in the Northeast, and it sold products through its retail store in the manufacturing plant located on John Anderson Drive in North Ormond on the east coast of Florida. It also sold its products by mail.

Jenny Barnes was responsible for the Plantation's operations. She was able to juggle her time between her responsibilities as a business woman and attending law school at the University of Florida, and after graduation she began work at a large law firm located in a bank on Grenada Blvd. in Ormond.

The law firm used Jenny as a rain maker. There was no one in town she didn't know and so clients flowed to her and the firm and she was a well-paid partner.

It had been expected that Jenny would practice law with Tom Night's firm, but Jenny was independent and wanted to go with the large firm at the bank. Jenny felt Tom's method of practice was out of date. He handled clients like family. Tom seemed to know everything about his clients. Jenny only saw clients for the initial visit when they were signed to a retainer contract. Afterward, the client was passed on to another lawyer in the firm and Jenny knew nothing about her client or the status or outcome of the case.

On rare occasions, if one of the cases she brought to the firm came to trial or a final hearing, Jenny was brought along to court; however, the attorney who had actually prepared the case for the client argued on behalf of the client to the judge.

Jenny became embarrassed on more than one occasion when she was asked a question by the judge and Jenny had to defer to co-counsel.

One time, the court dug in with a comment that Jenny needed to be better prepared if she was going to charge a fee for her services.

After that experience, Jenny decided she wanted to try cases. She didn't just want to carry someone's briefcase. Jenny was not encouraged by her employers in the law firm at the bank. She was advised that anyone can try a lawsuit. The key to a successful practice was bringing in the clients and the hourly fees. Jenny decided that was not what she wanted. She wanted to get in the pit and argue for the client.

Jenny talked to Tom and he said they had a place for a young trial attorney, but she would be working long hours and it was ugly work, most often dealing with honest to goodness criminals. Also, she would not be able to manage Plantation #7. She would not have time to do both. Last, she would have to move out of Marla's house on the grounds of the plantation in North Ormond Beach and move across the state to St. Petersburg. She couldn't practice long distance.

Jenny was excited. She was going to be working with James DeMarco. DeMarco was considered to be the premier criminal lawyer on the West Coast of Florida, (after Tom Night, that is). Jenny hired a manager for Plantation # 7 and she tried to keep up with the business using the phone and fax machine to communicate with the manager.

***

Both Jenny and DeMarco were single and they were thrown together for long hours working in a frenzy to obtain positive results for clients who mostly did not appreciate what was being done for them. At times, Jenny, on observing an inmate in the jail, saw a chimpanzee with its hands sticking out of the bars and its eyes glassy, as though tranquillized. The prisoner could not communicate any more effectively than the ape. She understood that the prisoner would be lost without her help. However the ape did not appreciate his predicament.

Jenny rented a house in the Old Northeast section of St. Petersburg. The new courthouse was located downtown and it had facilities for criminal cases. The courtrooms were large and with a deep gallery for court observers. The day Jenny came to work for the firm Tom told her to review a file. A client was charged with a misdemeanor – battery. Reading the file, Jenny realized the battery was a sexual battery; actually it was a rape charge. Apparently the State Attorney felt they could not prove the rape case through the victim and so they brought a charge of simple battery, which was a misdemeanor. So here she was, the first day on the job and she was in a criminal trial actually trying a case. Lucky for her ego, she won, hands down. There was no stopping her now.

***

James and Jenny had become attached at the hip for four years, trying cases across the State. Jenny was personable and beautiful and she always had a fresh comment for the media. Local TV news was developing, and part of the battle in a case in which there was press and TV coverage was that the defendant needed a response to the allegations the police made to the media. Capital cases, political corruption, and grand theft, were all cases where the police would call a press conference to rail on about a defendant and the horrible crime that was committed.

In those cases, if James and Jenny represented the defendant, Jenny was the face for the defense.

Chapter 7
Marla Reynolds

Marla stared into the mirror. It was her birthday. She was 47. Perhaps this would be the last declared celebration of her birth, she thought. She had lost her Mother this year. No one knew why she died. Marla's mother had been living at the Old House on the plantation in North Ormond Beach and she didn't wake in the morning. She passed in her sleep. She was a very private woman and probably had been ill, but did not complain.

Marla's husband James was unable to attend the funeral. There was an important board meeting. There were troubles at his company. American industry was under siege. Japan was a threat. Germany built superior heavy equipment and automotive products. The tag "USA" on a product connoted poor engineering and shoddy workmanship. America and China had their cultural revolutions. Both were failures. We had lost Viet Nam. Cambodia was a killing field. Laos was deflowered. The dominoes had fallen, but not in favor of any ideology. Religious folk were drinking Kool-Aid laced with poison. Even the infants and children were victims of their pastors.

What does the future hold for me, thought Marla? She continued her inspection as she stood nude in front of the full length mirror. She was still intact physically, but not mentally. The years in New York City had actually been boring. She wanted to have a conversation with someone that was personal and meaningful. Instead there was "all this fucking (excuse my French) noise."

You couldn't escape the clamor in the city. Even living on the edge of Central Park was cacophonous. She could look out the window if the window was closed and escape, but on the street there was angry noise at all hours.

The smell of the city was bad. It was cancerous. They should have sprayed Manhattan with vanilla to mask the odor of urine, but the City was bankrupt monetarily, emotionally, and morally. Times Square was a warren full of whores and pimps. It was like London during the late 1800's.

Marla did not like to go outside. She had lost her Florida tan.

As she looked closely, she could see the hair above her lip was turning dark. Her mother had a mustache when she was older. Marla always had fine hair, the same as her mother, but it was fair and blonde and invisible. Unless you got close and opened your eyes while you kissed her, you could not see the hair. "I have to do something about that," she said quietly.

Otherwise, her body was firm. She hadn't gone slack in her breasts, belly, or behind. Her hair was full and still vibrant. She was still blonde. She made no artificial changes. She needed more sun though. She would head to Florida again soon. Her husband couldn't go. He would be working. "These were times that tried men's souls," he said, quoting someone else.

Her soul, too. Women were up in arms.

The marriage wasn't doing well. Reynolds wanted a wife who was there when he needed a wife. Mostly, Marla was for show. She made him look good at parties and meetings and other public occasions. Otherwise, she was on her own ... left to her own devices. She was not a user or an abuser so she didn't cause him any embarrassment, but this was not what she had bought into. She thought she would be his partner. She would listen to him and give her advice.

"Hell, the President of the United States listens to me and I give him advice," he had said when she offered to listen. "I can't talk about it. It's an insider problem. It has to do with the business. Industry in America is dying. We are going to be selling each other insurance and 401K plans and nothing else. No one wants to buy our products. Even the military says the Kalashnikov is superior to the M-16. We lost a war, God damn it. The generals do not understand why we lost. We lost because we got involved in a civil war. An outsider has no control in a civil war. If you don't control the troops you will lose."

How do you partner with that? Reynold's is out of control, Marla thought. I gave him five years, Marla agreed silently. She wasn't going to wait forever.

He never considered that she would leave. She was sane and sober. At the time, they were living on the top floor of the tower overlooking Central Park, for Christ sake. Rent free. Why would she leave, he thought? But she did leave.

When she left, she said she was going back to the Old House at the Plantation to try to help out. She had gone there earlier in the year when her mother had died. She stayed two weeks. She missed the dinner at the Annual Meeting of the corporation. Now she's leaving again. The calendar is clear for a while, he thought, but I will need to say something to Public Relations. She could leave and how would that look? I need to get ahead of this, thought Reynolds. She's depressed over her mother's death and needs time. It would be better if she had a medical problem, breast cancer, something she had to fight. It would make a tighter story for the media. Well, PR will come up with something. I don't need to worry about it. That's what we pay them for – to make us look good.

***

Marla left all her things in the apartment in NYC. There was no divorce or separation agreement. She left quietly. She had never made a splash. Though she was on the list of the people to invite, and she was invited, it was usually her husband who was the one in the photograph in the society page of the Sunday Edition of the NY Times. After a while, she wasn't missed. They agreed that when she was absolutely needed by her husband for an event she would be there. He would send a jet. When she came back to the City she would stay at Corporate Headquarters in the JRD Building in the glass canyon in Manhattan. From the window she viewed the Seagram's Building. The towers were like sprouts of crystal rising from bedrock. Like something in a Superman movie. She would only stay in NYC a day or so. She supplied a body when her husband absolutely required her to be present to prove they were married. "What should I do, bring my girlfriend?" he would say. There was talk, but nothing but rumor was established. There was no hard proof Marla and James were not living as husband and wife.

It was expected that her husband would retire after 10 years as the head of JRD. He had a couple years to go. The successor had been vetted by the JRD Board of Directors but not officially announced. The matter of the marriage could wait until after the change in leadership at the company, thought her husband. That was best. PR agreed. There was no scandal. It was perfect. Beige or vanilla.

***

Plantation #7 had been left lying on fallow ground when Marla left. Jenny wasn't a hands-on administrator, and the business had grown competition over the years. Jenny had moved her interest to the law and she no longer even lived at the Old House. She was with James DeMarco now – heart and soul. They lived in St. Petersburg. They were partners but unmarried. A modern relationship.

Jenny had not watched the mail. At Christmas time everyone's mailbox was stuffed with catalogs. The catalogs solicited the sale of products for your home, in your home. You shopped sitting at the kitchen table paging through the slick magazines. There was no pressure beyond the best marketing ploys money could buy. The catalogs sold a product and the story of the business that produced and sold the product. These were all special items. Hand stitched shoes and boots. Jackets – fleece-lined. Colors. Modern and muted. Hand-picked boxed fruits. Steak from Omaha. These were products made in the USA. They were products "we" could be proud of.

Marla inquired of Jenny on several occasions, "Where was the catalog soliciting our jam and jelly? The guava jelly that was in the American home in the fall season to be spread on a biscuit over melted butter?"

Jenny missed the boat. Plantation #7 did not have a catalog, but a new company from Florida called "Plantation #9" did have one. #9 claimed their jelly and jams were made from fruit grown in their orchards in Florida and prepared by a family with homegrown values. #9 stole the niche from Plantation #7. If you looked at the label on the product, #9 was actually based in New York City and the people pictured in the slick brochure were actors. Regardless, #7's market share began to suffer and revenue declined.

After Marla left NYC, she was living in the Old House and she had nothing better to do, so she pitched in and tried to staunch the bleeding at Plantation #7. The company had begun to decline and when that happens, it can go quick.

Marla knew #9 had to be sued. #9 stole #7's logo. The only difference in the logo was the competition changed the 7 to a 9. The containers were the same. The labels were similar and the company colors were the same shade of brown. Marla called Tom's firm and talked to Darlene about the infringement issue. Darlene's mind was occupied by criminal matters but Alphonse Alesse would handle it, said Darlene.

Alphonse usually handled matters that were civil and not volatile, but he was up for the challenge. Plantation #9 did business in the State of Florida and had offices in Cocoa where they manufactured their jams and jellies according to the information Marla had dug up. She was still the quintessential para-legal. She could prepare a case file for a lawsuit with the best.

Marla had asked Alphonse for investigative services and was able to use Jim Faircloth for a couple of days. He went to the facility in Cocoa and sat in his car and watched as the crew at #9 unloaded guavas and oranges that were shipped from Central

America. #9 lied about where they grew their fruits. #7 could make a complaint for unfair practices to go with the suit for trade mark, trade name and business infringement and interference.

Jim Faircloth had asked Alphonse Alesse if he could make one more trip to Cocoa to obtain the license tag numbers of the vehicles at the manufacturing plant of Plantation #9. He wanted to see if there were any employees of the competitor who previously worked for Plantation #7.

Success.

One of the workers at Cocoa had previously worked for the Barnes' Family. Jim Faircloth talked to him in a bar on a rainy Friday afternoon and the worker bragged that he had access to #7's safe and took the list of #7's customers, copied the list and was paid for the list by the owners of the competitor.

Alphonse was happy with the case once he had the facts in front of him. He would file suit in Tampa in Federal District Court. Alphonse advised Marla that #9 had illegally obtained Plantation #7's proprietary information – #7's customer list. That was a criminal offense. That theft would have occurred in Volusia County. The competition had gotten into the safe at the office at the Old House at Plantation #7.

Marla still knew the Volusia County Sheriff and the State Attorney and all the judges. Now was the time to use her good name to see if Volusia County's local law enforcement would investigate the matter and determine if a law had been broken and come to the aid of a local business that had paid taxes for the last 80 years. If the law would take action, it would set #9 back on its heels.

If it wasn't too late.

Part II

The Hangman's Two Step

Chapter 8
Scientific Evidence

"So, the FBI says if we can find hair with substantial similarities to that of a victim on the person or property of the defendant then their experts will provide testimony that the defendant came in contact with the victim?" Rainey and McBride were discussing the conversation McBride had with the chief investigator for the FBI's forensic unit.

"According to the FBI, what is the probability that the testimony of the expert is in error?"

"Practically nil. Ten million to one."

"You're kidding," said Rainey. "That can't be right."

"It's a two-step process. First, the FBI will provide us with a forensic scientist who will determine if there are sufficient similarities in the hair from the victim found on the defendant or his property, like in his car or home. Then second, the FBI's expert will testify that the defendant had contact with the victim."

"Are you sure? If the defendant's hair is found on the victim the FBI expert will testify the defendant had contact with the victim."

"Yes."

"That could be conclusive, so far as a jury is concerned. It's scientific proof of guilt."

"Absolutely. It would be devastating to the defense. The FBI is also saying they can provide the same testimony with fiber evidence, shoe prints and bite marks. They will testify that they can connect a specific defendant to that type evidence.

"This sounds too good to be true. If it's not true and the appeal court reverses a conviction, we will be the ones who are devastated," said Rainey. Rainey was always the pessimist, or perhaps he was a realist.

***

Later, Sgt. Rainey and Lt. McBride sat with the three crime scene technicians who had worked the scenes at Indian Hollow Road and Paynes Prairie, looking at the clues and the evidence.

"We have blood?" asked McBride.

"Yes, it's all type A, which is the same blood type as Becky's. We found it in the right of way on blades of grass and in the dirt. The samples have some contamination from the elements and the environment."

"Do we have prints?"

"No fingerprints but we have shoe prints and some tire track evidence."

"What is their quality?"

"We have one really good heel print of the left foot of a boot, most likely. It's a man's cowboy boot, most likely."

"We have no other shoe print from any other scene of an abduction or burial site from another crime?"

"That is correct," said the technician. "This is the only shoe print we have, the one found on the right of way of Indian Hollow Road."

"What about the tread marks from a vehicle?"

"They are very faint. The vehicle needs new tires. The tread is thin and the side of the road on Indian Hollow is a mixture of grass and sand. It's a poor surface to capture an impression. We tried to obtain a plaster cast of one part of the tire track but we got nothing of value to use for a comparison. Out in the prairie on Bolen Bluff Trail where Becky was found, most of the area was covered in tracks from the fire trucks and the police vehicles that came to the scene. We walked back to see if we could find a set of tracks leading into the dirt trail but we found nothing."

"We have a sample of Becky's hair. We have her clothes, correct?"

"Correct," said the technician. "We also have a blood sample from her from the hospital. There was no foreign blood found. It's all type A serum. Even if we found foreign blood, there must have been 20 people who touched Becky. Everyone wanted to touch her to see that she was alive."

"Could you see anything on her clothes from the rescue scene?"

"No foreign hair or fiber was found on her at the prairie."

"What about the sweater and the backpack?"

"We found nothing from a visual inspection but the items were packaged and will go off to the FBI in Washington for them to examine."

"What about the rag?"

"It has an acetone smell. It's probably chloroform. We need to have a chemist test it. The rag was put in a sealed plastic container and it's on the way to the FBI with the sweater, the backpack, Becky's boots and clothes, and her hair and blood samples and photographs of the tire prints, as poor as they seem to be. Also, the boot prints, I have hope we will get more from the FBI. They should be productive."

"Good work, fellas," said McBride to the members of the forensic unit.

This was the first time the police had something more than desiccated flesh and bones to collect at the scene of a shallow grave. Maybe we will have some luck this time, thought Rainey.

***

Person entered the XYZ Lounge with no fanfare. It had been a week since he had been in.

The bartender noticed Person looked different, but he couldn't put his finger on what it was.

Person went to the video games. Missile Commander was his favorite and he didn't have to wait for a machine. It was Tuesday. A small crowd was at the bar watching baseball from Atlanta ... Hank Aaron.

Person bent over the video game and played four quarters worth – an hour and a half went by. A woman approached. He thought she had been his date sometime in the past. But they all looked the same.

"How ya' doin'?"

"You know, same old crap." His missile missed the mark and the game was over.

Person turned and smiled. He looked in her eyes. He might as well see if the lady would be his date for the night. He doubted if she would hang around until the early morning hours. Person thought he might as well make a move. Person couldn't fall asleep until the am hours and he didn't want to be chasing tail too early in the evening and then lie in bed in the dark waiting for 3:00 am. But maybe this could be a two-fer. They could screw and then they could have a meal and screw again.

"How's it with you?"

"Lost my job. I'm a little down," said the woman.

"Buy you a drink?"

"That would be nice of you." She added, "I'm broke, too."

Then I will have my way with you, me hearty, thought Person. He went and got her a drink. Some woman's thing. It was either a grasshopper or a stinger.

The bartender cursed under his breath just loud enough for Person to hear when he got the order. "I hate those drinks with crème de mint. I have to clean everything twice. It's so damn sticky."

"Yea, I know," said Person. "Chicks, what are you going to do?"

Person returned to the game. He handed the woman the drink, setting the cocktail glass on a napkin.

"I had to fight with the bartender to get him to make this," said Person.

"I'm worth it," said the woman. She reached over and grabbed his crotch and began to pat his cock-a-doodle-doo.

The barkeep had been watching. He slapped the bar top with the flat of his hand and said, "Take it outside."

The bartender stared at the pair. "The sign on the door says 'no soliciting', little lady."

Person and the woman got up. The woman downed her glass with one swallow. It stung. She straightened her dress and went out the side door to the parking lot.

***

"All I have is my work truck," said Person.

"Ok by me," said the woman as they walked to the little red truck.

Person slid in the bench seat behind the steering wheel. He still had his mug of beer. The woman slid next to him. The stick shift was between them.

"What would you pay me if I did anything that you wanted?"

"What do you have in mind?"

"I will do anything you want. But it will cost you."

"You mean money? I don't normally pay."

"But if I would do anything you wanted? Would you pay?"

Person looked at her. He was thinking.

"Just whisper in my ear," she said. "Anything you desire."

Person bent over and whispered in the woman's ear.

"Youuu," she said as she twisted up her lips. "You are a bad boy. What would you pay me to do that?"

"Fifty dollars," he said out loud.

Immediately after Person said the words "fifty dollars" the door opened on the passenger side and the woman exited the vehicle.

A man reached in the open driver's window and stuck his shield in Person's face.

"You are under arrest for soliciting an act of prostitution."

Person stared at the police badge. The detective continued, "You have the right to remain silent. You have the right to consult with a lawyer ..."

Person looked straight ahead. He did not say anything. There were three vehicles that had pulled up with their headlights facing the little red truck illuminating the parking lot. A crowd from the bar gathered. They were quiet. Person was removed from the vehicle. He did not resist. He looked at the group of patrons.

Person noticed a male friend and yelled, "Call my Aunt."

The friend nodded and walked back into the bar to use the pay phone.

One of the officers closed the doors to the truck and took the keys from the ignition.

Another officer had Person follow him to the front of the truck. Person still had the mug of beer in his hand. Person put the beer on the hood of his truck. The officer then had Person empty his pockets on the hood of the truck. Change, a few bills (maybe a five and three ones), and a wallet. That was it.

One officer advised that he was going to conduct a field sobriety test.

"I wasn't driving," said Person.

"Sir, you were in physical control of the vehicle. You were seated in the driver's seat and the keys were in the ignition. You had a mug of beer in your hand." The officer looked at Person and asked, "Have you been drinking, sir?"

"This is ridiculous." Person mumbled. "We just came out of the bar."

"Sir, drinking alcohol and driving are a very bad mix." The officer then explained the sobriety tests he wanted Person to perform. The officer told Person that he would explain and show him what he was to do.

"Do you understand?" the uniformed officer inquired.

"Yes," said Person.

The officer had Person recite the alphabet. Then Person performed the finger to nose test and he was required to walk a white stripe in the parking lot ... heel to toe.

"You performed those tests very well, sir," said the officer. "In my opinion you are not intoxicated."

"Am I still under arrest?"

"Yes sir. You are under arrest for soliciting prostitution. That is the only charge so far."

"What do you mean when you say, 'so far'? What does that mean?" asked Person.

"Do you have any contraband in your vehicle?" asked the officer.

"Contraband? Not to my knowledge."

"Is this your vehicle?" asked the officer.

"Yes, well, it's a company truck."

"If there is contraband in your truck, and the truck is in your control, then the contraband is in your possession, sir. That is the law."

"What do you mean by 'contraband'?"

"Weapons or drugs or pornography."

"No, to my knowledge there are no guns or drugs or anything illegal in the truck."

"Or weapons of any kind?"

"No, there are none."

"Is there anyone who can take the truck to your home?"

"No."

"Then it will be towed to impound" said the officer.

"Whatever," said Person.

Person was bent over the hood of the police car and the officer slid his hands over the outside of his clothes. No weapons were found.

"Is your full name really Mark Luke John Person?" asked the officer.

"Yes, that is my name."

Chapter 9
McBride and the Task Force

Since the task force was first created, Lt. McBride had convinced the sheriff that they would need extra help on the phones when there was a kidnapping. Solid citizens would want to express their concerns and offer advice and provide information that could be useful. The two man team could not answer all the calls. The sheriff contracted with an answering service to take calls related to an abduction, any tip, and pass the substance of the communication on to McBride or Rainey for follow-up.

After Becky was taken and the sheriff held his news conference, there were hundreds of calls where tipsters offered up the hated white male neighbor who owned a red truck to the police action line. The phone lines were crazy. Most of the notes scribbled by the operators, just said "red truck" and a phone number and nothing more.

Rainey had the duty to do the initial review of the notes from the operators. He put the notes that said nothing more than "red truck" in a pile and went to the other notes that named an individual as a possible suspect. A few of the notes were of interest. The most intriguing was one that identified the address of an unnamed individual who was seen washing his red truck inside and out on the afternoon of the day of the incident. The activity was suspicious to the caller because the truck was a common work truck for a carpet cleaning service. The truck was not a show car that would warrant special attention.

With all the clues from all the calls, it took a few days for Rainey to get to the note about the fastidious truck owner from the carpet cleaning service. When he called the number, the number was to a pay phone, but Rainey was so intrigued by the message that he looked in the yellow pages under "Carpet Cleaners" and found an ad for a company that touted their "Hot Service" in their little red Ford Ranger pickup trucks.

Rainey called and inquired of the manager whether one of the company trucks had been in an accident or had anything unusual occur to it. The manager said nothing except one truck got stuck in the mud. There was no damage, however. The manager identified the driver of the vehicle as Mark Person. He had worked for the company for seven years and he was a good employee with no complaints.

"Is there a problem officer?"

"No, just checking. When did the truck get stuck?"

"I remember the date because it was the day that little girl was kidnapped."

"Do you have an address for Mr. Person?"

"Sure," said the manager. "Let me get it for you."

***

Later that day Person's boss told Person about the call. Person had expected something like this was possible. He had dumped the girl too close to home. He had heard the sheriff's press conference. They were looking for a red truck. The girl was at Shands Hospital. That was the first time that information had been broadcast. They had a live victim-- a witness maybe. They knew where the kidnapping occurred. They probably had the sweater and the backpack and the boots. There was tangible evidence, he thought. He needed to clean up his mess the best he could.

After he was told by his boss that the sheriff had called, Person re-cleaned the truck. He used the carpet cleaning equipment on the truck to give a thorough cleaning of the bed of the truck, particularly the cavity where the hose was stored. He wiped down all smooth surfaces inside and out with a rag to eliminate any finger or foot prints. He cleaned the inside and outside of the tarp cover and cleaned the tarp and the bed of the truck and the exterior with Clorox bleach a second time. He flushed the contents of the tank containing the residue of the cleaning solution pumped out of the customers' homes with the vacuum hose down the toilet in his apartment. He was amazed how much hair was in the container. No telling whose hair it was, he thought.

He had to do something with the tires on the truck and he considered the problem. He could try to get his boss to change out the tires because they were worn and dangerous. Or he could change the tires himself, or he could distress the tires, cut them in some way to change the wear pattern and wear marks on the surface of the tires. He decided to do nothing after he looked closely at the tread. The tires were worn well down below the wear bars. There was very little tread. He decided to just drive the truck hard and hope the tread would wear down quickly or that his boss would change the tires of his own accord.

His boots, though, and his clothes, had to go. His clothes were at the uniform company. They would be cleaned and pressed and back to him in a week. He had to toss the boots. He hated to do it. He had worn those boots for years. The boots went to the Goodwill box. He had a pair of work shoes. They were black. He hardly wore them. They would have to do. He wore the black work shoes everywhere after that though they made him look shorter and Person felt self-conscious. He had lost a full inch in height switching to the black work shoes.

That left the souvenirs. He had to dispose of them. Up in smoke was the only solution. He could not take the chance they would be found in the back of the bottom drawer of the bureau in his room in the garage apartment. He waited until the afternoon when the neighbors were at work. He went to the front yard and raked the pile of leaves his aunt wanted him to collect and he put the pile of debris in the back of the house where they had a fire pit and he burned the panties with the leaves. He felt he could do nothing more.

Lucky for him, Person had acted promptly. He concealed and or destroyed the evidence the day before the police from Summer County began surveillance of his apartment after receiving the tip on the hot line. Person felt he was being followed and he kept everything low-key. He limited his travel to work and back home. He even stayed out of the XYZ Lounge.

***

In addition to the 24 hour tail, Rainey began asking questions about Person. The more he learned about Person's life at home and his term in the youthful offender facility and his aggressive behavior while in prison, the more he became intrigued. Rainey noticed that once the police put a tail on Person, it seemed like he was keeping a lid on his activities. Person went home and to work and that was it. The police felt he was too clean. He didn't even violate traffic laws.

Person felt he was being followed. He spoke to his aunt. He told her that he had been stopped by the police on Indian Hollow Road the day the girl was kidnapped. He told her he thought he was being targeted by the police. The aunt said she would set an appointment with an attorney.

"Just any attorney won't help." said Person.

"It will be different if we hire a good attorney this time. He will work for you." said the aunt.

"Whatever," said Person. "I think they are all the same."

***

Person's aunt called her Union representative from back at work up in Connecticut and got a recommendation for an aggressive attorney who would stand up for Person's rights. The Union representative called and set an appointment with James DeMarco on a date four days after Becky was abducted.

There was confusion when they first met. Jim DeMarco was not aware Mark Person was the client. The Union representative said the aunt would be responsible for the fee and DeMarco assumed she was the client. Once DeMarco understood Person was the client he excused the Aunt from the room and talked alone with Mark Person while the Aunt waited in the reception room.

Person and DeMarco had a long conversation. Person felt DeMarco was peeling his life apart like peeling the layers of skin off an onion.

Mark Person stated he felt he was being targeted by the police. He was being followed by an unmarked vehicle. They even followed today from my house to the law office, he said. DeMarco listened and took notes. Person felt the police were acting in an obvious, blatant way hoping he would do something that would allow an arrest so they could get him in the police station and interrogate him.

Person lied when he told DeMarco that he didn't know what he could have done that caused this attention. He admitted he had been in trouble when he was 17 years old and he was incarcerated in a Youthful Offender Program. He had not had any trouble with the law since he was a kid. He worked for the same company for the last seven years. That employment caused him to drive a red truck.

"Do you think that the red truck could be causing all this concern?" asked Person. "I have been stopped by the police three or four times in the truck."

"Could be," said Jim.

"What should I do about the surveillance?"

"Nothing, you can't stop the police from driving a car on a public road."

"What happens if they arrest me?"

"Why would they arrest you?"

"For kidnapping that girl the other day."

"You think?"

"Yes, I do."

"If you are arrested, go peaceably, be courteous. If they tell you your rights, tell them you want to speak to a lawyer. Call our office. We can be reached 24/7. We will come to the station and represent you."

"What will this cost?"

"It depends on what you are charged with. If you are right and the police are looking at you for the kidnapping of Becky Sue Painter, your aunt will need to deposit a $100,000 retainer in our Trust Account. That would just be the first installment. The total cost will probably be double that amount and could be more."

"That much huh? What about today. How much will this be?"

"Two hundred and fifty dollars for the conference today. Pay the receptionist. She will give you a receipt."

"Thanks."

Person and his aunt left the office. They got back in the red carpet cleaning truck and drove back toward Archer, Florida to their home. They were followed the entire way at a respectful distance by the unmarked police car.

"How much will it cost if they arrest you?" asked the aunt.

"Probably $200,000 if I'm just charged with the abduction of the girl, and it could be double that amount if they have to investigate the deaths of the other girls in Summer County."

"God."

"I know," said Person. "But DeMarco's the best. That's what everyone says."

"God." They drove in silence.

When they arrived at the house Person pulled in the driveway and dropped off his aunt. A large sedan pulled up in the street just off the aunt's property. They both stared at the 1973 Plymouth Road Runner that had followed them from St. Petersburg. The man driving the Plymouth stared back. The police wanted Person to know he was being followed.

"I'm going to the bar. I can't stand this anymore," said Person.

"I have the money. I have the full $400,000. It's just ... that's all I have" said the aunt. "That is my retirement money."

"Whatever, I'm innocent. You can help me or not. I think I'm cursed." Person began to tear up.

"I'll help you," said the aunt.

***

Jim DeMarco went in to see Tom Night as soon as he completed the consultation with Mark Person.

The only comment Tom had was, "Don't get us involved in this case unless you are sure we are going to be paid. We can't afford to be stuck with this case and not be paid."

***

Rainey took the radio transmission from the officer in the Plymouth. He described their day so far: The detective had followed Person to work at the warehouse. He loaded some supplies in the back of the truck and then drove to Hudson Beach on the Gulf Coast just north of Port Richey. He cleaned carpets at two locations and then was on the road to Brooksville, on US 41/301 and State Road 50. It was a long drive on roads through pine timber plantation and swamp. Person serviced a third account and then he was back in Archer at his house.

Next, the undercover detective in the Plymouth reported he watched Person's aunt enter the vehicle and then Person drove the truck on the Interstate until he got to Tampa, and then he took a left on US 92 and crossed the Gandy Bridge to 4th Street. The little red truck headed south to Central Avenue and then to downtown and Beach Drive in St. Petersburg. The detective watched as Person and the aunt went into the law offices of Night, Adams and Street.

The detective called in to report to Rainey.

Rainey listened to the report and shook his head up and down. "Great," said Rainey.

There were three detectives casing the movements of three different suspects who could have kidnapped Becky Sue Painter. Two of the suspects were in Pasco County and they were much less mobile than Person. The two Pasco County suspects had long records for lewd conduct involving children. Both were out of jail and both were staying in shelters for recently released prisoners. It was easy to track those men. Rainey was not that worried about the men who were in semi-custody. Rainey put his money on Person.

He's the one, he thought.

Two days before, Rainey had spoken to Person's boss. The manager thought he knew his men. To the boss, Person was a loser. He had no ambition. He was a barfly. He was at the XYZ every night, always chasing women. The women called work sometimes, said the boss. The women were skaggy, unwholesome. The manager was sure Person was an abuser of drugs and alcohol. He smoked dope mostly, he thought. He had seen the signs and smells. The boss had been in Viet Nam. Some of his men fighting in Khe Sahn smoked dope and shot up heroin to block out the constant tension of battle and the shelling. The boss admitted he smoked dope in Viet Nam. He knew a doper when he saw one, but he never saw drugs on Person. But he could smell it in the truck. One thing about Person, he loved that red truck. He washed it inside and out, like it was his baby. He had some blood in the fabric of the seat. He cut himself – said he fell down. Pretty bad, the wound was seeping blood. Person used the cleaning machine on the truck to clean the seat and then said what the hell and he cleaned the interior, the entire inside, of his boss's truck. Person said why not? He would do something like that. Sometimes he was friendly. But he had a mouth ... F this and F that ... but he did not curse, not around the customers. The boss never had a bad report in seven years. It's just that he was aimless.

To summarize, said the boss, "He's a loser. Do you know that cartoon character in 'Lil' Abner' that walks around with a dark cloud over his head? His name is Joe Blizflick or something. It's like Person thinks he's doomed," concluded the manager.

After listening to Person's boss a couple of days back Rainey called his contact in the Alachua County Sheriff's Department. Rainey would have to work through that office if he needed to conduct an investigation in Alachua County. Unless Rainey was in hot pursuit of a fleeing felon, he couldn't make an arrest in Alachua County.

Alachua County was conducting their own investigation of the Becky Sue Painter kidnapping because she had been found in Paynes Prairie which was mostly located in Alachua County.

Det. Peter Georges was quiet, thoughtful and wanted to help. He was with the "crimes against persons" squad in Alachua. He had no knowledge of Mark Luke John Person prior to the inquiry he received from Sgt. Rainey. Person was clean. His residence had not been the subject of any calls for assistance.

Rainey wanted to talk to Person badly, if only to test his mettle. Rainey wanted to see if his gut was right about Person.

"How do I do that?" Rainey asked Georges. "How can we talk to Person?"

"We run a sting for johns here in Alachua County. We might want to see if Det. Moran can elicit probable cause for an arrest of Mr. Person for soliciting prostitution."

"How would you do that, exactly?"

Georges explained that the Alachua Sheriff felt there was a problem with men soliciting women to commit sexual acts for money and they had recruited Det. Bessy Moran to act as a prostitute and wear a wire and go into bars and see if she was solicited for a sex act for money. She had been quite successful. Every Saturday the Gainesville Alligator, a rag of a paper, published the picture of every person arrested during the last week. Ten to twenty percent of the people arrested were prospective clients of Bessy Moran. They had been arrested for soliciting her for an act of prostitution.

"We could set up the sting in the XYZ Lounge. They haven't been a target of the operation yet. She can try to tempt Mr. Person if we know when he's going to be in the bar."

That was the plan devised to put Person in the hands of the police. The police would tempt Person with a sex sting. If he bit, Person would be arrested.

That night after Person and his aunt returned from visiting Attorney DeMarco in St. Petersburg, the detective who had followed them in the Plymouth reported that Person got in his little red truck and had driven into Archer and he was in the XYZ Lounge. Rainey called Georges. The sting was in operation that night at the XYZ Lounge. Georges had a photograph of Person which he gave to Det. Moran. There were three other members of the sting team who acted as back up and they would make the arrest. If Person was arrested he would be taken to the courthouse in downtown Gainesville for questioning.

Rainey got in his car and headed for the XYZ in Gainesville. Happy hunting he hoped.

Chapter 10
Person's First Appearance

Jim DeMarco thought little of the conference he had with Mark Person. He was just another paranoid individual worried about the police following him. But, he thought, maybe he was being followed by the police and maybe he was a suspect in the Becky Sue Painter case. He mentioned the interview to Tom Night.

The fact they might represent Person gave Tom more worry. DeMarco had a propensity to take a case without establishing the fee. Tom mentioned that fact to DeMarco. DeMarco assured Tom the fee contract would be in order.

DeMarco also told his girlfriend Jenny Barnes about the case. She said she hoped the case came to them.

"Watch what you wish for," cautioned Tom.

That night Jim and Jenny shared a bottle of red wine from California, R. Mondavi. They went to bed. Sweet dreams until 3 a.m. when the phone service called to report a message from the aunt. Mark Person had been arrested.

Jim called the aunt. She wanted DeMarco to represent her nephew. She said she could give him the retainer in the morning once she could talk to her broker. The money would be wired from her money market fund. Jim told her to contact Karen in the office for routing information. "I will head to Gainesville now."

The pair did not mention the amount of the retainer.

Jim got dressed. Jenny stayed in bed. She would cover Jim's hearing in the morning. Jim called the Alachua County Sheriff and left a message that he was Mark Luke John Person's attorney and that he was on the way to Gainesville and that his client was not to be interrogated unless he was present.

The desk sergeant took the note of DeMarco's call and gave the note to Det. Georges. The note was taken at 3:10 a.m. Georges and Rainey had been interviewing Person for six hours by that time. They would have to stop now or at least tell Person that DeMarco was on the way and see if he wanted to wait for him to get to Gainesville. Or should they just continue to talk? They would continue to talk to Mr. Person, they decided. When the detectives first started to interview Mark Person, Person had signed a written waiver of right to an attorney during questioning. The police would continue to question him, but tell Person his attorney had called and was on the way. If Person wanted to discontinue the interview the police would terminate the questioning. But the police would leave it up to Person.

***

When DeMarco arrived at the Sheriff's department it was 6 am. The office was built just behind the old red brick courthouse. Jim entered the new four story building; he went to the reception desk, and told the sergeant he wanted to speak to his client.

Jim was told to have a seat. He waited an hour and then asked for his client again. The Sergeant checked again and told Jim they would have him available shortly.

Then Jim asked when first appearance hearings would begin?

"Should be now," said the sergeant.

"Where?"

"In the courthouse. You have to enter through the door here. You will be searched."

Jim was patted down even though he was an attorney. The guards in Gainesville didn't know him from Adam. Jim rarely practiced law in Alachua County.

There were no private attorneys or family in the courtroom. There was a bailiff and clerk in the small courtroom. Jim spoke to the bailiff. He said he was there on behalf of Mark Person. The bailiff wrote down Jim's name on the sign-up sheet and Jim gave the clerk a business card.

The court reporter entered the room a few minutes before 7 a.m. She was an older woman. She entered through the judges' entry and the judge followed. He was an older man. He was in a long sleeve white shirt. He had no robe or suit coat or tie.

The judge saw Jim in his suit and asked him to introduce himself for the record.

"Jim DeMarco, of Night, Adams and Street, from St. Petersburg. I'm here on behalf of Mark Person."

"We're a little casual here. I'll try to get to you soon," said the judge and he asked the bailiff to bring in the prisoners.

Jim looked carefully at the men all cuffed together but didn't see his client. The judge called for Mr. Person to step before the bench. The bailiff whispered to the judge that Person wasn't there yet.

"He'll be over shortly, Mr. DeMarco. You'll have to sit with us awhile," said the judge.

The judge began to call the names of the prisoners and explained the charge for which they had been arrested and talked to them about bail and whether they had counsel. If the charge was a misdemeanor or one for public intoxication, the judge resolved the case with a day or two in jail or a small fine.

This took about an hour. The judge inquired about Mr. Person again. While they waited there was time for small talk.

"I know Tom Night, your partner," said the judge.

"He's been around awhile," said Jim. "Everyone seems to know him."

The bailiff came back and announced that Mr. Person was not going to be brought over.

The judge asked the bailiff to find out why.

"What is Mr. Person's status? Tell the State Attorney to send someone over here so I can find out what's going on." The judge turned back to Jim and said, "We are having budgetary problems here in Alachua County. The State Attorney (SA) does not provide an assistant to handle first appearance hearings unless there is some problem."

"Do you want that on the record, judge?" asked the court reporter.

"Yes, of course," said the judge. "I made the statement in the courtroom."

The Assistant SA entered the courtroom and the judge explained the problem.

The Assistant SA got on the phone and spoke to his office and listened and then hung up.

"I don't know what to say, Judge. They have Mr. Person in custody but they are not ready to bring him over."

"Mr. DeMarco, what do you have to say?" asked the judge.

"Mr. Person is my client. I called the sheriff's office and spoke to the desk sergeant at 3 a.m. after being informed by my answering service that he was in custody. I told the desk sergeant that I was representing him and the police were not to question him until I got here. I arrived at 6 a.m. after driving directly from my home in St. Petersburg. I was told to wait to see my client. At 7 a.m. I came here figuring he would be brought before you for First Appearance Hearing."

"Was your client arrested?"

"That was the message. My service said he was arrested and apparently he's with the police now, so I assume there has been an arrest."

The judge looked at his list of new prisoners that had been provided by the jail. Listed was "Mark Luke John Person" who was charged with "Soliciting for Prostitution".

The judge showed the jail list to the Assistant SA and the SA got back on the phone and said loudly enough for everyone to hear, "Mr. Person is to be brought over. The judge wants to see him."

***

Mr. Person was brought into the courtroom with his hands shackled and he was in leg irons.

There were two uniformed deputies with Mark Person and two detectives followed. The detectives were dressed in white shirts, slacks and ties. They had ID attached to their belts. The uniformed officers were armed.

Jim went over to his client and Person looked at him and greeted him with a smile.

"Can I have a minute, judge?" asked Jim.

"Of course," but you will need to stay in the courtroom. Sit over there at the table in the corner," said the judge. "Do we have paperwork for the prisoner?"

Jim and Person spoke for a short while. Jim then asked the court if the charges could be read.

"The paperwork says he was arrested for solicitation for prostitution."

"Am I correct that the charge is a misdemeanor here in Alachua County?" asked Jim.

"Is that correct?" the judge asked, looking at the SA. "This isn't some new charge."

"It's a misdemeanor," replied the SA.

"Why is there no bond on a misdemeanor?" asked the judge.

"I don't know," said the SA.

"That can't be right," said the judge. "Is this a sting operation with Det. Bess Moran?"

"Appears to be," said the SA.

"Was there an attempt to escape?"

The SA spoke to one of the detectives. "No, there was no escape attempt."

"Unless you can explain why the man is in shackles and irons, the restraints are to be removed," said the judge.

One of the detectives leaned over and spoke to the SA.

"The man is a suspect in the kidnapping of Becky Sue Painter," said the SA.

There was a titter in the courtroom. Everyone recognized the name Becky Sue Painter.

"Mr. DeMarco, response?" asked the judge.

"The restraints should be removed and the court should set a reasonable bond on the soliciting charge. If bail is posted, my client should be released. Being a suspect is not a charge," said DeMarco.

"Agreed," said the judge. "Take the man out of restraints and if he posts a $500 bond he's to be freed unless he's charged with kidnapping, and then he is to be brought back before me. If he's charged with kidnapping the bail will be considerably higher."

***

At 11 a.m. DeMarco met with Mark Person at the sergeant's desk. His aunt posted a cash bond, $500.

There was a crowd outside the reception area at the jail. There was a commotion with people shoving one another to get a good look at the person who kidnapped Becky Sue Painter and killed the five girls. The area just outside the door to the reception room was restricted, but you could see there were cameramen and reporters with note pads; they were loaded for bear.

"Are you sure you want to go out the door?" asked the sergeant.

"It might be safer in here," said DeMarco. "But we will brave the press."

The pair went outside and they were crushed against the door.

The sergeant had mercy on them and re-opened the door. He asked Jim where he had his car. Jim gave him the keys and the sergeant left and then was back in five minutes.

"Follow me."

Person and DeMarco were taken to a tunnel that led under the street next to the jail. DeMarco's car had been parked at the entrance to the tunnel across the street and on the opposite side of the sheriff's office from the entrance where the press and the locals had gathered.

DeMarco drove from the jail to Person's garage apartment in Archer, in Alachua County, but as they approached the apartment in the car they could see a mob in the street.

DeMarco turned his car around and pointed the car toward St. Petersburg.

***

DeMarco got on the Interstate and headed south after passing several university buildings. It seemed there was always new construction in Gainesville, even in a recession. University of Florida's Blue Key Society produced most of the state's politicians and as a result UF was the best funded university in the State. As Jim turned his car onto the interstate he noticed a 1973 Plymouth Road Runner behind them. The car looked like an unmarked police car. Jim mentioned the car to Person.

"Yeah, that car has been following me for three or four days. That was the car I told you about when we met. It followed me and my aunt all the way to St. Pete and back when I saw you at your office."

"So, where is your truck?" asked Jim.

"It was impounded by the police when they arrested me."

"Do you have any ownership interest in the truck?"

"No, the truck belongs to work."

"When we get to my office you can call work and tell your boss where the truck is located."

***

Both men were silent for the first 10 miles.

"So, we have three hours before we get to my office. Do you want to talk about the case?" said DeMarco.

"Can they hear us talk? The car that's following us, I mean. Can the deputy in that car hear us?"

"What are you saying?"

"Do you think the desk sergeant put a bug in your car when he moved it?" Person was deadly serious. He was convinced the deputies who arrested him had put a listening device in DeMarco's car.

"I can turn on the radio if you want," said DeMarco. "We can listen to a good old country station." And he turned the nob and searched for a station. It didn't take long to find some rock-a-billy.

"So, tell me about the arrest."

Person leaned over to Jim's ear and spoke directly but quietly: "After my aunt and I went to your office and I dropped her off at home I went to the XYZ Lounge. I had a couple of beers and played the video machine for a couple of hours and a lady comes in and comes on to me. She says she was just fired and she was broke and I felt sorry for her and I bought her a drink. She grabbed my crotch and said she could make me happy and we went to my truck. She starts asking for money and she's rubbing my leg. I told her I didn't pay for sex. Then she asks me what I would pay if she would do anything I wanted. What did I want? And I whispered in her ear and she asked how much I would pay if she let me do that and I said $50, and that's when the police came to the car and told me to get out of the car and I was under arrest."

"What did you whisper in her ear?" asked Jim.

"I asked her for anal sex."

"Is that what you said, that you wanted anal sex?"

"No."

"What were your exact words?"

"I said she should 'give up her poop chute'."

"Where did you hear the term 'poop chute'? Was it in prison?" asked DeMarco.

"Yes," said Person.

"Are you homosexual?"

"I guess I am bisexual. Being in prison at 17, I was broke in by men. I still see men sometimes for sex, but not that much."

"Do you have trouble finding a female partner?"

"No," Person laughed. "Not hardly. Women love me. And if there are no women, I've got men, and I always have myself to make me satisfied. Prison taught me well, sexually. The government will make criminals of us all."

"What do you mean?" asked DeMarco.

"It's like the IRS. My aunt's husband says the IRS makes thieves of us all – liars, I guess he means – we all cheat the government on our taxes. The government makes you a criminal. As far as me, the state putting me in prison didn't give me many choices, sexually. I didn't grow up like normal people."

"Do you think you are different?"

"Sure, look what they say I did."

"You mean the kid thing?"

"Yeah."

"Is that you?"

"I don't want to talk about it."

"Ok, when you are comfortable."

DeMarco turned off the radio and they drove to St. Petersburg in silence followed closely by the 1973 Plymouth Road Runner. The deputy driving the unmarked car made sure his presence was obvious.

Chapter 11
The Conference

As DeMarco rolled into his parking place behind the offices of Night, Adams, and Street, his car was attacked by reporters. He told Person to stay in the car and DeMarco exited the vehicle and confronted the Press. "Why are you trespassing on my property?"

"Are you representing Mr. Person for the deaths of the girls in Summer County?" the reporters asked.

"Mr. Person has not been charged with homicide. You need to leave. I have to be able to enter my office with Mr. Person," said DeMarco. "You don't think we intend to discuss this matter in the driveway?"

"Can we talk to Mr. Person?"

"He has nothing to say at this time," said DeMarco.

"Did he kill all those girls?"

"Are you kidding? This is ridiculous. I have no comment," said DeMarco. "You need to leave the law firm's property. You are trespassing. I have given you fair warning. You will be arrested."

The reporters gave DeMarco enough space to walk around the car to the passenger door and he motioned the crowd back. He noticed there were others besides the press who were clambering about. DeMarco didn't recognize the people. It would be very bad if some angry parent of a deceased child started shooting at Mr. Person, thought DeMarco.

DeMarco grabbed Person's arm and the two of them shoved through the crowd to the side door of the office. Jenny Barnes had seen the mess of people outside and she anticipated DeMarco would head for the side door. As the pair got to the door, Jenny opened the side entrance and DeMarco pushed Person inside and then stood outside giving Jenny time to lock the door. DeMarco then walked to the front of the building ignoring questions that were shouted at him as he went through the parking lot and into the front door.

Jenny took Person to Jim DeMarco's office and sat him down in a chair with a cup of coffee.

Person took a sip. "It's good."

***

The crowd continued to swell outside even after Jim was inside. What DeMarco hoped for was the security and the safety of the building. All the entrance and exit doors had been locked. Tom Night called the police to report a disturbance. The police arrived and pushed the press out to public property (the sidewalk) and, using a bull horn, advised that arrests would be made of anyone who entered upon private property or anyone who blocked the public ways.

The crowd dispersed finally with a little coaxing.

Karen had hired security guards and they arrived and the police left.

"I've never seen anything like this," said Tom.

DeMarco wanted Tom to come in his office and speak with Person. DeMarco went ahead.

"I'll be right there." Tom turned to Karen and asked if the bank had received the wire of the $100,000 retainer from Person's aunt.

"We received a wire for $400,000. It's more than we asked for."

"Put the money in the trust account. We will sort it out." Tom began to walk to Jim's office, then had a second thought and followed Karen back to her office.

"Karen, we need to make sure that Mr. Person signs the standard fee agreement. Everyone in the office who works on the Person case has to keep full and complete time records in this case. It will be a headache, but it will be necessary." Karen said she understood.

***

There weren't enough empty chairs in Jim's office for Tom and Jim and Person. Jim's office had numerous chairs but each one was piled with case files and law books and file folders. So they moved to the library and sat across an oval table. The top of the table was made from a single slab of mahogany that Tom had purchased in Belize.

Person rubbed the table top and he looked across at the two men. Tom was 63 and Jim was 34. Person felt that they offered his best hope against the charges he would be facing.

"Why did they release me?" asked Person as he looked at Tom.

"They may not have enough evidence at present. They could be waiting for the opinion of experts, the FBI perhaps," said Tom. "Or they want to see what you do. If you run, the fact that you run could be used in your trial as evidence of your guilt."

"Did you speak to the detectives last night?" asked Jim.

"Yes, they had two or three detectives talking to me all night after I got to jail in Gainesville."

"Did the police ever tell you that you were under arrest?

"Just once, when I was in the red truck, with the undercover policewoman at the XYZ's parking lot. The officer said I was under arrest for soliciting for prostitution."

"Did they tell you you're Miranda rights – that you had the right to remain silent and the right to an attorney?"

"Yes," said Person. "They told me my rights when I was first arrested when I was in the red truck."

"Did you speak to the police after that?"

"Yes, the officer said he wanted me to take a test to see if I was drunk. The officer spoke to me and I answered his questions. They said I was not intoxicated. After that they took me to jail and they kept talking to me and I answered their questions."

"Did you ask to call me?" asked Jim.

"Yes, I remember I asked them to call you and I gave them your business card."

"Who called you, Jim?" asked Tom.

"I thought it was the aunt," said Jim. "Did you talk to your aunt?"

"No, I never got a phone call," said Person. "But when I was being arrested I yelled to a friend at the XYZ to call my aunt. My friend must have called her."

"What did you and the police talk about?"

"My life," said Person. "They started from when I was born and just kept asking questions."

"Were you truthful?"

"Yes, mostly."

"What do you mean?"

"When the detectives started to ask me about any crime other than the soliciting prostitution charge and that arrest I refused to answer."

"What do you mean?"

"They asked if I kidnapped Becky Sue Painter and I asked them if I was under arrest for that crime. When they said, 'not at this time,' I said I will talk to you if you arrest me for that crime but otherwise I will not talk to you."

"How long did the questioning go on?"

"From about 9 pm 'til 8 a.m. the next morning when they had to take me to court."

"Was there a recording made of your conversation with the police?"

"I think so. There was a court reporter taking notes on a machine. I asked if I could get a copy of her notes. They said they were investigative notes and I would have to get a court order. I said I would ask you to do that."

"Did the court reporter put you under oath – ask you to swear to tell the truth?'

"No. Why would they ask a suspect to tell the truth?"

"Why do you ask?"

"Wouldn't they expect a suspect to lie?"

"I get your drift," said Tom, smiling. "Did they ever re-state the Miranda warnings, that you had a right to a lawyer and that?"

"Yes, at about 3 a.m. they said that Mr. DeMarco called and said he was on the way. They told me my rights again. Then they asked me if I would sign a piece of paper regarding my rights. I read the paper and signed it."

"Did you feel you were being forced to talk to the police?"

"Not really," said Person. "Actually, they were very respectful. We just had a conversation. They said they didn't know me and we just talked about me, my family, where I grew up and what I thought about things."

"Like what?"

"Like my philosophy about life."

"What did you say?"

"I told them I didn't have a philosophy about life. They asked me a lot of questions that seemed to come from a test. I have taken personality tests before and the questions were like those test questions."

"Have you heard of the MMPI, the Minnesota Multiphasic Personality Inventory exam?" asked Tom.

"Yes, I took that exam before I left prison. It had a lot of questions. That's what the questions were like that they asked."

"Did you answer the test questions the police asked you truthfully?"

"Yes."

"Have you ever had an IQ exam?"

"Yes."

"Do you know what your intelligent quotient exam result was?"

"I don't, but my aunt does. She says I'm very smart."

"What other crimes besides the kidnapping of Becky Sue Painter did they ask about?"

"They named a number of other names. I asked if I was charged with those crimes. If I was under arrest. They said, 'not at this time,' and I said I wouldn't answer questions about things I wasn't arrested for."

"Did they get angry or upset with you?"

"No."

"Did they yell?"

"No."

"Can we talk about Becky Sue Painter now?" asked Jim.

"Not now." Mark Person looked around the room. "Where am I going to stay?"

"Our investigator, Mr. Faircloth, is trying to find you a place to stay as we speak," said Tom.

Person looked embarrassed and then smiled. "Thank you for taking my case."

Tom looked directly into Person's eyes. Person did not look away. Who are we talking to, thought Tom? Mark Luke John Person was not the man who Tom thought he would be.

Karen interrupted and brought in a fee agreement for Person to review and sign. Person read the agreement carefully and then signed his name Mark Luke John Person and Karen and DeMarco witnessed the signature.

Part III

Pick 'Em Up Sticks

Chapter 12
Agate/Cement

Tom Night had told Bob Barnes that he would not be able to go back to Belize for a spell. He explained that he would need to help Jim DeMarco and Bob's sister, Jenny Barnes, with the law firm's case of the century involving a possible child killer. Bob told Tom he would handle Belize.

Bob and Marla had renewed their relationship. They were back living together at Marla's house on the Plantation. Marla and Reynold's were still married.

Bob asked her if she would accompany him to Belize, to the south of the country, to the Belize Resources' lime rock operation near Big Creek. Marla was unable to go. James Reynolds needed her. She had a duty as a corporate wife in NYC.

The trip to Big Creek was awful. You had to fly into the International Airport at Belize City and then drive to the Capitol, Belmopan, and then drive on the Hummingbird Highway to Stan Creek and then south on the Southern Highway past Monkey River Town to Big Creek.

Belize Resources had purchased the port at Big Creek from the Atlas Corporation. Atlas had closed down operations and was now a "corporation non grata" in the country. The government had changed political parties again, all be it peaceably, via an election, and Atlas was out and Belize Resources and the Barnes' Family was all in so far as the port was concerned.

Bob and his brother, Albert, had engineered and constructed the largest lime rock pit in the Americas at the port. The company had constructed the pit a few hundred yards from the port and dug the mine directly to the west (inland). First they had cleared the overburden and then, using dynamite to fracture the agate type rock, the material was removed with huge power shovels and transferred by conveyor belts to a series of crushers at the port which reduced the size of the rocks to about the size of a grape. Then the processed rock (called agate) was loaded directly into the hull of a ship. From there the ships transported the lime rock agate to cement factories in Mexico and the United States on the Gulf Coast.

The mixture of agate and cement was then shipped to the eastern and southern US and was used to surface Interstate highways that had been originally constructed during the Eisenhower Administration and were now being re-surfaced, re-routed and rebuilt. The agate/cement was a superior product that outlasted that of all competitors and Belize Resources had difficulty keeping up with its orders. The main problem was finding workers who wanted to deal with the heat and the dust and the grind of the mine at Big Creek.

Belize Resources had almost gone bust because of difficulty maintaining lines of credit, but Marla had come through by convincing her husband that JRD Corporation should make loans to the lime rock operations for its heavy equipment, and to act as a factor and make loans against receivables and provide lines of credit for continuing operations. Frank Barnes (the father) and Bob and Marla had agreed that if Belize Resources was to succeed it had to remain a small company subsisting on road contracts in Florida, or it had to become a big corporation that other international companies depended on. They decided to try to build the company into the largest agate producer in the hemisphere.

The entire family participated in the operation. Albert Barnes had been sent to Belize to run the mine. He was sent to the site with his bag of pills to combat schizophrenia. Albert's mom, Bea, worried that he might not take his medicine, but she was assured that he was taking his medicine because it was doled out to him by a nurse at the small hospital the company built in Big Creek.

***

The Belize Government regulated the operations at the mine and the government required that a hospital be built. If there was an injury, the worker would need treatment and until the small hospital was established there was no medical care in the south of the country, not even a chiropractor. Anna Hernando, MD, operated the hospital as a satellite to her hospital in Belize City.

Tom had known Dr. Hernando for years now. Her husband Rick had been his pilot in the 1960s. Tom still flew with him when Rick carried cargo from Florida to Central America. But it was rare that their schedules were compatible. Since Tom had finally quit drinking he worried less (less paranoia) about being stuck in Central America without his own personal pilot and trans-portation to escape danger. Tom now felt he was safe to take commercial flights.

Belize International Airport was truly an international airport. Delta had flights in and out daily. Albert had a small plane that he could fly to the private airport in Belize City if a worker had to be evacuated to Dr. Hernando's hospital in the city. The main hospital in the city had an operating room and a surgeon was on call 24/7.

The Belize Government regulated the lime rock operations closely. Tom, Bob and Albert did not object because the government was even handed and did not try to run the operations. So long as they received their royalty payments for natural resources from the company on a timely basis the government did not interfere with operations.

Bob and Albert were pleased with the last change in government. As a bonus, Andrew Prince Jr., Esq., an attorney who was a partner with Tom in the Belize law firm named Night, Adams, Street, and Prince, had been elected a Member of Parliament and his political party was in control and had formed the new government. So Tom and his firm had a direct line to the government.

In the past, Tom had been thrown out of government offices. Times had changed. In fact the person with whom he had, had the most trouble, Andrew Prince Sr., Esq., the former Solicitor of Belize, was now working at Tom's Belize law firm in their office in Belmopan lobbying for the firm's clients. The water had flowed over the dam or under the bridge, or whatever. Andrew Senior was proud of his son and he was paid well and didn't have to worry where his next dollar was coming from. Tom felt he could trust Andrew Senior now. The Belize firm was run by his son, so if Senior crossed Tom he also crossed his own son.

Since Tom and Andrew Junior had become partners, the company the Senator, Frank Barnes' father, purchased, which was known as Belize Estates, had become lucrative. In addition to the lime rock operations that were owned in the Belize Corporation's name, they harvested lighter knot stumps for resin production and they cut pine saw-timber that was transported to the Mennonites at their mill in the Spanish Lookout. The pine lumber was used in most houses constructed in the country. Last, they had taken the old steam sawmill on the Belize River near the international airport and it was being converted into a condominium community.

Belize Resources was in a sweet spot. The country was growing and that aided the Barnes company.

Now it was Bea's turn to worry. Things looked too good. Their drive-through dairy business, trade name: "Homestead Creamery", was very successful. They made money "hand over fist" said Frank. "It's obscene, really. The drive-through dairy stores are a 'cash cow'," said Bob. His parents made so much money that Bob didn't feel bad when his Dad and Mom threw money at Bob and Albert's lime rock business. The lime rock business was always on the edge of profitability and, conversely, disaster. Frank believed the lime rock business would ultimately be more successful than their timber business had ever been.

But Bea knew in her heart that they were set to be knocked down a notch.

***

Marla and her husband, James M. Reynolds, the president of JRD Corporation, were in sync though they were separated. They had an open marriage. They had their own separate lives but they only met when convenient and necessary, mainly for business. And when they met, they shared. It was Reynolds who tipped Marla off that the Barnes' drive-through operation was in trouble. The company, Homestead Creamery, had slipped a bit in its credit rating. The main creditor was JRD Corporation.

"I didn't think Homestead had borrowed any money," said Marla. "Bob tells me they get buckets of money each month from the company."

"Those are dividend payments. That's the officers and the directors paying money to the shareholders to keep them happy," said Reynolds. "Frank and Bea don't know what's happening with the day to day operation of the company. The company has borrowed heavily for its operations."

"What do you hear?" asked Marla as she snuggled closer to her husband to encourage the disclosure of inside information from a man who counseled the President of the United States.

"JRD Capital was approached by the Chief Financial Officer of Homestead Creamery about the possibility of a bridge loan, and then permanent financing. The inside dope is that the franchisees who run the individual stores are not making any money and they are turning the stores back to the franchisor. The CFO said the board of directors had voted to take the business private. That means Frank and Bea's stock will shrink in value and they will probably be bought out or forced out."

Marla had invited Reynolds over for the night and they were staying in JRD's corporate residence suite in the office in the JRD Building in Manhattan. Marla fluffed up the pillows in the bed in the apartment as Reynold's removed his tie and pants and shoes.

"I don't think that the creamery itself is in danger, but it will become a rotten investment for Mr. and Mrs. Barnes. Their dividends will shrink to nothing," said Reynolds. "I would hope they have saved some money during the time the business has been fat against the lean times to come."

Marla said nothing, knowing that the entire Barnes Family had bet all of the monthly dividends to cover the cost of the improvements to the lime rock mine owned by Belize Resources. The family knew how to do nothing but take risk. Marla simply said, "I will remind them they need to be cautious."

Marla helped her husband undress and they crawled into bed. Marla turned off the lights in the apartment and she opened the curtains. The windows were glass, 12 feet from floor to ceiling. A person with a fear of heights would be startled. They were treated to a view of the canyon with all the lights in the towers in the core of Manhattan blazing. The Seagram Building was a jewel.

"Why is the Seagram Building so stunning?" asked Marla.

"It's the color of the glass. There is just something about that color."

Reynolds considered the view. "If I could have, I would have traded this building for it. If I could have, I would have, but my time at JRD is almost over. It's too late for a trade."

"You could come down to the plantation and cook jelly with me," said Marla.

"What would you do with Bob Barnes?"

"Yeah, there's Bob," said Marla. "There is always some baggage, isn't there?" Marla moved closer to her husband. They snuggled. Reynolds wasn't that bad. He will be a prize once he is retired. She could have James Reynolds all to herself.

Chapter 13
Plantation #7

Upon her arrival at home at the plantation after her recent trip to New York City, Marla was greeted with a newspaper article reporting the arrest of the President and Treasurer of the company known as "Plantation #9". The article had been sent by courier from Alphonse Alesse Esq., who was spearheading the effort to enjoin the company from using the name Plantation #9 because it was so similar to Marla's company (Plantation #7) that it caused confusion in the market place and interfered with the trade name and business of Plantation #7.

Marla and Alphonse had discovered that one of #7's former employees had stolen #7's customer list and sold the list to #9 and the police had been called. The investigation was over and the police had made an arrest.

We are well on the way to resolving that problem, thought Marla.

***

Bob Barnes was flying in from Miami on Delta. He would be in Daytona at 8 p.m. with a headache. Marla wanted to share the information she learned from her husband about the creamery when she was in NYC, but she knew she needed to take it slow and give Bob a chance to decompress after spending two weeks in near jungle conditions in Big Creek.

"Nice tan." Marla greeted him with a hug.

"The tan only goes to my neckline." He smiled and lifted her up and kissed her on the lips. She was light as a feather, he thought.

Passersby were a little shocked by the kiss on the lips. The two looked more like son and mother rather than husband and wife. Marla noticed they were noticed and she blushed deep red.

From the airport, they went to a Polynesian restaurant on Atlantic Avenue in Ormond for dinner. Marla still used the Senator's old Packard. It drove fine. They were familiar to the wait staff at the restaurant and they were seated quickly, as though they had reservations. Bob enjoyed the food, vegetables that were sticky and sweet. He had been eating tough beef and yard chickens while he was in Belize and he was tired of protein.

They had a leisurely dinner and afterward Bob drove the old vehicle down on to the beach and headed south to Daytona with the Packard's head lights on, driving in the hard packed white sand. Bob was watching for pedestrians who were walking in the sand heading to their hotel rooms or a bar. The lights of the old Packard passed over the waves that were starting to come in with the high tide. Bob drove off the beach at the Hartford Approach and then drove north on A1A to Granada, then west to John Anderson and then north to the plantation and to bed.

***

Bob and Marla slept until 11 a.m. Both were tired from their plane trips and their busy schedules while they were away. Bob woke first. He went to the shower in the master bath located in the corner of the large bedroom. He brushed his teeth while the stream of water in the shower warmed. He looked in the mirror and his face was creased from the cotton sheets after a long and fitful sleep that gave him no rest.

Bob brushed his teeth and walked into the shower. Marla had created a shower head of her own design. It was a spout that allowed the water to stream like a rivulet lazily flowing from the wall. Marla had tried to imitate water cascading from a rock in an oasis in the large bath. She had seen something similar to the shower in Morocco when she visited North Africa during her month in the South of France. The shower was relaxing. The water fell by its own weight on your body. The water was not forced out at great speed, beating your skin.

Marla gave Bob his privacy and then while he dressed in shorts and sneakers and a polo shirt she completed her constitutional.

They met in the kitchen. They ate cornflakes and agreed they needed to clear their heads with a brisk walk. They went out the back door and walked by the Senator's grave and continued east past the jelly factory. Marla popped in on the workers and saw that all the rendering vats were in operation and the line was moving filling jelly jars with jam. The smells made them salivate.

They walked through the grove of citrus and came to A1A (Atlantic Avenue). This far north the highway was only a two lane road that separated the Atlantic Ocean and the dunes from the peninsula and the Barnes' orchard. Bob didn't expect that the highway would remain only two lanes for long. US Steel Corporation had built the infrastructure for a new city on the coast to the north about 15 miles away near Flagler Beach. Thousands of homes were to be built in Palm Coast. That development would put further pressure on Plantation #7 to convert its grove land into homes and condos. Bob did not mention the thought. Marla considered the future, and was saddened by the idea.

Bob and Marla held hands and crossed the road quickly. It was dangerous as cars sped by this area where there were no buildings and no traffic lights. There was a beach access trail and a small area on the right of way where cars were parked. They were old cars, mostly rusty with surf board racks attached to the car roofs. You needed sneakers as you followed the trail through this area of scrub oak trees along the coast. The path was covered in sand spurs and apple cactus with spines like porcupine quills. The spines would infect your skin if they became imbedded. Care was needed to avoid the plants.

As they came down the dune with the thick growth of oak they could hear the surf. It was heavy and crashed on shore. There were big rolling swells moving sequentially from the sea as though pushed by a machine. As the swells met the bed of coquina rock below on the sea floor, about 200 feet off of the shore, they crested and the onshore wind stood the wave up and presented a surf rider with a smooth face on the wave to ride to the shore.

***

Bob and Marla sat in the sand. It was brown, red and gritty, unlike the white hard packed sand in Daytona Beach that you could drive a car on. The sand where the pair sat watching the surfers would stick to your skin. The sun was almost overhead but the air was still cool to warm. The ocean was cold. The surfers were dressed in black, rubberized wetsuits.

The waves were becoming sloppy and the only people left trying to catch a ride were the diehards. The waves were now simply coming to shore and crashing, closing out all at once. The waves had no face for the surfers to ride. Marla could smell the pungent odor of weed that was being lit and smoked by the boys as they discussed their morning surfing. Possession of even a small amount of marijuana was a felony but the surfers were oblivious to the potential penalty.

It was time to move on and north away from the surfers. Bob and Marla removed their sneakers and they walked north along the shore with the surf chasing up and over their feet and ankles. They caught the chill of the surf and moved higher on the beach and out of the water.

After walking about a mile they came to the first of the outcroppings of coquina rock on the shore along the coast. The first stone they saw was propped on another rock like a table. They sat there on the rough coquina and looked out to the ocean.

"So how bad is it?" asked Bob.

"Is it obvious?"

"You have been very quiet."

Marla told Bob what Reynolds had told her. Bob listened quietly as Marla slowly doled out the facts she had learned from her husband.

Marla cautioned that the information could not be shared with anyone. It was insider information. If it got back that Reynolds revealed the information he would be fired. If Bea and Frank knew the information and sold a large portion of their stock in Homestead Creamery to avoid a downturn in the value of their stock, they could be sued by the SEC and maybe even prosecuted criminally. The only way Marla thought the family might be able to use the information would be to start immediately to save as much of the stream of cash they were receiving in dividends as possible before the stream of cash was halted by the company. But that would have other consequences. That would mean his parents would no longer be making an infusion of cash to Belize Resources.

"Belize Resources owes a large chunk of money to JRD Corporation. If we don't receive funds regularly from Frank and Bea we can't make our payments to JRD," said Bob.

"Then you will have to sell something or take on a partner in Belize" said Marla. "Do you have any ideas?"

"I need to think. This is the problem with operating a company in a poor nation like Belize. There is no one in the country who can lend us the kind of money we need to survive."

"Then you will need to 'greed' someone in this country (the USA) who has the money into making the investment," said Marla.

"What do you mean by 'greed someone' into a decision?"

"You will need to find someone with the money here in the USA who will loan you the money you need, who thinks they are stealing the company from you. They will have to believe that the loan is well collateralized and that Belize Resources is worth way more than the loan. Their greed will sell them on the deal."

"The company has a major cash flow problem," Bob admitted for the first time. "Honestly, if someone stole Belize Resources from us it would be a good thing. Bea and Frank are owed about 40 million dollars. Albert and I have ten million each in the pot and you are owed a million. If we got a loan that just paid all the debt, including the debt owed to the family and the debt owed to JRD Capital for operations, we would be in good shape."

"I have someone in mind who has the money, is greedy and who would want to steal Belize Resources from you," said Marla.

"Who?"

"Think Savannah."

"Oh yeah, Thompson Timber Fund. I hated that man. What was his name?"

"Thomas N. Thompson," said Marla. "Mr. TNT."

"Let's head back. I want to get on the phone with Dad."

"You can't tell him what Reynolds told me."

"No, I won't tell him what Reynolds said. I am going to give Frank an unvarnished report of the true situation in Belize. He will come to the idea he needs to reduce his risk on his own. He will call Mr. Thompson."

They put on their sneakers and sprinted back to the house.

Chapter 14
Henry T. Logan & Michael Grant

After a man turns 60 years of age and has practiced a profession in the same location for over 30 years he becomes used to attending funerals. The rites were for the living, not the dead. Tom only knew clients and other attorneys, so when one of them died he rarely knew the family of the deceased. So, if he attended the service he would have to explain who he was. He could really offer little solace to the survivors. Tom was a reformed drunk, and he had worked hard when he was sober and he was oblivious when he was intoxicated. As a result, he had few close friends in the profession and fewer still who could make him attend church for a funeral.

So it was unusual when Tom was asked where he was going, and he said he was going to church to a funeral. Tom had received a call from Anna Logan, the mother of Henry T. Logan, an old client. He had been killed in prison. Mrs. Logan had said the authorities in Florida State Prison in Starke, Florida, believed it was a hit. He was killed with a shiv to the belly that destroyed some vital organ, and he was left to bleed to death by the other inmates.

No one called for medical assistance. He was a snitch.

Logan had complained to Tom in a letter that word had gotten out among the other inmates that he had testified in the trial in Clearwater about the escape in the Pinellas County Jail that had resulted in the death of a guard and four prisoners.

Logan and his cellmate, Michael Grant, had both testified for the State against other men who had planned and facilitated the escape attempt. There were five men in prison for life who blamed Logan and Grant for their sentences, and there were at least a thousand men in Florida State Prison who were willing to carry out the death sentence that had been issued because the two men had testified, and were snitches.

Michael Grant had been lucky. When he agreed to testify, he was released to the custody of his friend, who took him back to New York State. After he testified, Grant was given a sentence of time served and he was living with his friend again. He had managed to go straight.

Logan's predicament was more difficult. He was thought to be a hit man for a drug cartel and was implicated in three murders. The State would not agree to release him from jail. One charge arose from a murder of a drug dealer at an outdoor concert in St. Petersburg. The case was being tried when the State moved for a mistrial. Logan's case was on appeal when the escape attempt in the county jail occurred.

After Logan testified, the State agreed to allow Logan to plead guilty to three manslaughter charges. He would be sentenced to ten years on each charge. The sentences would run concurrently (at the same time).

Logan had been in prison for about two years between the time he was waiting to be extradited to Florida from Carolina, where he was arrested, and the time he was in jail in Florida waiting for the ruling on the State's appeal. He was given credit for the time he served so with credit and gain time he should have been out five years after he was sentenced. But he never got out. He had served four of the five years when he was attacked.

Logan's mother wanted Tom to go to the funeral. Tom told her he would and offered to drive her and her daughter and another family member. Logan's father was deceased.

The group at the service was no larger than the mourners that arrived in Tom's car. The service was held in a small chapel in Largo near the county jail and Logan was buried in a pauper's grave. There was no headstone or flowers.

"They killed him. They can bury him," his mother pronounced. Mrs. Logan felt the State had failed to adequately protect her son from the five men he testified against.

Tom could say nothing but agree to her assessment. Tom became depressed. When he became depressed, he had the temptation to drink. It happened every time.

Tom had promised Darlene he would not slip and hit a bar on the way home. He had been good. He had not had a drink since their marriage. He figured there was no sense in starting to drink again now. And as he considered the importance of Logan's death to the scheme of things, Logan's death was no reason to waste his sobriety. No ... not for Logan. Logan had made his bed. The State had offered to hold him in a wing reserved for police officers who had been sentenced to prison, but he wanted to go in with the general population and take his chances. He had almost made it. It was his choice.

***

Back at the office, Tom grabbed a cup of coffee. The coffee beans were from Indonesia. Tom was used to Folgers. If it was made in a percolator, Folger's was as good as anything, he thought. But he had to admit the java grown in Indonesia was tasty.

Tom headed to Jenny Barnes' office. Her room was dark, with the curtains drawn. She had a banker's lamp on her desk, which concentrated the light on what she was reading. She used the light when she studied to help her concentrate on the subject at hand.

"Turn on the lights, Tom, please. So I can see you."

Tom was Jenny's model attorney. She wanted to think like him. She was out of school now for five years and she had a bad start. Her name had been used by a law firm in Ormond Beach to attract clients and she had not learned any law. She could do lunch or talk about what the Supreme Court's latest case meant, but she had gained no practical knowledge.

"Jim asked me to research the effect on the case if Mark Person had Dissociative Personality Disorder."

"Which is?" asked Tom.

"A split personality, a person with at least two distinct identities or personalities that control their behavior," said Jenny like she was reading from a book. "A Dr. Jekyll and Mr. Hyde type."

"What good would that do the defense?"

"It's a recognized personality disorder," said Jenny. "We could show he has a psychiatric disorder."

"If the State proves he is a multiple child killer, everyone will believe he has a mental disorder, but that will not save him from the electric chair."

"What will save him?"

"The only mental disorder that would offer a true defense would be one that precludes him from knowing right from wrong. Mark Person knows right from wrong from the conversations I have had with him."

"What if he has one personality that does not know the difference between right and wrong?" asked Jenny.

"Are you asking if one personality is the child killer, and if that personality does not know the other personality committed the homicide, does the child killer know right from wrong and can the personality that is the child killer who does not know right from wrong be found not guilty by reason of insanity?"

"Well, yes."

"It's too many steps. It needs to be simpler for a jury. It won't play for the guilt phase of the trial when the jury determines whether Person is guilty or not guilty. A personality disorder might be something to present in the penalty phase of the trial. I think we put it on the back burner and wait and see if the police arrest him for the crime of kidnapping or homicide."

"Don't you think we should research it now?"

"If Person is convicted of being a child killer, there will be no mitigating factor that will save him in the penalty phase of the trial."

"Jim says Person was very nice."

"I think Person was just playing with us. He has plenty of time to show us who he really is. I don't think he has decided to show us who he is yet."

"Okay."

"We will hire a psychiatrist if they charge him."

"Okay."

Tom smiled. Jim is wrapped a little too tight, he thought. It's hard to loosen up with a case like this.

"Are you feeling some pressure?" asked Tom.

"A lot." Jenny was tearing up.

"Don't do that to yourself, Jenny."

Tom could see what was happening. Jenny was not prepared for the reality of representing a man who had killed five children. The only way she could justify representing him was if she thought he was crazy (legally insane). Any normal person could only rationalize Person's crimes by allowing that he was insane.

Tom knew the feeling. There was no possible sentence that could be imposed that could right the wrong committed by Person. It was like he was a war lord who had killed 50,000 humans. Who is worse, a man who kills five innocent children or a politician who murders 50,000 civilians in a religious war? It seemed that both were equally vile. Worse, there was no likelihood they could make restitution for their sins as they only had one life to give.

Such evil only has one purpose and that is to offer proof there is a God and an afterlife. There has to be an entity that can mete out justice to the child killers and the war lords after they die.

There has to be an afterlife to allow some all-powerful God a place to right the wrongs and the chaos man inflicts on his brothers on earth.

***

Tom talked to Darlene about Jenny's mental predicament. Darlene asked Alphonse if he needed some help with the theft of proprietary rights case he was working on for Marla and Plantation #7. He said he could use a hand. Darlene spoke to Jenny and told her Alphonse needed help for Marla's case.

"Would you mind?" asked Darlene.

"No," said Jenny.

Tom explained to Jim DeMarco that he agreed to partner with him instead of Jenny; that he, Tom, would devote full time to Person's case.

Jim DeMarco did not understand what was going on with Jenny, but he agreed to work exclusively with Tom on Person's case.

Chapter 15
Faircloth

The law firm's investigator, Jim Faircloth, was known as "Faircloth" to prevent confusion when he and Jim DeMarco were in the same room. Faircloth was given the job of finding a place for Mark Person to stay while they waited for the State to decide if they were going to charge their client with something more than Soliciting for Prostitution.

Faircloth had been able to easily shake the tail of the police officer in the 1973 Plymouth Road Runner. He had been a police officer and he was adept in such matters. After avoiding the tail, Faircloth first tried to take Person back home, but there were reporters who were still waiting there.

Faircloth spoke to Tom and Person and it was decided it might be best to forget about hiding and just park Person close to the firm's offices in case Tom needed to speak to him. The Safari Beach Hotel, a small inn with a coffee shop, was directly on Spa Beach on Tampa Bay in St. Petersburg. It was a short walk from the beach venue to the law office of Night, Adams, and Street. Tom knew the manager of the Safari, Jasper Lee Smiley, and explained the situation to him. Mr. Smiley had been a client who Tom successfully defended on a charge of killing his girlfriend. The old client still felt he owed Tom and his deceased partner, Roger Adams, a favor for what they did for him. So long as it wasn't illegal, Mr. Smiley had no objection to taking in Person on Tom's word he would not cause trouble.

Besides, the motel was going to be demolished by the City soon. The City was buying up the downtown waterfront as it became available and was turning the land into waterfront parks. The Safari's property was right on Tampa Bay and fit the profile of property the City desired.

Because the property was under contract, only the coffee shop and a few rooms were open for business. The hotel was not occupied except for a room occupied by the manager, Mr. Smiley. The manager agreed to open a second room and let Person stay in the motel while they waited for the State's decision whether to file a kidnapping charge in Person's case.

Tom figured correctly, that the State would be frantic when they learned they had lost contact with their suspect. Tom called the sheriff in Summer County and made a deal. "I will tell you where Person is staying and you can follow him all you want, but don't tell the press where he is."

The sheriff had been more than frantic when they lost Person. He was ready to fire staff. The sheriff had not been in full agreement with the task force allowing Person to be bonded out. He wanted to arrest him for the kidnapping and also for the five homicides. His men had argued they did not have sufficient evidence to convict Person and if they made an arrest, the defense would know the proofs were weak as soon as they obtained discovery. The police would be required to disclose their evidence to Person's attorney if he was arrested.

The proof against Person was weak. The police had no ID of Person from the latest victim. When Becky was shown his picture she just shook her head. Person had not confessed. The FBI had not made a preliminary match of the tire tracks, or the boot prints. There were no fingerprints or fluid matches.

In short, all the police had was an anonymous caller who said Person washed his truck thoroughly the day of the attack on Becky Sue Painter. The police also knew he drove a red truck and that it got stuck in the mud on the date of the kidnapping and was observed by a highway patrolman near the Wildwood exit of the Interstate on the same date. Further the same patrolman had stopped Person on Indian Hollow Road on the day of the kidnapping, but because of the ground fog, the patrolman did not know exactly where on the road Person had been stopped.

The sheriff was advised that if they arrested Person, the time would begin to run on the Speedy Trial Rule, and if the State could not make their case and convict Person in 180 days from the date he was arrested, then he would be free for all time. They couldn't take that chance. It was better to release him but keep him under surveillance until they had a solid case.

The police had arrested Person for solicitation of a sex act and not murder and kidnapping. The police wanted to try to obtain a confession from Person after that arrest but he did not oblige them with a confession or incriminating information. They had to let Person go. The sheriff knew it was bad politics but good legal strategy.

The idea was that they would let Person go and follow him. They would also tell the newspaper reporters where he was. The press would hound him. He might make a mistake and run. Flight would be evidence of guilt. They would use the time to wait for the final reports from the FBI forensic experts. Person would be under pressure if he was under constant surveillance by the deputy in the 1973 Plymouth Road Runner and the reporters. Maybe Person would crack and confess.

This strategy unraveled when Faircloth eluded the tail and Person was secretly housed in the vacant hotel.

Tom waited a day and then proposed the solution allowing the sheriff to know where Person was so long as the sheriff did not tell the press or make Person's whereabouts known to the public. Tom and Jim were worried their client was in danger from the families of the victims or from vigilantes as much as they were worried about the press trying to coax a statement from their client.

Tom and Jim explained to their client that they proposed to tell the sheriff where he was staying. Person understood the logic of the proposal and he agreed. Person smiled. He was amused that he had gotten one on the sheriff. Tom and Jim also explained that they would agree to turn Person in to the authorities if an arrest warrant was issued. Person agreed with his attorneys that he would go voluntarily if the warrant was issued. Person told Tom and Jim he understood it was in his best interest to turn himself in if he was charged and not attempt to run.

Person however was lying. Person did not intend to volunteer himself to an arrest ever again.

***

Thereafter, Person stayed at the hotel and spent his free time on the beach (Spa Beach) getting a tan. He grew a beard and let his hair grow. He stayed by himself. He conserved his strength, knowing he had to steel himself for the ordeal he would face if he was charged. When he was asked, he presented himself promptly to the office of his attorney for conferences. He received reports on legal research, the investigations Faircloth was conducting, and information on court matters and copies of the time sheets for the firm's legal representation and the firm's billings.

He was at Tom's office for hours and hours daily preparing his defense.

***

Tom had filed a motion to require the State to produce the court reporter's transcript of Person's statement to the police after his arrest for soliciting. Person had advised his attorney that after his arrest in the parking lot of the XYZ Lounge he was taken to the jail behind the courthouse in Gainesville and he was interrogated for 11 hours. Person claimed the detectives questioned him about the Becky Sue Painter case and the other child killings and the missing children. Person told his attorneys he refused to talk about those cases. The police told him he was not under arrest for those cases "at this time" and Person wouldn't talk about those cases.

Tom felt he could get a lot of information about the State's case if the defense attorneys had a copy of the transcript of the interrogation. But when he made his demand for discovery on the soliciting charge the State did not give him the transcript, even though the rules of criminal procedure required the State to produce the statement the defendant made to the police.

The State Attorney in Alachua County realized he would probably have to give up the substance of Person's statement, that is, what he admitted to so far as the soliciting charge was concerned, but the SA wanted to hold back as much of the transcript as he could.

The judge ordered the State to produce the entire transcript. The judge reasoned the entire statement was taken after the arrest for soliciting and if the defendant was not arrested for the kidnapping, or homicide, then the entire statement concerned the arrest for soliciting and the entire transcript had to be given to the defense so long as the defense paid the reasonable cost of copying the transcript.

Tom and Jim paid the State ten cents a page times 2028 pages for the copy and they drove back from the hearing to their office. As Tom drove, Jim read the transcript aloud. They couldn't understand anything in the statement that was inherently incriminating. In fact, it was pretty much what Person had described. There were four detectives that participated in the questioning and they would ask questions and repeat questions that had already been asked. Person's answers seemed consistent. They wouldn't know if the statement would be damaging until all the evidence was in. Person denied that he had driven any middle school age kids in the red truck. If the police found a fingerprint of Becky or one of the other victims on a surface in the truck that denial would be incriminating. But Person had also explained that he didn't drive this particular red truck all the time. The drivers could switch around depending on the job and the type equipment that was needed for a particular job. So, he explained, other drivers could have used the truck and those other drivers could have let a victim in the vehicle.

The statement went on like this. Person explained everything. Yes, he had driven on Indian Hollow Road. He had been on the road many times. He had been stopped by the police on the road.

His truck was stopped on the right of way heading west. The highway patrolman had said he was driving too fast for conditions. He did not get a ticket. The patrolman had inspected the vehicle inside and out. He looked in the bed of the truck and he wanted to see the work order to show why he was on Indian Hollow Road heading for New Retirement City.

Hours of the interrogation involved questions that came from psychological tests. Person's answers to those questions did not concern Tom. A psychologist's conclusions based on the test would only be admissible if Person claimed he was insane or if he claimed diminished capacity as a mitigating factor if Person was found guilty of the child killings.

When Tom and Jim returned to the law office from court, Person was there. Faircloth had picked him up from the Safari and brought him to the office and the '73 Plymouth was in the parking lot.

Tom and Jim gave Person a pad and pen. Karen Xeroxed three copies of the transcript. The original copy went in the file and Tom, Jim and Person each got one of the copies. Person was put in a small room with a desk and chair and his pad and pen and told to read the transcript carefully and make notes of anything that he thought was important and they would discuss the notes.

Tom hoped Person's notes would spur a conversation between them about Person's involvement, if any, in the killings. To date Person neither admitted nor denied any involvement in the child killings or the abduction of Becky Sue Painter.

***

Person was in the small room for three hours. He came out to use the restroom. He went back in for another two hours. It was 5 p.m. Tom and Jim said they would wait for Person to finish. Faircloth went out and told the deputy in the '73 Plymouth that it was going to be a while. The deputy had a paperback novel and said no problem. He was used to the drill. Sit and wait and wait some more.

At 8 p.m. the door to Tom's office opened. Jim and Tom were inside talking. Person pushed open the door and he was holding the pad, pen and reams of copies. He laid the papers on Tom's desk.

"Sit down," said Jim.

Person sat in front of the desk next to Jim. Tom looked at the pad and passed it to Jim. There was nothing written on the pad.

"You didn't make any notes?" asked Tom.

"No, the court reporter got it right," said Person. "She didn't make any mistakes. She got everything that I told the detectives."

"Did you think there was anything in the transcript that could cause a problem?" asked Jim.

"No, I think I covered us alright. What do you think our next step should be?" asked Person.

"We wait for the FBI," said Tom. "Is there anything else you think we should know before the State obtains the final reports from the FBI?"

"No, you know everything you need to know for now," said Person.

"Ok, Faircloth will take you back to the hotel," said Tom. "Are those accommodations working out alright?"

"Yes, I like it much better than my garage apartment. I enjoy the beach," said Person as he walked out the door.

***

"What is going on?" Jim asked Tom after Person left.

"He's not going to tell us his story until all the cards are on the table," said Tom.

"Why?" asked Jim.

"He wants to know all the evidence the State has before he will tell us what his defense is. He thinks he can lie around any evidence the State finds."

"I still don't understand," said Jim.

"It's a matter of control. He is controlling the case, or at least he thinks he is controlling the case," said Tom. "He is controlling us by keeping us in the dark."

"I don't think that is very smart," said Jim.

"It's his dollar." said Tom.

Chapter 16
A Taste of Prison

On his release from the Youthful Offender camp, Mark Person swore he would never return to prison if he could avoid it. He knew that if he returned to a prison the chances of a successful escape were minuscule. He was now at risk of returning to lock up and he began to make preparations.

When Person asked the likelihood the SA would bring him to trial, Tom told him there was a 50/50 chance the State Attorney would procede with the murder and kidnapping charges. Therefore it was to Persons advantage to wait and see what the SA did. The SA might choke and miss his chance to successfully prosecute the guilty party.

But by waiting and not running now Person was missing his best chance to run and get ahead of the law. But Person felt a 50/50 chance of exoneration by the SA was worth the risk and so he would wait.

However Person would be proactive.

Person had spent long hours considering the chances he could succeed in an escape attempt immediately after his arrest. He knew the authorities who would attempt to make the arrest would want to have time with him when he was vulnerable to try to obtain a confession or statement. He would be vulnerable to make a statement when he was arrested. He could slip up and say something incriminating.

Person's ability to escape would depend on the amount of security assigned to cuff him and to transport him to jail. At the time of his arrest in his motel room he had the best chance to take action before he was placed in the police vehicle and driven to jail.

Person had not anticipated his arrest inside his truck in the parking lot of the XYZ Lounge and he had not been prepared to escape at that time. Now he was staying at the Safari Beach Hotel and he needed to return to his garage apartment to make preparations for his escape. He had to return home and go to the glass jar that was sitting out in the open on his dresser in his apartment.

Person felt he would know a lot about the police if he was able to look in the glass jar.

The police should not have been in his apartment. He was not arrested in his apartment and so his rooms could not be searched incident to his arrest. There was no search warrant issued. He would have been aware of that because he would have been served with a copy of the warrant and the inventory. Further, the warrant would have to be posted on the door of his apartment and his aunt would have told him. His aunt said the police asked her husband and his aunt for permission to conduct a search of the apartment but they refused.

The police had no right to enter his apartment, but Person felt sure they had violated his constitutional rights. Someone in the police department would not be able to stand the fact that there was probably evidence of crime in his apartment just at their fingertips that they could not seize. The urge to conduct an illegal search would be more than the police could stand.

Person knew that the detectives that interviewed him would not have made a surreptitious search as they knew the consequences of an illegal search. If a search was found to be illegal by the court, the evidence seized would be inadmissible in Person's trial. In addition, any other evidence that was discovered as a result of the illegal search would also be inadmissible. The evidence would be the fruit, or result, of an illegal search. But Person believed someone with the police had searched his living quarters. It would have been someone in authority who would order a trusted underling to search. Then the cop who violated the law would reveal what he saw to his superior.

Person had left no obvious contraband in his apartment, not even a little weed. He had burned his souvenirs and disposed of his clothes. The glass container of coins and loose buttons and keys and marbles did not contain anything that was inherently illegal. Person could possess everything that was contained in the jar. But since Person was now under surveillance he could no longer go to a hardware store and obtain what was in the apartment that would help him escape. He was always followed, even though Person and the primary surveillance officer, Deputy John Bose, had become friends.

Person needed to get back home. He had a driver now and he had a direct line to his aunt's money. Faircloth was his chauffer, paid for with the money his aunt paid to the law firm.

Person called Tom and told him he needed to go to his apartment. He refused to say why other than to say he needed clothes. Tom did not press the matter. He had other more important matters to contend with. Tom agreed that Faircloth would drive him but made Person agree that Faircloth would enter the apartment and stay with him inside. When they left, Faircloth would put an evidence seal, yellow adhesive tape, over the door and windows. That way they could see if the room was disturbed by someone who entered without permission after Person and Faircloth entered the apartment.

Person said he had no objection to the rules Tom laid down.

***

Faircloth watched their client closely during the visit to Person's apartment in Archer. Person obtained clothes, mostly. He got a suit and a white shirt and tie for court. He also went in his drawers and got socks and underwear, pants and T-shirts.

Person dumped all the perishables from the refrigerator and collected the trash. Person told Faircloth to give the trash to the deputy in the 1973 Plymouth Road Runner. Faircloth asked why. Person said he noticed the deputy was collecting his trash at the Safari Beach Hotel. The trash from the ice box in his apartment was messier than the trash at the hotel. And the trash was moldy. Person realized that anything he threw out, such as his garbage, was fair game for the police to search and confiscate. The deputy had been given the dirty job of rooting through the trash. Person tried to make it easier for the deputy. He was trying to establish a rapport with the officer. Person knew Deputy Bose worked long hours and he was not well treated by his superiors.

While Faircloth delivered the bag of garbage to Deputy John Bose, Person went to the glass jar. Faircloth did not see what Person retrieved from the jar. Person put the object, a small key, in his mouth. It nestled perfectly between his cheek and gum.

They drove back to St. Petersburg with Faircloth and Person in one car and the deputy following in the Plymouth.

All the way back to the Safari Motel, Person manipulated the small key with his tongue turning it between his cheek and gum. Occasionally Person smiled. The cops are so naïve, thought Person.

***

Faircloth reported to Tom on their return that he had taped the doors and windows with yellow evidence tape as instructed.

"What did our client retrieve from the apartment that was so important?" asked Tom.

"Nothing that I saw that would hurt or injure anyone. It seemed like it was only clothes. He said he needed a suit for court if he needed to go before the judge or a jury. He wanted to look presentable; at least that's what he said."

"Anything make you suspicious?"

"He looked in a glass jar when we first came in the living room."

"Did he take anything from the jar?"

"Not that I saw. When I looked in the jar after I was away from him and he was in the bedroom getting his clothes, I didn't see anything important. Mostly pieces of metal. Coins and such," said Faircloth.

"You need to be careful dealing with this man," said Tom.

"I know," said Faircloth. "He's very cagey and smart."

"He would kill one of us as soon as look at us," said Tom.

"I looked close. He didn't get anything from the apartment except his clothes," said Faircloth. "He did not get a weapon."

Tom again reminded Faircloth that he had already been to a funeral for one of his investigators who was killed in the line of duty and he didn't intend to attend a funeral for Faircloth.

Part IV

An Explosive Character

Chapter 17
TNT

Thomas Nathaniel Thompson had called and left messages for Frank Barnes three times in the last week. Thompson admitted he was desperate to place a loan with one of the Barnes companies. He was looking at Plantation #7 as a potential borrower of funds from Thompson's investment company. Better still would be Belize Resources. Both companies were closely held and not publicly traded. Both companies had hard assets and an income stream from an ongoing business. Both companies also had legitimate reasons to borrow.

To Thompson they were the perfect companies with hard assets to have as a customer for a loan from the Thompson Timber Fund (TTF). The value of the Barnes companies could be massaged so that his investors could see a profit whether the businesses generated a profit or not. Thompson could assign any value that he wanted to the assets of the company by using appraisers who were in his pocket. An appraiser from the MAO (Made as Ordered) Appraiser Group would issue a report that would give a generous value to any business that TTF owned or loaned money to. By pumping up the value of the company any loan amount to the company could be made to look reasonable.

Thompson was required to make a quarterly accounting to his investors, who were called "unit owners". MAO appraisals never failed to show a positive return on the investment made by his unit owners. Thompson Timber Trust investors were known as qualified investors. These were rich folks who had had investment assets valued at more than a million dollars (not including their residence). Because they were rich they were not protected by the disclosure requirements of the State and Federal authorities.

Thompson was not an honest man. His fund needed to acquire new assets, or loan money to companies with the cash investments made to TTF by his unit holders. If he failed to make loans or purchases his fund could not grow. He was paid a fee equal to two percent per annum of the overall value of the fund. Therefore, in order for Thompson to profit personally the fund had to grow.

***

When Frank Barnes' mother was dying of consumption his father, the senator, did not want Frank to see her die. His mother would die a long and lingering death the doctors said, and Frank was packed up and sent off to Georgia Military Academy for the duration. Frank was in eighth grade when he was sent off to school and it was anticipated he would finish his high school education at the academy.

The academy's purpose was to teach its students discipline and also give them a first rate education in math and the sciences. Discipline was taught by drilling the all-male student body from the moment they awoke until they went to bed. Frank fell into a routine and the rubric of marching to breakfast and then to class and then to lunch and then drilling in the afternoon after classes.

The discipline was not offensive to Frank. But to others, including his roommate, Thomas N. Thompson, the drills and the marching and the discipline tore the soul from their being. The discipline made them rebel. When they had a moment from the academy they would wreak havoc to cool down. These renegade students were known to the local police and they were under surveillance as soon as they left the gates of the school and entered the town.

Thomas Nathan Thompson, who was known by the nickname "TNT", ran the local constabulary ragged. He was especially well known for detonating cherry bombs and black cats (firecrackers).

In the spring there were no fledgling birds that survived in their nests for the fact they were destroyed by an explosion.

Thompson was sly. He was rarely caught in the act but was always suspected of being the culprit who caused the harm if a pond had fish floating from one of Thompson's malicious deeds. He would combine charges of cherry bombs so that multiple devices were molded into one to cause a single enormous detonation. The result could be dramatic.

Thompson's family was from middle Georgia. His father was a widower and he would rather have his son at home, but he was unable to control his son. He was told by the juvenile authorities in Macon, where they lived, that if Thompson was not put in military school they would have no choice but to send him to a state detention school for incorrigibles.

The worry of the juvenile judge was the cruelty Thompson exhibited in his pranks. He left small animals maimed. The judge had sat on the bench long enough to know that Thompson would kill someone if he wasn't broken of his evil proclivities.

The judge confided to Thompson's father that violence to small animals was a sign of later criminal activity.

"You need to break the boy now or you will spend your retirement visiting him in prison."

Thompson Sr. understood and he sent his son to military school beginning in the fifth grade. Thompson hated the regimentation of the school, but like all attempts made by society, the mistake was that the effort to segregate the criminal element to one location gathered all the rotten apples of society into a single barrel. Further, the rotten apples did not heal each other. Instead, the rotten apples taught each other new tricks.

The school had normal students who were there for a reason that was benign. And the academy had students like Thompson, who were there because they were criminals.

The question was whether the criminals would be broken or, in the least, if they could be taught the discipline that would allow them to function outside the walls of the institution without causing physical injury to the general population.

Frank Barnes remained at Georgia Military Academy until he was in the tenth grade and his mother passed. Then the senator brought him home. During the two and half years Frank was at the academy, TNT was Frank's roommate. The teens got along well. Thompson did not practice his meanness on Frank realizing that it was not a good idea to foul his own nest. He left Frank alone and Frank thought Thompson to be a good friend.

Thompson appeared to change during the time he was in school with Frank. Rather, Thompson learned to hide his malevolence. Thompson learned to behave while in Georgia Military Academy. The school's administration congratulated itself and he was touted as an example of the theory that if you drilled a boy sufficiently you would make him into a man one could be proud of.

Thompson repeated the habit of good behavior after he graduated and went on to University of Georgia and graduated at the top of his class with a degree in Economics. Thompson used the Great Depression to establish himself as a pillar of the community. He married well, into a good family to a beautiful and faithful wife.

There was no work in Macon except backbreaking manual labor. Thompson was well educated and wearing blisters on his hands was a waste of talent. His dad scraped together what money he could and told Thompson to find a better home for his family.

Thompson searched Atlanta for work but there was nothing there for him. Besides, the city was too big and it was confused and lost. Atlanta was a commercial hub, but there was no commerce. The financial fire of the Depression had burned the heart of the city again – another Sherman.

Thompson realized he had to find the essence of the State of Georgia. He had his roots in Georgia. He found work in Savannah as an investment counselor and stock and bond trader. There was little work, but rent was cheap and his wife taught school. They had children. Thompson dedicated himself to his family and the community. Thompson was the Boy Scout leader and the church deacon and the school board member and a city commissioner and a Wizard in the KKK.

Every year Thompson sent Frank a Christmas card. In the card Thompson would include a letter to all his friends. In the beginning the letter was mimeographed. It was copied to over a hundred people at first and then the hundred became hundreds and then over two thousand of these Christmas cards were sent out to friends of Thompson. And on and on, Thompson's business grew.

In the letter, Thompson would expound on his thoughts about the future. He was optimistic that things would get better. His philosophy was that Georgia had resources. The trees and the rocks and the soil gave lumber and paper and gravel and food.

Thompson always closed his annual letter with the following:

"We can survive with the grace of God. Your friend in Christ, TNT."

Frank always anticipated the letter in December and, in the letter, he read the progress his friend had made in the preceding year. The letter would list the achievements Thompson and his company had made. Each year Thompson announced the value of the investments made with and through his company. Every year the value increased.

Every year Frank would respond to Thompson's letter with a hand-typed letter of his own, telling his old roommate the news. He had married, had a son, went to Stetson, lived on a dairy farm, managed a timber farm, adopted three children, and on and on. Thompson read each reply to his Christmas letter. The replies were like the harvest he reaped from the seeds sown with the words in his letter. Thompson received hundreds of replies to his Christmas letter.

As Frank gained more assets, Thompson began to write a personal note along with the annual "report" which was now printed on thick quality paper and signed in ink by Thompson himself. The report was on the letterhead of Thompson Timber Fund. The note was a solicitation. Thompson promised he would personally handle his friend's accounts if he would "trust me".

Through Frank's correspondence, Thompson followed Frank Barnes and his company, CCC. Thompson knew the ups and downs the company was experiencing and he stayed in touch. He invited Frank and Bea to the Georgia/Florida Football Classic in Jacksonville and the 500 mile stock car race at the tri-oval race track in Daytona. Frank and Bea begged off, but thanked Thompson for his thoughtfulness.

Finally, after years of solicitations, an opportunity to do business arose. Frank had control of CCC and Frank, Tom and Albert were in Atlanta to negotiate a sale of CCC's timberlands and sawmills to Withlacoochee Lumber Corporation (WLC).

During the negotiations Albert became very ill, but in spite of the illness, Tom negotiated a purchase of 65,000 acres of land by CCC from WLC. The deal came in reverse order from what had been planned. Instead of selling its assets, CCC was buying. Frank needed to borrow some money quickly to close the deal with WLC and he called his friend TNT for a loan.

Thompson was happy to make the loan. Frank trusted Thompson and did not study the loan documents, but relied on what his friend promised. As usual, Thompson said one thing when he talked to a potential client about the terms of the loan while the documents said another. In particular, the loan documents stated clearly that the loan could be called at TNT's whim and the borrower would only have 30 days to repay the loan from the date notice was given.

If payment was not made according to the terms of the loan papers, Thompson Timber Fund could foreclose and take the collateral (in this case 65,000 acres of land). However, Thompson denied that he would call a loan and take a borrower's collateral.

Further, Thompson's clients believed him and ignored the terms of the documents. The client's even believed Thompson would reinstate the loan after the foreclosure notice had been filed of public record in the Atlanta Constitution newspaper.

By making a promise like that, even if it was a lie, TNT tended to relax the borrower who had lost his farm to Thompson Timber Fund.

Thompson always said, "So long as I hold the paper (title) to your farm, I will sell it back to you. Just catch up the payments and pay my costs and the property will be yours again." Thompson would even rent the farm to the former owner at a reasonable rent.

The foreclosed borrowers believed TNT would hold their land. But Thompson did not wait to sell the farm. When a purchaser was found, the farm was sold. Thompson wrote a note to the original owner saying he was sorry. He had waited as long as he could but there were "market necessities that had to be resolved". The former owner still got his annual report. They were still part of his "investment family" as he called it.

Thompson never called a loan unless he felt he could do it without there being a fuss. He had to feel he knew the borrower would be placated by more promises.

However, Thompson had misread Bob and Marla. They had taken over CCC from Frank after Albert became ill. When they came to see him in Savannah to discuss the loan on the 65,000 acres CCC owned, Thompson thought they were an easy nickel. He could make another loan, eventually make loans on all CCC's operations and eventually control CCC's operations, or own it outright. Instead, when Bob and TNT had a dispute as to the true terms of the loan, and TNT called the loan, Marla was ready for that. She had the money in the bank and they paid off the loan in full.

Thompson looked like a fool. He did not like it. It caused him to double his efforts to bring the Barnes Family back into the Thompson investment family.

Chapter 18
Strangled by Debt

Frank Barnes listened carefully as his son, Bob, explained the family's plight. Yet again they were in danger of bankruptcy as a result of being strangled by debt.

Regardless of how they arrived at this position, they had to refinance the debt in Belize Resources and repay at least some of the money Frank and Bea had invested in the lime rock mine in Big Creek, Belize. Homestead Creamery was not the cash cow it had been, and Frank and Bea could not depend on the stream of dividend payments they had been receiving from the company which they in turn loaned to Belize Recourses. Without that inflow of loans from his parents, Bob would have to close the operation in Belize. If the mining operation closed, Belize Resources would go into bankruptcy and Homestead Creamery franchise would be at risk next. JRD Capital was the primary lender to the franchise company. Frank and Bea co-signed the loan between JRD Capital and Homestead Creamery. Frank and Bea would have to file personal bankruptcy if JRD Capital foreclosed. Further, Plantation #7 was at risk because of the theft of proprietary secrets and customer lists by a competitor. Plantation #7 was barely paying its bills as they came due as a result of the thefts.

The Barnes Family had one hope. In spite of this bleak outlook, Thomas Nathanial Thompson of Thompson Timber Fund was willing; in fact he was desperate, to loan money to Belize Resources.

Bob and Frank visited Savannah to meet with Thompson. Before the trip, they had been able to get five minutes with their old company attorney, Tom Night, for a phone conference. His advice was to not lie about the family's financial condition. They should be honest. They had assets but the cash flow from the assets would not cover the debt as it came due.

"Do not lie to a banker, he will put you in jail," said Tom. "Tell him the truth and give your true and correct financial condition to the banker in writing. If he doesn't give you the loan, you won't have the bank's money but you won't be in jail for being dishonest."

Based on that advice Bob completed an in depth loan disclosure questionnaire to present to Thompson. The document laid out all the financial dirty laundry of the Barnes Family's holdings and industry. Nothing was left out.

The day before Bob and Frank met with Thompson at his office in Savannah the original disclosure questionnaire was delivered to TTF's offices and Thompson personally signed for the delivery. The receipt was given to the courier and returned to Bob and Frank. Bob had complied thoroughly and completely with the advice he had been given by Tom. Complete disclosure had been made to TNT and Thompson Timber Fund.

When the meeting occurred, the first question Thompson asked Bob was why he had sent the disclosure statement.

"To make you aware of our financial condition," explained Bob. "We have short term debt that needs to be converted to long term debt so that our loan payments are in line with our income. As you can see, the mine in Belize will not be able to rely on loans from Frank and Bea in the future."

"Well, why didn't you just say that?" said Thompson. "I didn't need to see it in writing."

"We were trying to do the right thing," said Frank. "Our attorney told us to provide you with the truth."

"That's the same fella that got you and me off on the wrong foot, isn't he?" asked TNT.

"We have had him as our attorney for over forty years," said Frank. "We try to follow his advice."

"He's probably used to dealing with banks. TTF is not a bank. I am not a banker. I am an investment counselor," said Thompson. "Rich people, and only rich people, what they call qualified investors, (and TNT made a gesture with his fingers as though to put words 'qualified investors' in quotation marks) come to me to invest their capital. They come to me expecting me to put that capital at risk using my expertise to find investments that will produce a superior return."

Thompson then stood up and shouted, "If they wanted a safe investment, they could put the money in a bank. They know TTF is not a bank and there is no guaranteed return on their investment. In fact, they sign a piece of paper that says their money, principle and interest can be lost. The money is at risk." Thompson's face was red. "Do you understand?"

What Bob and Frank understood after watching TNT scream at the top of his lungs was that he was crazy. However, what they said was, "Yes, we just don't want a fight over whether we were honest about our situation," said Frank. "We are too old to fight those battles."

TNT sat down and sat forward in his chair. "Let me tell you why I see the Barnes Family businesses as a good investment for my clients."

"Fine," said Bob.

"It's one word: 'collateral'. Belize Resources is a subsidiary of Barnes Lime Rock which supplies just about all the lime rock that meets DOT specifications throughout Florida. If a paving contractor cannot meet Department of Transportation specifications for road base materials, the contractor can't bid for the contract with the State to build the road. TTF sees the Barnes Lime Rock business as a valuable asset and I would expect you to put up Barnes Lime Rock as collateral for any loan TTF makes to Belize Resources."

"How much are you willing to lend if Barnes Lime Rock was collateral for the TTF loan?" asked Bob.

"What do you need?" asked Thompson.

"We will have to pay off the loan we owe to JRD Capital. They have lent us money on our receivables and on our equipment in Florida and in Belize. We owe them thirty million dollars. JRD has a mortgage on the lime rock and they will not let TTF take a position in the collateral unless they are paid off. Every dime that comes in, JRD has to be paid first."

"And you never have enough money to improve your facilities?"

"That's right. JRD Capital always starves us," complained Bob. "They let us have just enough capital to pay their loan back. We get nothing to improve our operations or our mines. That's why we are so cash poor." Bob was not blowing off steam. He felt JRD had hurt the Barnes companies.

"If you could improve the mines, would you attain profitability?"

"Yes, I believe we would," Bob emphatically replied.

"If I let you stretch out your payments by giving you long term money, would that help you succeed?"

"Yes it would."

"Then that is what I will do," said Thompson. "TTF wants you to succeed. That is how we will give our investors a superior return."

"This is what we need, Dad," Bob said to Frank. "This will free you and Mom up from loaning the lime rock operations any more money."

Frank realized that they were just digging a deeper hole and he turned to Thompson. "Will you invest enough money to allow the family to be repaid the startup money we have invested to date?"

"How much is that?" asked Thompson.

"Forty-one million."

"Are you willing to give up some of the equity in the lime rock companies?"

"How much of the equity?" asked Bob.

"Fifty-one percent," said TNT.

"We would lose control of the lime rock companies," said Bob.

"I will let you buy control back for so long as TTF owns its interest in the business," said TNT. "And remember, if the lime rock business makes a profit and declares a dividend, your family will receive forty-nine percent of the profit."

"The family would be repaid the forty-one million dollars we loaned to Belize Resources and TTF would refinance the debt Belize Resources owes to JRD Capital and we give up fifty-one percent of our investment," repeated Bob.

"That's my offer," said TNT. "I have the paper work here. My attorney drew it up. We just have to fill in the dollar amounts. If my math is correct, that's seventy-one million dollars."

"Can we think it over?" asked Frank. He was not sure this was a deal they should make.

"Sure" said Thompson. "But you have to be aware that TTF may not have this amount of money available to loan in the near future. You are asking us to commit seventy-one million dollars in capital and keep it in the bank for you. There are other op-portunities available to our investors. They could withdraw their commitments. You need to act now or forget it, is my thought," said Thompson.

"Well, do we have five minutes and a small room in which Bob and I can talk?" asked Frank.

"No, I don't think so. You know what you want and need to do. Seize the day," said TNT.

"You're right," said Frank. "Sign the papers, Bob. You're the president."

Bob had been reading the paperwork. It seemed in order. It was short but not so sweet. With 51% control, TTF could cut the family out of all of their equity in short order. It wasn't the investment in Belize so much as it was the business in Florida that Bob hated to loose. But what could he do? His mom and dad would be repaid and he and Albert would have enough money to start again and Marla would be repaid her one million dollar loan.

Bob signed on the dotted line.

"I just love to make people happy," exclaimed TNT. Especially me, he thought.

Chapter 19
Albert Barnes

Bob and Frank Barnes knew that Albert would have an adverse reaction to the sale of the controlling interest the family held in Barnes Lime Rock and Belize Resources to Thompson Timber Fund. However, they did not expect that when he heard the news, that Albert would load a suitcase with clothes and go to Barkley's Bank in Belize City and withdraw his savings in US dollars, that he would fuel the gas tank of his two-seater Piper Cub Special and fly out of the airport in Monkey River Town and head south. Bob thought he would at least have an opportunity to speak to Albert in person before Albert did anything. Albert failed to tell anyone where he was going. The Piper aircraft had a range of 350 miles.

Bea became very upset. She knew Albert would immediately quit taking the drugs that suppressed the effects of his schizophrenia. Bob did not want to tell his mother that Albert had already quit taking the Risperdal that had been prescribed for his mental disorder.

Albert explained that when he was in Belize he felt free and when he felt free he did not have hallucinations and did not hear voices. He felt wonderful. At least, so he claimed. Albert refused to take the drugs, even though he and Bob had fought over the issue.

But even if Albert took his drugs as prescribed, he still acted like he was under the influence of the mental disease. He insulted people without knowing that what he said was hurtful. He spoke quickly and his words collided with one another. He made rash decisions. A good example was hopping in his plane and flying away when he heard news he disagreed with.

Marla told Bob he should have spoken to Albert in person about the sale and not sent him a telex.

Marla was angry with Bob anyway. She disagreed with the decision to sell the family's controlling interest in the Florida lime rock. To Marla the asset was very valuable. The DOT number certifying Barnes Lime Rock was unique for a company that had a presence throughout the State of Florida. Marla had agreed the Barnes Family should negotiate a loan with Thompson but not to give up equity in the companies.

Bob's view was that the entire State of Florida sat on top of lime rock. Lime rock was everywhere. It was not unique.

Marla countered that when Barnes Lime Rock controlled all the paving business in Florida and Belize Resources controlled the cement factories on the Gulf of Mexico, and Bob drove on any road in the State, he would feel regret in the pit of his stomach because the road he was driving over could have been built by his family. But instead, Thompson would own the road because Thompson controlled Barnes Lime Rock and Belize Resources, albeit after paying $71,000,000 for the 51% interest in the two companies.

"That is a low thing to say," Bob spat back at her words. "We are dying here, hanging on for dear life and I am trying to keep our heads above water and you say something like that."

You are mean as a snake, Marla. Mean as a snake, thought Bob. He was angry.

Bob left the old house at Plantation #7 and moved into the farm house on the Homestead. He was in the dog house there with Bea, but she kept her mouth shut. Bea did call Marla and she asked her to please go to Central America and find Albert. Bob's thought was to leave Albert alone. He would return on his own. Bob had no intention to search for his brother.

***

Bea prevailed on Marla to go to Central America to find Albert. In the winter Belize is temperate. At night it is cool, in the low 70's, and though it is warm in the daytime the humidity is low.

Marla had talked to Tom about Central America, but she had never visited. She remembered what Tom had said about the weather so she knew the best way to dress was casually, loose, in khaki slacks and shirt with closed-toed walking shoes and a straw hat.

Marla was met at the airport in Belize City by Rick Ibn and Anna Hernando and their three daughters. Dr. Hernando had one child every three years after her first child was born five months after their wedding. Anna had never met Marla, but she had heard from her husband that she was beautiful. Anna came to the airport with the girls because she wanted Marla to know that Rick was spoken for.

Marla would have to rely on Rick to find Albert so they would be spending time alone together. The plan was for Rick to find Albert by flying south and checking the airports. Marla was to accompany Rick and then once they found him she was to convince Albert to return to Florida.

Rick had worked as a mechanic for both TAN and TACA airlines and he still knew the chief mechanics for the companies. Rick was told that a small plane had crashed near the airport in Tegucigalpa and the pilot was in a private hospital. That pilot could be Albert, thought Rick.

The morning after her arrival in Belize City, Rick and Marla flew commercial on Tan Airways to Tegucigalpa, Honduras.

When they got to the hospital in the capital of Honduras, the nurse was reluctant to talk about their patient. Marla had Albert's birth certificate and adoption papers and Bea had given Marla a recent picture taken of Albert over Christmas to prove that they were there on behalf of the Barnes Family to rescue Albert and take him home.

The nurse spoke to the doctor by phone. Rick was listening to the conversation, which was in Spanish. He asked to speak to the doctor. When the doctor got on the line Rick identified himself as the husband of Anna Hernando, MD. The doctor knew Dr.

Hernando. They spoke about Anna's hospital in Belize City and the clinic at Big Creek.

The doctor no longer felt threatened and he identified their patient as Albert Barnes. The doctor wanted to be sure Albert would receive treatment by Dr. Hernando. He said she should be prepared for a patient with a serious mental disease, schizophrenia.

"Did he have any physical injury?" asked Rick.

"No. He was babbling in English when he landed his plane and he was delivered here. We handle mental cases," said the doctor.

Rick asked if they could leave Albert there while Rick went to the airport to look after Albert's plane.

"There is no need to check the plane. The plane is operational," said the doctor. "I flew it myself."

Rick surmised the doctor was concerned about payment of the hospital bill. Albert had no money when he was brought in to the hospital. The plane was collateral for the cost of Albert's medical care.

Marla paid the bill and the doctor's lien on the plane was released. They went in and spoke to Albert. He seemed pretty clear-headed. The doctor had started him back on the Rx Risperdal, and he was calm and happy to see Marla and Rick. He wanted out of the hospital. He said he was put in restraints at night.

In the cab to the airport the three decided that Rick and Albert would inspect the plane. Marla would get tickets for her and Albert on the next plane back to Belize City with connections to Miami and then Daytona Beach. Rick would stay with the small plane and fly in it back to Monkey River Town. Monkey River Town was only 10 miles north of Big Creek and the lime rock mine and crushing operation. Rick's wife had her clinic there for the locals and the Belize Resources workers. The plan was that Rick would hitch a ride from the clinic back to his home. He would catch a ride back to Belize City with the full-time doctor who practiced at the clinic at Big Creek.

Rick was familiar with Albert's plane. Rick and Albert had piloted the Piper Cub Special from Florida to Big Creek. Albert was peculiar about the plane. The Piper PA 11 was built in 1949. It was a two seater. It had a small economic engine. Albert kept the plane in tip top shape. The family had purchased it to fly between their landholdings in the Southeast US when they owned CCC Corporation.

The question Rick had was whether anyone had begun to strip parts from the plane while it sat unattended at the airport. Rick checked the plane thoroughly and took a short test flight before gaining altitude and heading back to Monkey River Town. The plane responded well during the flight and he had no incident on the trip back.

***

Marla decided she was not going to take the chance of Albert bolting from her and running away if they took a taxi into Belize City after the TAN flight landed. So they stayed at the airport and ate a lunch of tamales under the Royal Poinciana tree out in front of the customs area and waited for the connecting flights on Delta. The Delta flight would take them to Miami and then to Daytona.

Marla assured Albert they were going home. Everything would be alright. He would see Bea and Frank and Bob and Jenny.

While they were sitting on a bench under the Poinciana tree Albert shared his experiences in the hospital. The facility treated mental patients. They were all in one large room divided by curtains. Some of the 10 or so patients were awake but restrained in their beds. Albert was also restrained at night. He was not allowed to communicate with the outside world. He had asked to see the American Counsel but he had no proof he was an American. His wallet was taken with his identification and money. He had left Belize with over $10,000 but when he awoke in the hospital he had nothing.

***

"There was one man who only had the whites of his eyes. He had no pupils in his eyes. I don't know what was wrong with his eyes," Albert tried to explain. "He was frightening to watch. Most all of the patients were attached to some type of tube and they had catheters to eliminate their waste. I never want to go there again. The people being treated were zombie patients."

Albert said that at night the patients were restless and spoke to themselves. He was kept awake all night.

Albert saw a doctor and he was given his medication. He was able to explain to the doctor that he normally took Risperdal but he had not taken his medication regularly. The doctor had Risperdal available. He became better, less frantic and he spoke slower and with more comprehensible speech after taking the drug.

The flight from Belize back to the USA was uneventful. In the winter there were few storms in the Caribbean and there was little turbulence. It was a three hour flight. Albert slept the entire trip with Marla sitting in the seat next to him. He was very grateful Marla had saved him from the hospital in Tegucigalpa.

Albert did not resist. He wanted to go home to the farm house and sleep in his own bed.

***

Bea was unable to sleep while Albert was lost to her in Belize. And even when he was back home in his own bed she had the same feeling of unease and disquiet that she had when her son Jimmy was still alive.

The feeling was one of intense anxiety that made her want to run away and hide. She was upset with Bob and Frank that they failed to understand how important it was to explain to Albert the business difficulties that resulted in the necessity to sell a controlling interest in Belize Resources and Barnes Lime Rock. Bob and Frank failed to realize that Albert put his soul into his work and he had to make a supreme effort to overcome his mental disorder. Albert had to fight past the demons who spoke to him in order to accomplish meaningful progress at work.

Albert fought his disorder and now he was fighting the effects of the drug that allowed him some normalcy. He had a tendency to be overweight from the drug but now he was developing breasts like a woman and his doctor did not know what to do to reverse the effect except to discontinue the drug. The Risperdal appeared to cause the side effect. The only option was to place him back on Phenothiazine. Phenothiazine was not as effective as Risperdal and it had a more pronounced side effect causing greater weight gain than Risperdal. So the doctor left Albert on Risperdal.

The weight gain and the gynecomastia affected Albert's confidence. He felt he stood out, that he was seen as someone different, and he spoke of his dislike, even hatred for the person who he had become. He could not find companionship, male or female. He wanted a wife or a girlfriend, but he had never established a relationship where he was loved except for the relationship with his mother. He did not feel sexual attraction to Bea, he saw her appropriately as his mother. He didn't need a mother, he needed a wife. He needed to be normal. He wanted to have a wife even if marriage led to a divorce. He wanted to be able to establish a relationship, but that seemed to be impossible.

Bea understood. She tried to talk to Albert's doctor, but he was more interested in the chemistry of Albert's disease than the emotional effect it had on him. Bea decided Albert needed a new doctor and she tried Jacksonville and then Atlanta trying to find help for her son. She was never satisfied with the psychiatrists. She even tried alternates to a medical doctor.

Tom suggested a counselor named Rosemary Ferlita. The law firm had used her to help with clients who were incompetent. She had a degree in psychology. Tom felt she was caring and she would be someone Albert could talk to. Tom felt she was someone who tried to find practical solutions to emotional problems or mental defects. She charged hourly but even if she devoted herself full time to Albert's care, she would be much less expensive than Scientology or a psychiatrist.

Rosemary Ferlita practiced in St. Petersburg. At first, Bea drove Albert across the State from Holly Hill to St. Petersburg. Then, when it appeared Rosemary was doing some good, Darlene and Tom let Albert move into one of their two condos. That way Tom and Darlene could keep an eye on Albert. Darlene always liked Albert, and she had known Rosemary Ferlita for a number of years and she felt Tom was right, Rosemary was very practical.

Rosemary was perfect for Albert. After their first session Rosemary suggested Albert take dance lessons at the YMCA. Albert was shy but Rosemary insisted and she accompanied Albert to the lessons and was his partner if the dance required a partner. Otherwise the dances were acts of self-expression and more exercise than routine. Albert threw himself into the lessons.

Rosemary suggested that Albert exercise when he complained about his weight and she started him on a diet. The exercise was available at the old YMCA and they had rooms for rent for men. Rosemary had been against the idea that Albert stay with Tom and Darlene. She agreed to the arrangement only as an interim measure. She expected Albert to find a place of his own within a month after he moved to town. Albert said he would stay at the "Y" for the time being. It had small studio apartments. Rosemary agreed, but after they spoke, Albert realized that he needed to broaden his scope and find another place to live. He was spending all his time at the "Y".

He got the newspaper and went through the want ads and got addresses for apartments and borrowed Rosemary's car and looked until he found an apartment on the water that had a dock. Albert loved to fish. When he stayed downtown at the YMCA, he went to the municipal pier and rented a rod and reel and bait and fished for hours. Passersby would talk to him and ask him if he had any luck. Yes, he had luck. He caught a few. He was happy that people felt he was normal and spoke to him.

Albert bought a small white truck, a Datsun. He had mobility and independence. He could visit the Homestead if he wanted but he really didn't want to. He had a phone and he spoke to Bea to keep in touch. He rarely asked how the business was doing and when he did he had a vacant feeling like he was talking about the ancient past.

Albert still fished on the public pier on the bay. Downtown he had the company of passersby and the conversation, but most times, after he rented his apartment, he liked to fish on the dock behind his residence. He was able to spend time thinking about himself and for himself. He liked his apartment. He invited Rosemary over for dinner. She asked him where he obtained all the furniture. Albert confided that he liked to go to thrift stores and sometimes he found things on the side of the road. He found a TV that way. It was abandoned. It worked. He was intrigued by the device. He was the first member of the Barnes family to own a television. Living at the Plantation or the Homestead you were in the woods. There was such poor reception that a TV wasn't a good buy.

Albert rarely watched the shows, the sitcoms. He didn't understand the humor. It was lost on him. He liked the local news. He watched at 6 p.m. and again at 11 if he was still awake.

Albert fell into a routine. He liked his life. It was the first time ever that he was at ease.

Otherwise, the Barnes Family was suffering from the turmoil of the loss of their hard won businesses. Everyone was being sued.

Part V

The Main Feature

Chapter 20
The Bell Bar

Mark Person could only be good for so long. Thirty-seven days after he moved into the Safari Beach Hotel on Spa Beach near the municipal pier in downtown St. Petersburg he sneaked away from John Bose, the Summer Deputy Sheriff who was surveilling him. It was after midnight. Person went out the back window of his room and out to the beach and then he was on Beach Drive and he went into the Old Northeast section of town and he was away. It was dark and quiet. He went to the Bell Bar.

The Bell Bar was a biker bar populated by felons and failed members of twelve step programs. If you wanted to be bad you went to the Bell. You could find any perversion or avenue of escape from reality you desired. The bar was like a magnet drawing Person into its field; it had a tractor beam.

The Bell Bar had a few upstanding patrons. Members of the Florida Bar, lawyers who stopped in for a beer on their way home after a late night of research or while they waited for a jury to come to a decision. The Judicial Building was only a few blocks away. The bailiffs at the courthouse knew the number for the tavern. When the verdict arrived the bailiffs would call the bar and the barkeep would announce the jury was in and the lawyers would curse and leave the bar.

Person pushed open the door in the rear of the bar. The door was the emergency exit to the alley behind the establishment. The entrance was unlit and it was 1 a.m., two hours 'til closing. Just enough time to down a few brews. Person went to the bar and ordered a draft and a shot of whiskey. He took a sip of beer and then downed the 2 ounce shot of bourbon. He cradled the beer in his fist and waited as the hard liquor burned as it raced down his esophagus into his belly.

No one spoke to Person. He was acknowledged by the bartender with a nod and then he ordered and the bartender moved on and left Person alone to his thoughts. Person had been waiting for word from the FBI. He didn't expect that he would be given a copy of the report of the experts, but he would know if he had been connected to the kidnapping of Becky Sue Painter. He would be arrested and taken into custody.

It was a waiting game. Every day he called and spoke to Tom or James and he was told the same thing. They didn't know whether he would be arrested or not. Each time they gave him the same advice. If he was arrested he should say nothing to the police. He should ask to speak to his lawyers. Either Tom or James would come to jail and be present if he was interrogated.

After finishing his beer, Person walked into the back room. Two men were shooting pool. Their money was on the small table next to the pool table. Others waited to play. They deposited their ante in cash to reserve their place. The antes were lined up one after another, about seven deep. Person would not be able to get a turn to play a game before the bar closed.

Person watched the game awhile. He really didn't understand the finesse needed to play the game. He liked to slam the balls into one another. He rarely won a game, which was good, because he made a good player angry. Person just wasted a pool shark's time shooting pool. He was no competition for a good player.

Person rubbed his belly and walked back in the bar. He was looking for a little excitement. He worked his way toward the front door. The bar was full now, standing room only, with customers looking to get a drink before last call. Person spotted the twenty-something tucked in the corner booth in the front in the dark. She had her hair in a bun and she was wearing a pair of odd glasses. The rims of the prescription lens were purple. The rims of her glasses matched the purple pull over that announced the female's big breasts. Person sidled up to the booth and asked if he could sit down.

"No matter to me, I'm leaving."

"Stay a bit. Can I buy you a beer?"

"I've had a few. Are you looking for a party?"

"What's the deal?"

"Twenty bucks," she said as she looked over the rims of her glasses. "I've got a room down the street."

"It would be a short date."

"Yah, an interlude," she chuckled.

"Do you want a drink before we go?"

"No, save your money. Visit the john and get some protection. I'm out of rubbers. Get some colored ones. I like purple."

Person went to the toilet and inserted three quarters into the machine that dispensed condoms for medicinal necessity only. He got three purple condoms, he slipped them in his pocket and collected his date. Person downed the dregs of his beer. She had donned her coat and hoisted her large purse, which was the size of an overnight bag, and they went out the door.

The Bell Bar was on 8th Avenue and 4th Street. Streets ran north and south and avenues ran east and west. A simple grid system. The couple walked north on 4th about two blocks. There were small mom and pop businesses along the street. Most of the businesses were motels with 10 or 12 units. They catered to business people and couples on vacation looking for a cheap place to stay the night.

Person's date had a room in the Owl Inn. The neon sign flickered and the vacancy sign was still lit. They walked past the office. The manager was behind the desk. He acknowledged the woman with a shake of the head. Business was good, thought the manager, the Shriners must be in town.

The manager got a good look at Person. He was tall and white.

Miss Purple took a motel key from her bag and inserted it in the lock in the door handle and opened the door. She sat at the small table in the room that had a pen and writing paper imprinted with the motel's logo. She was trim. Her face was flush with alcohol and she had pock mark scars on her face below her ear lobes. She loosened her hair and pulled off her top. She had hairy pits and wore no bra. She kicked off her shoes, slippers with no socks. She wore tight knit pants, black. She stood up and shook them off and she was nude. She climbed into bed.

"Put the money in my hand and then get into bed. Oh, and hit the light."

Person looked around. There was a dresser in the corner with framed photographs of children and adults. Maybe she lives in the room, thought Person. He went into the bathroom. He removed his clothing and piled his belongings in the corner. He ran some water and threw a few drops on his face, spritzed his upper torso and dried with the sole raggedy towel in the room. He left the light on and closed the door. The light from the bathroom bled into the main room of the unit.

Person had a bill, legal tender in his hand and he gave it to Miss Purple. She lifted it up and stared at it in the gloom of the room and took both hands and snapped the bill. "Sounds like a twenty."

"It is. I wouldn't cheat you."

"Me either." She reached between Persons legs and grabbed his cock. He was excited. She rolled over on top and began to work. She had at it a while but had no success. It was taking too long.

"What do you want?"

"How about a little head?"

"That would be more dough-re-me."

"How much?"

"Ten more."

"I don't want to sound like a lawyer but you said $20 not $30."

"I didn't realize you would be so much trouble. I didn't charge you for the room."

"What are you talking about?"

"I had to pay for the room."

"You can't tell me this is the only time you used this room for business tonight."

"That's none of your business. You need to pay me. The local rate does not include the room. The room is $5 extra."

"Nickels and dimes ... I'll remember that next time."

Person rolled on top. "Forget the blow. I'll do it myself." He began to hump the lady and she began to get into it. Person pushed up so his chest was off her body. At first he shifted his weight onto his elbows and then he got up on his hands and she slid down into the bed. Person was on his knees and he continued to pump. Miss Purple began to grunt. Person laughed when she grunted. She cursed him and slapped his face. Person moved his hands around her throat and he began to grapple her neck. At first she thought it was good but then she panicked. She tried to push him away but could not remove his hands. She could not scream. Finally she grabbed his breast and twisted with her last bit of strength. Too late. She was dead.

Person did not let go of her neck. He kept pumping. He was in agony and ecstasy at the same time. He finished his business.

Person pushed her away. His lover's body was slack and her neck was limp. Her tongue protruded from her mouth. Her tongue was purple. Her face was red and blue and then black. He threw the covers over her as he got out of the bed.

"Shit."

***

Person had looked everywhere in the room for something that was flammable. He was looking for an accelerant that would cause a fire hot enough to consume Miss Purple's body. He found cleaning fluids in the closet in the bath.

Person took a shower and used the single towel to wipe down the bathroom walls and mirror and toilet and tub. He piled everything he thought would burn on the bed on top of the corpse. He pulled up the carpet so air would penetrate the mass of textiles, rayon, nylon, all petro-chemicals that would burn. There was a window in the bathroom in the back of the room and a window in the front. He opened both and the early morning breeze began to push through the room.

Person got dressed. He looked at the labels of the cleaners from the closet to see which were flammable. He soaked the carpet with the chemicals and then he waited five minutes and struck a match and lit the pyre. Person remained in the room to make sure the materials caught fire. When the blaze had reached the ceiling he left the room with the door open so the oxygen outside the room would feed the fire.

Air, fuel and flame, Person had the prescription for a conflagration that consumed the entire contents of the room.

It was 4 a.m.; the manager had gone to bed. All the bars and their whores had gone to wherever and there was no more business. Then the manager heard the banging on the doors and he ran out and saw the flames. The front picture window had exploded out of Miss Purple's motel room and the flames were shooting up to the roof and the tar and roofing shingles had caught fire. The whole building would go, he thought. He ran in to use his phone but the line was dead.

Who was here? he thought. What rooms were rented? The manager ran outside. He began to bang on the doors of the rooms closest to 4th Street. The first fire engine arrived. The lieutenant called for backup. The police arrived. The police were told to alert the neighbors and bang on doors.

Person helped. He banged on the doors of a motel to the south of the Owl Inn called the Blue Bird Inn and then he slid into the moonless night.

***

Person returned to the rear window of his room in the Safari. He used both hands to push the window open. He wiped his prints off the outside of the window and climbed in and rolled onto the floor. He was nude. His clothes were in the dumpster.

He showered in the dark. He cleaned himself thoroughly, dried and got into bed. He slept soundly, immediately, like he was in a coma.

He was at ease, totally at ease.

***

Was it a dream, Person thought? Someone was banging on the door with their fist.

"Mark Person, Mark Person, come to the door."

Person shook himself awake and went to the door. He was wrapped in the sheet from the bed.

"Where have you been?" shouted John Bose, the Summer County Deputy Sheriff.

"Here, I've been here, asleep."

"I saw you go out the front door last night."

"That wasn't me. I have not been out. What time is it?"

"Eight a.m. You never sleep this late."

"I was tired. Couldn't get to sleep. I kept hearing sirens."

"There was a big fire last night. Two motels burnt to the ground on 4th Street. There were fire engines from all over the county. Tampa Fire Department even came over to help."

"Anyone hurt?"

"I haven't heard."

"You know I would not get you in trouble. I promised you I would not leave my room without telling you," said Person.

"That's what you said. After last night, I didn't know if I could believe you." said the deputy.

"I promise you I did not go out last night."

"Okay, okay, I believe you. What are you doing today?" asked the deputy.

"I don't know what's on the agenda but I'll call the attorney and find out if I'm going in there today."

Person turned on the television to Channel 8, local news.

"Here's that fire," said Person to Deputy Bose, and he invited him into the room.

The deputy sat on the edge of the bed and watched the black and white TV. Person reached up behind the deputy and casually began to rub his back.

"Not today," said the deputy.

"We are still friends." said Person.

"Yes," said the deputy. "We are still friends."

Person grabbed his clothes from the dresser and went into the bathroom to dress. He inspected himself in the full length mirror that hung behind the door. He had no bruises or cuts or scratches except on the nipple of his left breast where Miss Purple tried to rip off his breast. She had left a black and blue swatch on Person's chest but the mark was mostly hidden by his chest hair.

"What are they saying about the fire?" Person yelled out from the shower.

"The reporter says it's the worst fire in years. It took 11 engines to put it out and wet down the adjoining buildings to keep them from igniting."

"Anyone hurt?"

"They aren't saying," said the deputy. "There's probably a body. They aren't saying one way or another. Looks like it's still hot. Smoldering."

Person finished buttoning his shirt and then went to the desk and called Night, Adams and Street. Tom wanted to see him as soon as he could get in the office.

"I have to see my lawyers," Person told the deputy. "You want to give me a ride or do you want to wait for Investigator Faircloth to get here?"

"I'll take you," said the deputy. Deputy Bose had started to take Person in the police vehicle if it was a short drive. The two men had regular conversations and Person listened attentively as Bose told him about his history when he was up north. They were both transplants from Connecticut. They were almost friends. They were lovers.

Chapter 21
Good Work, Detective

The law offices of Night, Adams and Street were on Beach Drive and 8th Avenue. As the crow flies, the office was six blocks from the fire at the Owl Inn and its companion motel the Blue Bird Inn. There was still a heavy smell of burned petroleum ... thick, black and suffocating ... that hung in the air when the deputy dropped Person off at the office. The deputy parked the unmarked cruiser and sat in the car to wait. Person went inside and took the stairs to the second floor.

Tom brought him into the office as soon as he arrived. "We should know something on whether the State Attorney will proceed in your case soon. James was before the court yesterday afternoon and the State Attorney told him they had been in communication with the FBI."

"Soon," repeated Person. "That will be good. I'm getting tired of that hotel."

The pair again discussed what Person was to do if he was arrested. He was to be cooperative and say nothing. He was to ask for his attorney. Although James had given him the same advice before he was arrested in the parking lot of the XYZ Lounge, Person had failed to follow the advice and instead he had spoken to the police detectives for many hours.

"Do you know anything about the fire in the motels?" Person asked Tom.

"Not much yet. Faircloth is over there poking around. We think we represent the company that insures the two motels. They are a total loss. We think there is at least one fatality – a lady who keeps a room in the Owl. She services the sexual appetites of about half the members of the police force who are married, and all of the bachelors. The lady is named Pricilla Bonnet. They call her 'Pierce'."

"Who's handling the case?" asked Person.

"The SPFD arson investigator and a homicide detective, I don't know what his name is yet." Tom thought the questions were strange but Person was "strange". Tom set the question aside and asked Person if he had any other questions about his case.

"No, I'll ask the deputy to take me back to the hotel. We were watching the TV about the fire."

Why is he so intent on the fire, thought Tom?

***

That evening, detectives from the St. Petersburg Police Department were interviewing patrons of the Bell Bar. Paddy, the bartender, had been on duty until 2 a.m. He said he saw Pierce with a guy. "Actually," he said, "she was with a few different men that evening."

"How many men?"

"You know how it is in here, it's really busy and they don't give me no help so I don't know her business. But it was more than three or four times that Pierce was in and out."

"Was she drinking?"

"Yes. The usual. She sat in the corner. Someone would buy her a drink. She has scotch/rocks. Let's the ice melt. She could nurse a drink for an hour."

"When did you see her last?"

"She left with a tall guy at about 1:30 a.m. Just after last call. They threw the drinks down and walked out the door. She did that thing she does. Ya know. It's like she is Gary Cooper where she points her finger at you and blinks and she's out the door."

"What time was that?"

"Jeez, am I a suspect now? You're repeating your questions. I already told you. It was 1:30 a.m."

"Did you recognize the man?"

"No, I only saw her. She was wearing that purple top that shows off her breasts. I was concentrating on her breasts. I didn't see the guy. He was taller than her and bigger than a bread box and that's all I'm sure about. It was busy and it was last call."

"How long was the man in the bar?"

"An hour at most. He had a Boilermaker. Beer and a slug of bourbon. Then he went back to the pool table. Then he sat with Pierce and she did her business and set a date, for all I know."

"Who controlled the pool table?"

"Eddie. He was winning like he always does. No one could beat him. The big man was only back there a minute. He left a five dollar bill on the bar next to his empty glass when he went back in the back. I hate it when a customer leaves money unattended on the bar. I didn't want anyone to flinch the fiver and there would be a fight. So I watched the money."

"Where's Eddie staying?"

"I don't know. He will be back tonight most likely. He left here a winner, unlike Pierce."

***

The detectives had spoken to the manager of the Owl Inn. He didn't remember that much about Pierce's date. He was tall with a good build. He saw his face but he was plain looking. There was nothing to distinguish him from any other white man. The thing that was unusual was he thought he saw him after the fire banging on doors warning people.

"I thought when I saw him beating on the doors that Pierce had gotten out of the room. If he was out beating on the doors, she had to be outside too. That was my thought. She was a good person." The manager started to cry. "But I guess she didn't get out. Pierce was the only female in that room. I saw her come back and walk past the office at about 2 a.m. with a man. If there is a female body in the room it has to be Pierce."

"Do you think we could get an artist up here to see if you could describe the man and we could get a drawing of the man?"

"I would be happy to help."

***

The arson inspector for the St. Petersburg Fire Department called the Florida Department of Law Enforcement in Sanford, Florida for assistance. The FDLE arson inspector located the source of the fire to be the bed of Pricilla Bonnet's motel unit in the Owl Inn.

"Could Pricilla Bonnet have been smoking in bed, dozed off and her cigarette lit the bed on fire?"

The instructor from the fire college said no.

"The fire was too hot and too quick." The instructor had brought his dog and the animal could smell accelerant where the bed was located.

"It was arson." That was the inspector's opinion.

***

The homicide detectives walked across the hall at headquarters and spoke to the detectives who worked undercover the night before.

"Was anyone working undercover duty last night in the Bell Bar?"

Two of the detectives admitted they were in the bar late.

"Did you see Pierce?"

"Yes, she was in her usual seat in the corner."

"Was she with a customer?"

"Not sure, we were looking for new blood, dealing drugs."

"Did you see a big guy, tall, non-descript sort of a guy with Pierce?"

"Maybe."

"We'll have a drawing of the perp later. We want you to look at it."

***

Two hours later, the homicide detective delivered the drawing to Vice and Narcotics.

"That guy in the drawing was with Pierce according to the manager of the motel. He bought her a drink at last call. They left the bar together," said the homicide detective to the vice detectives.

The undercover Vice detectives mumbled that they agreed the man in the drawing was the man who left with Pierce.

***

Homicide gave the drawing to the TV news and the press. The next morning the newspaper ran a picture of the drawing on the front page. The TV broadcast the picture on the 7 a.m. news. It was the only story. Yesterday the fire was the story and today the "be on the lookout for" the suspect was the story.

Homicide received 27 tips by lunch. They were running down the leads but none were that promising.

***

Person woke early the day after the arson. It was 7:00 a.m. and he was in his hotel room staring at the TV. There was the picture of the drawing of the suspect on the screen in black and white. The drawing resembled Person. He could see himself in the picture. He had a panic attack.

After he saw the broadcast of the sketch Person was determined to stay in his room. He did not eat. He was panicky and used a bag to control the panic attacks – breathing in the bag and then inhaling the CO_2 from the bag. He became dizzy and he lay in bed and curled up. He resolved to keep his mouth shut this time. Let his lawyer handle it.

Person was convinced he would be arrested. But no one came to the door and he received no calls.

Person watched the TV and absorbed the news all day long.

Then in the news that night at 11 p.m., there was a report that the police had made an arrest in the arson/murder case.

The TV news reporter had an exclusive. The suspect who was arrested had been identified in a line-up. The man had been charged after he confessed. He had been in the Bell Bar and he went home with the victim to her room in the Owl Inn. They got in a fight and he hit her and killed her. He threw her in the bed and then he set fire to the room to cover up the crime.

Person listened. He was flummoxed. How could this be, he thought? It was a trick. The police floated this story to trick Person to go outside his room so they could arrest him. It can't be this simple. Could he escape justice just because the wrong guy was charged?

***

James DeMarco had also been watching the news all day. He expected an arrest in the arson/homicide at the Owl Inn. But he thought the individual who would be charged would be their client, Mark Person. When DeMarco looked at the picture of the drawing of the suspect on the front page of the newspaper, he saw a distinct resemblance to a person he knew. DeMarco thought the suspect was Mark Person.

DeMarco spoke to Faircloth about the drawing.

"I saw the similarity," conceded Faircloth. "I even talked to the deputy from Summer County. The deputy said Person was in his room at the Safari all night. The deputy is Person's alibi. The deputy said he saw him in the morning and he didn't leave his room all night.

"Our guy is in the clear," said Faircloth, rubbing his hands.

"Amazing," said DeMarco.

***

Deputy John Bose had worked 40 hours straight. He was the lead detective in charge of the surveillance of Mark Person at the Safari Beach Motel. After working 40 hours straight he thought he would be off for at least one day but he was told to report to the Captain of the Guards at the Summer County Jail for special training.

The sheriff anticipated there would be an arrest of Mark Person soon because the forensic reports were back from the FBI.

The sheriff had one more nasty job to heap on the back of John Bose. He was to be trained to conduct body cavity searches. When the order to arrest Mark Person was given, the sheriff intended to have his men harass Person with a body cavity search in an attempt to demoralize him and hopefully cause him to say something incriminating. The arrest team would include three very large deputies. John Bose would be the one to perform the search and the two other officers would know how to grapple Person to cause him pain during the arrest.

A body cavity search is an extreme invasion of privacy and there needs to be a reason for the use of the procedure. The State Attorney and the sheriff thought that the crimes charged, murders and kidnappings, would be sufficient to warrant the search just for the protection of the officers. The arrest, particularly if there was injury caused to Person during the search, might open the door to the defense to argue that any incriminating statement that resulted from the arrest was coerced.

The State Attorney felt there would be less likelihood that the judge would throw out an incriminating statement if the officer who conducted the body cavity search was trained in the procedure. Therefore, John Bose was told to report to the jail to meet with the warden and the Captain of the Guards for training on his day off.

Although Bose was able to put a smile on it and joke with the captain about rooting around in Person's anus, this was the final straw. John Bose did not feel that the use of the procedure was fair to the accused, particularly since he could see the search was not being conducted for the protection of the arresting officers but instead it was intended to force a confession out of Mark Person. The authorities knew they needed an incentive since they had not been otherwise able to obtain a confession in 11 hours of questioning Person after the soliciting arrest.

Once Bose understood what the sheriff had in mind for Person, the deputy decided to even the playing field and tell Person exactly what was going to happen to him when he was arrested. Person would be prepared and keep his mouth shut.

Deputy John Bose was also upset that he was being ordered to act in an illegal way. But he shut his mouth and marched forward.

Chapter 22
Jesse Lee Rice

There was a call for James DeMarco. It was the Office of the Public Attorney. The Public Attorney said they had a conflict on a case and wanted Night, Adams and Street to take the conflict case. The Office of Public Attorney represented a man who was a witness in a case. That client was a witness against a second man they represented and so they could not ethically represent the second man. The second man arrested had been charged with killing Pricilla "Pierce" Bonnet.

DeMarco said he would have to call back. He had to speak to the partners before agreeing to take the new case.

Tom was against the appointment. He called the Public Attorney back and told him the firm could not take any more free cases, particularly now with the case load they were handling. He reminded the Public Attorney they were handling the Mark Person case.

Later that day, Tom had a call from the Chief Judge. "I intend to appoint your firm to represent this arsonist and murderer that was just arrested for killing Pierce Bonnet."

"We can't handle the case. Why can't some silk stocking lawyer take the case? Give it to my wife's ex-husband."

"Tom, you know he only handles civil cases."

"That's no excuse. He can read up on criminal law. I handle civil cases and I still practice criminal law."

The judge wasn't having it. "Quit screwing with me, Tom. I'm going to appoint you. You can appeal the order of appointment if you want, but as of this moment you are the attorney on the case."

Tom knew he had a losing hand with the judge. He had to make the best of it. He was able to get the court to appoint Faircloth as the investigator and pay his fee separate from the attorney fee. Also, the judge agreed that the State had to provide copies of all reports without charge and the court appointed an arson expert to consult with the defense. That was the best Tom could get from the judge. Otherwise, the law allowed Tom's firm to be paid a flat fee of $1,500. That was not enough to pay the secretary for her time working on the case. It was not enough to pay Tom.

***

Tom brought Jenny Barnes into his office. He explained that she would be lead attorney on the case of State vs. Jesse Lee Rice. He told her to work with Karen to get the file together and to get out on the street with Faircloth and see what she could dig up. He would give her some advice if she needed it. It would be an easy case. "Everyone says the guy is guilty," said Tom. Then Tom added, "Just kidding ... just kidding."

***

While Tom waited he took a call from the Summer County State Attorney. The SA wanted to meet in Glade City that afternoon.

"Do I need to bring my client?"

"No, not yet."

"What do you mean, 'not yet'? Are you going to arrest him or not?"

"Just come up here alone. Bring DeMarco and whoever else you want but we don't want to speak to Mark Person at this time."

Tom rang DeMarco and told him to clear the calendar. They were going to Glade City.

Tom walked into Jenny's office. Karen and Faircloth were with her preparing to go out on the street.

"I need the three of you to get a handle on what the State has against this fellow, Jesse Lee Rice." said Tom. "He is supposed to have killed Pricilla Bonnet. I think everyone knew her as 'Pierce'. She was a prostitute who worked out of the Bell Bar.

"Faircloth, you go with Jenny to the jail. I want you to do the talking, and Jenny, you listen." Tom nodded at Jenny.

She nodded back.

"Faircloth, I need to know if he confessed like they said on TV," said Tom. "If he confessed find out if he still says he killed her. Find out why he did it and if she provoked him." Tom thought a second, then continued.

"With the name 'Jesse Lee' he's probably been around the block a few times. We also need to look at mitigating versus aggravating circumstances. Jenny, bring the list of death penalty circumstances from the Florida Statutes so you can refer to the law and ask questions.

"My guess is this guy has rocks for brains. See if he has mental problems and if he has any learning deficiencies, shaken baby syndrome, you know."

"Ok, Boss," said Faircloth as he began to leave the room.

"I'm not done talking. Faircloth, take Jenny to the scene of the fire. Jenny, take a camera and take pictures. I expect you to burn through 100 or 200 pictures. You are going to show those pictures to the arson expert we hire. Karen, you call Greg Jones, the PhD at the Fire College in Ocala. See if he will handle our fire investigation. Set up an appointment tomorrow. Tell Greg to go out and look at the scene. Tell Greg the state is paying his fee so he will need to pad his hours."

"Last, I need you two, Jenny and Faircloth, to go talk to the bartender at the Bell Bar. His name is 'Paddy'. Tell him I sent you. He owes me. Tell him I said to tell you everything he knows about the case. He will want a witness fee. Bring a crisp $100 bill."

Tom left the room. He was all tensed up.

Jenny turned to Karen. "Did you write all that down? I can't remember what he said after 'I want you to ...'."

"I wrote it all down," said Karen. "I'll type the list and make copies so we all know what to do."

***

Tom and James DeMarco rode in James' small, socially conscious VW automobile to the Summer County Sheriff's Office. Tom always complained that he didn't have enough room in the car. James just smiled. "We could take your car."

Tom scrunched his arms together. He hadn't been driving. He became too upset with other drivers and got in screaming matches at intersections. Darlene took his keys. It wasn't normal to start a fight out on the road. She wanted him to see a neurologist and she spoke to Tom's general practitioner about a referral. Tom refused to go to the neurologist so Tom's GP wrote a letter to DMV (Department of Motor Vehicles) stating Tom was unfit to drive and the agency revoked Tom's driver's license. Tom could not drive until his doctor wrote a letter stating that he was able to drive.

As a result, Tom agreed to an appointment with a neurologist in a month. So far, he followed his doctor's advice. He wasn't driving.

It was hell to get old, thought Tom.

"Why are we going to Glade City?" asked DeMarco.

"I don't know. They wouldn't say. They wanted to see us in person without our client. That's all I know."

***

Jesse Lee Rice was still locked up in the St. Petersburg Police Department holding facility awaiting transfer to the Pinellas County Jail in Clearwater. He was a big man, 6'2" tall and strong. He could break a man's arms. He was nondescript. A white male 30 to 32 years of age. He had no distinguishing marks or scars or tattoos. He was a petty thief and a druggie and a drunk. He had no arrest for a violent crime until the murder of Pierce Bonnet. He worked in construction hauling dry wall when he wasn't claiming his back was injured. He grew up in St. Petersburg. He failed to complete 9th grade and left school when he was sixteen years old. He had a dull look and was slow speaking. It wasn't a drawl, he was just slow to put one word to another. People had a tendency to finish his sentences and he would just nod in agreement. He had no family in town. His mother was up north. He lived in a cheap motel room with some other men when he was working. If he wasn't working he was on the street living in a cardboard box.

Faircloth asked Jesse if he killed Pricilla Bonnet and he said, "They said I did."

"Do you think you killed her?"

"Well, uh, no."

"Did you confess to killing her?"

"Confess?"

"Do you know what I'm asking you? It's simple." Faircloth bored in, pressing Jesse Lee. "Did you kill a lady two nights ago and burn down a motel on 4th Street or not?"

"No," said Jesse Lee. He was shaking.

Faircloth and Jenny obtained all the information Tom wanted from the new client and they left the holding facility and headed for the crime scene.

***

Faircloth had been at the scene of the fire the day before. Tom had told him to get pictures. Tom thought their law firm represented the insurance company that insured the Owl and the Bluebird. Tom was wrong. The firm had not represented that company since Roger Adams had been alive.

Faircloth explained to Jenny that he had taken a ton of photographs but that Jenny should take pictures of what she thought was important without being influenced by him.

Jenny used the old 35 mm camera that Marla had given her for graduation. Tom told her to take 100 to 200 photos and she did what she was told. They took the film to the Photo-Mat for one day service so they would have the pictures developed for the expert to review the next day.

It was good they came to the scene when they did, the City had condemned the site and both buildings were to be demolished and removed by the end of the day.

***

It was 6 p.m. The late shift at the Bell Bar would be on duty. Jenny asked Faircloth to let her ask the questions this time. Faircloth agreed.

"So," said Jenny "are you Paddy the bartender?"

The bartender looked around like he couldn't hear who was talking to him.

Faircloth reached across the bar and touched his arm. "Come on Paddy," said Faircloth. "Tom needs some information about Pricilla Bonnet. He sent Jenny and me over to ask some questions about Pricilla's death."

Paddy just swirled the towel in his hand around on the top of the bar. He was still deaf and dumb.

Faircloth took out the crisp one hundred dollar bill from his wallet and laid it on the table. Paddy scooped it up, shoved it in his pocket, grabbed a bottle of Crotty's Bourbon and three glasses and headed to the booth in the front so he could watch everything happening in the bar. He yelled to the back. "Eddie, come watch the bar. I have to talk to some folks."

Eddie came out of the back with a pool cue. He turned on the TV, poured himself a draft beer and watched the news on Channel 8.

Paddy poured three drinks to the rim of the glasses.

"So what do you want to know, little lady? Where I'm sitting is the last place Pierce sat when she was here. Fact is, this is where she always sat. She sat on her gold mine, so ta' speak."

"What do you mean?" asked Jenny.

"She was a whore. She sat here on her twat. We're going to be interviewing for Pierce's replacement later tonight. Do you want to have a go?"

Jenny ignored him. "When did you see her last?"

"The morning she died, 1:30 a.m."

"She say anything?"

"She was blotto I think. She gave me her sign, a wink and she pointed at me with her trigger finger and she left with the man that they say killed her."

"Do you know Jesse Lee Rice?"

"That thieving rat. Yes I know him. He lives in a cardboard box around here someplace close by."

"The police haven't released this yet, but they say Jesse killed Pierce."

Paddy pressed forward on his elbows. "I admit Jesse Lee looks like the man who left with Pierce at 1:30 a.m. but Jesse isn't the same man."

Jenny looked Paddy in the eyes and said, "We got the police reports and there were two undercover cops in here that night and they identified Jesse as the killer. Picked him out in a line-up. They said Jesse was here and left with Pierce."

"Those cops couldn't pick snot from their nose. I saw those cops. They were drunk and wasted. I had to get Eddie to drive them back to the station." Paddy yelled down the bar. "Eddie, you drove those two undercover cops back to the station the night Pierce was murdered?"

"Yeah, I drove them."

"They give you a tip?"

Eddie blew a heavy breath out of his mouth and said, "Yeah, Shamrock in the fifth race at Aqueduct."

The two men laughed. Great joke, they thought.

Paddy poured three more bourbons to the rim.

Eddie yelled. "Hey Paddy, look. They got a picture of Jesse Lee on the TV screen. He's being arrested. They say he killed Pierce."

"Eddie, did you see Jesse in here the night Pierce died?"

"No, Jesse wasn't there that night."

"How long were you in here that night?"

"I was winning shooting pool. I never left," said Eddie.

Paddy turned back to his guests. "See? What I tell you? Jesse wasn't here. The guy that left with Pierce wasn't Jesse. Jesse isn't innocent, he's a thief, but Jesse isn't a killer, he didn't kill Pierce."

Paddy collected the glasses and the bottle. "That'll be nine dollars," he said.

Faircloth threw a ten dollar bill on the table. "Keep the change."

Chapter 23
Glade City

Tom had not driven to Glade City in a number of years. The town was small. The primary industry was a juice plant that made orange juice concentrate. The plant was constructed in the center of thousands of acres of rolling hills planted with citrus trees. The oranges were picked and delivered to the plant for processing into concentrate.

The acreage was fully maximized by agriculture uses. If the land did not have an orange tree growing on it, there was a cow, bull or steer feeding on the Bahia grass pasture land, or there was a grove of pine or cypress trees being grown for timber to be cut into lumber at the sawmill in the town of Lacoochee, located north on the Withlacoochee River.

Glade City was the county seat for Summer County. The county maintained its 100-year-old court house and government buildings in the city. The buildings housed the offices of the sheriff, the clerk, the tax collector, the property appraiser and the state attorney.

Tom had forgotten how beautiful the scenery was on the drive to the courthouse. DeMarco didn't see anything but the road, which was winding over hills and around lakes. The road had numerous sharp, 90 degree turns. If DeMarco was on the interstate he could use the driving time to think about his cases. The interstate was designed to allow a driver sufficient time to react to a dangerous condition. But on the curving, narrow, two-lane back roads leading to Glade City a driver had to be alert for school buses, horses, wild animals and cattle on the road.

The lawyers arrived at the State Attorney's office safely at 3:30 p.m. They didn't have an appointment. They were asked to get there as soon as they could.

The SA's office was run much differently since John Hale had died. Hale had been a very uptight individual. He was hard to deal with. It was difficult to resolve a case without a trial or a plea bargain with the judge. Hale refused to participate in plea discussions. He used that fact when he ran for office. The voters liked the fact he didn't agree to sentences and he never lost a race for office. No one knew why he had killed himself because there was no note, but the coroner had ruled his death a suicide.

Tom and John Hale had been absolute enemies. Tom got along with the man the governor appointed to fill the balance of Hale's term. Charles Young had worked for John Hale for 15 years. Young came along behind Hale picking up the pieces of one contentious prosecution after another. Because of that experience, Prosecutor Young knew how to resolve matters quickly and efficiently. If he couldn't prove a case he got rid of it. He was very careful to state the reasons why he did not proceed. His decisions not to prosecute (called a Nol Pros), were sometimes very lengthy, stating that a witness had gone back on their testimony or that expert testimony disagreed with eyewitnesses identification. He wanted the public to understand why he was not prosecuting a case. It was not because of some whim on his part.

Young was a short man. He was shorter than Hale. Unlike Hale, he was quick with a smile and a firm handshake. He could laugh at a joke and understand the pain of his victims and tried to dispense justice on their behalf.

Young liked DeMarco. They were close in age. Young had a fear of Tom Night. The SA Office had a losing track record with Tom when they tried cases against him. To gain an edge, Hale tried to hide evidence from Tom, but the tactic backfired. Young learned from that mistake and he was particular in his requirement that his assistants give the defense the evidence that might lead to defenses or proof of innocence, along with the evidence that would damn the defendant to prison.

At the meeting regarding Mark Person, besides Prosecutor Young were the Sheriff of Summer County and Lieutenant Jim McBride and Sergeant Joseph Rainey.

"So," asked Tom, "why are we here?"

"The purpose of this meeting is to talk to you about the evidence we found so far in the kidnapping of Becky Sue Painter," said Prosecutor Young. "The FBI forensic reports are in. The DNA typing shows a match from a sample of the perpetrator's blood found on Becky's dress with a sample of your client's saliva found on a coffee cup your client discarded in our undercover vehicle when he was a passenger."

"DNA Fingerprint evidence has not been admitted as evidence in a criminal case in Florida," said DeMarco. "It is not considered reliable."

"That's correct. Mr. Person's case could be the first."

"Do you have anything else? Any admissible forensic evidence? Finger prints for example?"

"Not so far as the FBI analysis is concerned. No, we do not."

"Do we get the reports to share with our client?"

"Of course." said the deputy. "Copies will be made available."

"Is there anything else you want to discuss?" asked Tom. "You didn't bring us all the way up here to discuss the fact that you have no admissible evidence that ties our client to the kidnapping of the young girl Becky Sue Painter or the murder of the other five girls."

"You might ask your client if he would agree to plead *Nolo Contendre* (no contest) to a single false imprisonment charge. We would reduce the kidnapping charge. The kidnapping charge carries a life sentence. The False Imprisonment carries 30 years. We would expect Mr. Person to agree that he would receive the maximum sentence of 30 years. We would agree not to pursue the five open homicides so far as your client is concerned."

"Anything else?" asked DeMarco. "What about this soliciting prostitution charge?"

DeMarco has to be kidding, thought Tom.

"That case is in Alachua County. My understanding is that the defendants are given a $500 fine or time served. Your client was in jail for a day. He could receive time served."

"Am I correct that Mr. Person would only be subject to prosecution in Summer County? Alachua County would waive any rights it might have to prosecute Mr. Person for the old cases involving the five girls?" asked Tom.

"That is my understanding from the conversation I had with the SA in Alachua County."

"See if you can firm that up while we are here and we will take the offer back to our client," said DeMarco.

***

Tom and James DeMarco sat in a room by themselves waiting for word from the State Attorney in Alachua County. As Tom thumbed through a magazine looking at pictures of the latest in bass boats he asked, "Where are the courts on this DNA Fingerprinting?"

DeMarco leaned forward and whispered, "The courts haven't permitted the use of DNA evidence in court in Florida. The test was developed in England. There is a case moving through a court in south Florida involving a rape committed during a burglary. The defense and the prosecution are waiting for the case to make its way on appeal. There is also movement in the legislature to pass a law allowing the introduction of the results of DNA testing in criminal trials."

"What is your opinion? Will this become a new type of evidence the prosecution can use to obtain a conviction?"

"Yes, the legal question is whether the test will meet the standard for admissibility of expert testimony."

"Do you think DNA Typing will meet the scientific standard?"

"Yes," said DeMarco. "I believe the test can be shown to be scientifically reliable."

"I think I need to retire," said Tom as he scratched his head. "This would be a first for me, to plead a client guilty to a crime when the only evidence available to the state to convict my client is evidence that was inadmissible at the time of the plea."

"You are taking an awful chance not to recommend to our client to take what the state is offering." DeMarco's face flushed. "I think we would be doing our client a disservice if we did not accept this deal."

"Mark Person has not admitted any of these crimes to us. It would be easier to push him if he had said he kidnapped Becky or killed the other girls. We are opening ourselves up to a Rule One, an incompetent counsel inquisition," said Tom.

"I do not see how our advice to Person to plead under these circumstances would be bad advice." DeMarco was upset. "Tom, you have not been trying any cases lately. Juries have no sympathy for people charged with crime, particularly the kidnapping and murder of an innocent child."

Tom shut his mouth. He went back to reading his bass fishing magazine.

***

Based on what SA Young disclosed, the only evidence the state had against Person was a DNA match that was not admissible. True, if the court allowed the DNA evidence to be presented to the jury as competent substantial evidence, the jury would probably find Person guilty of kidnapping and he would be sentenced to life in prison. In addition, Person would be open to prosecution for the five murders of young girls. That would give the state five chances to impose the death penalty.

***

There was a knock on the door. Prosecutor Young entered the room.

"I spoke to the State Attorney in Alachua. He will agree to the same disposition in Alachua as in Summer County. He will Nol Pros the solicitation charge so long as your client enters a plea to the False Imprisonment charge and receives a sentence of 30 years. He will file no charges in Alachua County."

"Ok, we will get with our client and get back to you soon," said DeMarco.

On the drive back DeMarco was upbeat. He thought the plea bargain being offered was great for the client. Tom was not sure the State was offering anything. To Tom the offer to close the five homicide cases meant that the State Attorney had no admissible evidence of any kind to prove Mark Person murdered the children. Tom was not sure just how strong the DNA match would be as evidence to prove guilt when the DNA evidence was the only evidence of guilt and there was nothing else (Fingerprints, confession, eyewitness testimony, et cetera) to tie their client to the crime. Tom would not feel the same if Mark Person had admitted the crimes to them as his attorneys. But Person had admitted nothing. Tom and DeMarco had no leverage to induce Person to plead.

It was a long quiet drive back to St. Petersburg. When the pair arrived and DeMarco parked the car Tom said, "I apologize for my attitude. You need to provide me with the research on DNA evidence. I may not fully understand how strong the evidence is and just how likely it will be admitted in the near future."

"I will do that."

Chapter 24
Press Conference

The receptionist at the law firm had gotten so many calls from the news media asking for interviews involving Jesse Lee Rice that she begged Karen, the office manager, to talk to the attorneys about holding a news conference. Tom said that was a good idea; however, when it was time to meet the press, Tom was nowhere to be found. Jenny and Faircloth spoke to the press outside in front of the office.

The reporters shouted questions all at once.

"This isn't Miami," said Jenny scolding the press. "Ask your questions one person at a time and identify who you are associated with and give us your name."

"Did your client confess?" was the first question. The reporter, Lucy Hale, daughter of the late State Attorney, ignored Jenny's rules.

"I have no knowledge that my client made a knowing, intelligent confession. Our client has little education and appears to be retarded, so I don't know anything about a voluntary confession."

Lucy Hale followed up. "Didn't two cops ID your client in a lineup as being the last person to be with the victim before she was murdered?"

Jenny replied, "I have information those two undercover police officers, who were drinking while they were on duty at the Bell Bar, observed the deceased leave the bar with a white male. These officers, who were drunk and sitting 40 feet from the door in a smoky bar, made an ID of our client. We believe the officers are mistaken. Our client was sleeping in his cardboard box at the time the victim was picked up in the bar. Our client was not in the Bell Bar that night according to the bartender and other witnesses."

"You contend your client was not the perpetrator of this crime?"

"That is correct."

"You contend your client was not with the victim?"

"That is correct. He hasn't worked in a month and was living in a cardboard refrigerator box. He didn't have the money to pay the lady for her services."

"That's a little mean to say that about the victim," said Lucy Hale, trying to put Jenny on the defensive.

"It is what it is. You want the truth, don't you?"

There was a moment of silence. Faircloth stepped in front of Jenny and said the press conference was concluded.

During the conference, Jenny was looking at the crowd of people in the back of the reporters and noticed her brother, Albert, in the crowd. She went over to him.

"You did good sister. You shut them up." Albert hugged Jenny.

"I don't think they will print anything other than the fact our client denies the charges. That's good enough," said Jenny. "What are you doing down here?"

"I was fishing on the pier and I saw the crowd and I came over to investigate."

"You are looking good."

Albert blushed. He had lost weight, about 20 pounds and he was fit and tanned from the time he had been spending fishing on the pier.

"I have been doing a lot of walking and jogging. My doctor has me doing a lot of exercise and getting out in the sun. I feel really good."

"Have you been to the Homestead?"

"No, it makes me nervous. I'd rather stay here and fish."

"What happened to your plane?"

"It's here in St. Pete at the airport downtown – Albert Whitted Airport. I haven't flown the plane in a while. Do you want to go up?"

"No," said Jenny. She was afraid of flying, especially in small planes. "Did you get your money from the lime rock sale?"

"Yeah, everyone got paid. Tom is handling my money. Like I said, I would rather be fishing. The business is all behind me now, I hope. I don't want to go back to work." Although those were the words Albert spoke, deep down he wanted to return to the mine at Big Creek in Belize.

"You don't have to work now," said Jenny." You are rich." Jenny was embarrassed she saw so little of her brother. "Would you like to go to lunch?"

"I'm not hungry," Albert smiled. "Good to see you."

"You too, brother."

Jenny watched as her brother retrieved his fishing gear ,which was in a shopping cart like the ones old ladies used to tote groceries. Albert had customized the cart to carry his rods and reels and tackle box. Albert could pull the cart out on the pier and all his equipment was close by.

Albert had an odd look about him. His clothes did not match. He had a T-shirt and an open, unbuttoned checkered shirt and shorts with a herring bone design. He wore a floppy hat and black army boots. St. Petersburg had an assortment of odd folk and Albert fit right in. No one would know he was worth $5,000,000.

Albert did not seem to care that he was no longer involved in the Barnes Family business. Jenny did feel guilt for letting the business of Plantation #7 slide and then be overtaken by a competitor that stole their customers.

Jenny was helping with the litigation Marla and Alphonse Alesse were championing. It looked like they would win the proprietary theft suit. The competitor had failed to respond to the complaint Marla filed in Federal District Court in Tampa. The competitor had given up. Marla and Alphonse had requested a complex remedy in the litigation including money damages that would repay their company for what they had lost monetarily and also punitive damages and injunctive relief so the competitor would be out of business.

Jenny felt the same as Albert so far as the Barnes' family businesses were concerned. Homestead Creamery was on its last legs and Thompson Timber Fund was destroying Florida Lime Rock. She no longer wanted to participate. Jenny was 30 years old now and she wanted to settle down and raise a family. She hoped James DeMarco would join her in matrimony but he had not asked. He was always totally engaged in his law practice. Jenny thought the only way she could get his attention was to leave the firm, but she was afraid he might not notice she was gone. Consequently, she did nothing.

***

Mark Person had read every word written about the murder of Pierce Bonnet and the fire that destroyed the Owl and the Blue Bird motels. He also watched TV for the latest bulletin and became enraged as he watched the press conference with Jenny telling everyone that Jesse Lee Rice was innocent. He destroyed a box of tissues. He had a terrible head cold and he was dripping and coughing and his throat was raw. That old whore gave me the flu, thought Person.

Person tore more facial tissues to shreds and spread the fibers around the room.

He dialed the phone and when the receptionist at Night, Adams and Street answered he said he needed to speak to Tom immediately.

"Mr. Person," said the receptionist, who was now familiar with his voice, "Thank you for calling. Mr. Night wanted me to call you to come in this morning. Is that possible?"

Of course it's possible, thought Person. I have nothing to do. I spend all my time waiting for my attorney to call or for the deputy to arrest me. Person suppressed the anger. He said he was happy to oblige.

The receptionist set the appointment for the meeting. Person apologized for the way he sounded. He explained that he was ill.

***

When Jenny Barnes got back to her desk after the press conference there was a message from a man who said it was important he talk to her about her client Jesse Lee Rice. The message was from the former manager of the Owl Inn.

Jenny called the manager immediately.

"You have information about Jesse Lee Rice?"

"Yes, I know Jesse."

"How do you know him?"

"I was the manager of the Owl Inn before it burned down. I'm out of work now."

"Sorry, what do you know?"

"Well, Jesse used to stay at the Owl sometimes with some of his buddies when they had the money, so I know what Jesse looks like. The night of the fire I saw Pierce come back with a big, tall man at about 2:00 a.m. I got a look at the man's face. That man was not Jesse Lee Rice."

"Did you recognize the man? Had you seen him before?"

"No, I told the police I had never seen him and I didn't know who he was. I did help an artist draw a picture of the man who was with Pierce."

"Is that the picture that was in the newspaper?"

"Yes.

"Can you give me your address so I can have our investigator come over today and take your statement?"

"Fine, I want to cooperate."

***

Jenny went to give Tom an update on what her investigation had turned up. "It looks like I have the privilege of representing an innocent man," she said.

"Not another one? Tell me what you know."

Jenny explained their defense. "Some other dude did it." She told Tom what the witnesses she interviewed said and she read him the reports of the witnesses the police had located.

"Looks like the killer is still at large," said Tom. "Watch your back, Jenny."

Chapter 25
Back to Basics

Dr. Rashindra Solomonga was a neurologist who was recommended to examine Tom for problems he was having with irritability. The tests had come back normal, or marginally abnormal, and Dr. Solomonga ordered repeat image studies of Tom's brain. The results were back and they were negative for any growth, infarct or bleeding in the brain.

Darlene insisted there was something wrong. Tom, who had always spoken quickly, now seemed to have difficulty forming his mouth to make words. He would grope to position his mouth to correctly enunciate a word. This affect happened when he was tired and when he first started speaking. Once he got going he was fine until he had a long phrase or word and then the difficulty would return.

The doctor had given a preliminary diagnosis of Apraxia of Speech, although the image studies had not located a lesion in the left hemisphere of Tom's brain.

The speech problems were embarrassing. Tom's method of coping was to gesture or shrug or limit answers to a yes or no.

Darlene had noticed the problem for some time and realized Tom was good at hiding the condition and there were times that he did not seem to be bothered by the disorder. Other times, he had gotten in disputes and had no patience, especially while driving an automobile. Darlene had put an end to Tom operating an automobile.

Otherwise, no one seemed to know he had a problem with his speech.

***

Mark Person arrived at Tom's office much earlier than the scheduled 8 a.m. appointment. He walked the four blocks up to the office from the Safari Hotel with the deputy following behind in the car. Person refused to ride in the police car after Deputy Bose told Person he had been trained to conduct body cavity searches and that the training was for Person's benefit when he was arrested. Person was angered by this information.

Also, Jasper, the manager of the motel, had told Person he was going to have to move out soon. The City was about ready to demolish the hotel and build more water front park in its place.

Person had a lot on his plate. He wanted to discuss the possibility of him returning to his garage apartment in Archer along with other issues. Person would not tell Tom that Bose told him he would be arrested soon. Or that Bose told him he would be handled roughly during the arrest and be subject to a body cavity search in an attempt to get Person to confess.

A taxi pulled up to the side of the law office and Tom got out. Tom recognized Person leaning against the side of John Bose's car and called him over so they could enter the door at the side of the building. Once inside, Tom put on the coffee. The water and coffee were in the machine and it was his job to push the "on" button.

They went in Tom's office. Tom had a pile of reports that he had copied for Person. They were all the FBI forensic reports that had been disclosed by the State Attorney. Person began to page through the reports while Tom turned on the lights in the common areas.

Tom explained to Person what the reports stated. He also told Person Tom's opinion as to the future admissibility of the DNA testing. Tom had received all the information on DNA matching from DeMarco and he now agreed that if the evidence was admitted there was at least a 50/50 chance Person would be convicted of Kidnapping. Tom explained it was his opinion the State could prove DNA Testing was scientifically reliable and that it was Tom's opinion that the DNA match would be admissible in his trial.

Tom then explained the relevance of the test if the results were admissible in the trial. If the State could match a specimen of Person's DNA on the dress the victim was wearing when she was attacked, the evidence would be compelling. If Person's blood was found on Becky Sue Painter's dress it would be substantial proof of guilt. "How would we explain that away?" asked Tom. "Our only argument would be that the test itself was not reliable."

Tom then went on to tell Person that the State had made an offer to a reduced charge from kidnapping if Person would enter a plea of guilty to the crime of false imprisonment. "Thirty years."

Mark Person listened patiently and then calmly said, "I do not intend to plead guilty to any crime, period."

"Period," repeated Tom. "You won't plead to time served?"

"No."

"Alright, I will tell the prosecutor." Tom looked at Person intently and then said, "It's easy to act with bravado if you are not sitting in the electric chair. I would like you to take the time to read the FBI reports and the legal analysis we prepared for you before you make your decision."

"I'll do what you ask. You are my attorney. I will listen to your advice, but I am not inclined to plead to this charge."

"You understand, the plea would preclude the State from proceeding against you for the murders of the five missing girls."

"I understand."

"Do you also understand that Florida has the death penalty and has actually executed inmates?"

"I understand."

Person was so blasé that Tom became angry, but he suppressed the feeling. "Is there anything else you would like to discuss?"

"Yes, this fellow Jesse Lee Rice. Are you representing him?" asked Person.

"Yes, I was appointed by the court to represent Mr. Rice and I have engaged the firm to assist me. Jenny Barnes is the lead attorney."

"You are going to have to resign. You can not represent Rice."

"I was appointed by the court. I can't just withdraw without a reason."

"Well, you have to talk to the court because you have a conflict."

"How do I have a conflict?" asked Tom.

"Think about it. You're a smart man. If you defend Jesse and contend he didn't kill that hooker and set fire to the motel you have a conflict of interest with me and you cannot represent Jesse Lee Rice."

"I'll think it through and we'll talk." Tom understood. Person had just admitted he killed Pierce Bonnet and set fire to the motel.

"I don't want to talk about it. I want you to withdraw from representing Jesse Lee Rice. I do not intend to change my mind."

"I could withdraw from your case," said Tom.

"Not according to the Bar rules. You represented me first," said Person.

"I will talk to the Florida Bar Association and get their opinion. Perhaps I will have to resign from the firm. I will represent you and the firm can represent Jesse," said Tom.

"I'll think that through and we'll talk about it." Person stuffed the paperwork Tom provided into an accordion folder and carried it out of Tom's office and then out the door. Person waited outside until a taxi came to the door and he rode away with the car driven by John Bose following closely. Person refused to ride with the deputy.

***

Tom went to Darlene's room as soon as Person left the office. He repeated the conversation he had had with Mark Person.

"Did Person actually admit he killed Pierce Bonnet and set fire to the Owl?" asked Darlene.

"Not in those words, but he certainly implied he was the culprit. How else would there be a conflict between our firm representing Mr. Person and Mr. Rice?"

"I hated the fact we were appointed to represent Jesse Lee Rice. I didn't want the firm to represent Pierce's killer," said Darlene. "I represented Pierce on a prostitution charge."

"When was that?"

"Back before I knew you," Darlene explained. "The police would charge her with prostitution but not charge the 'john' for soliciting the sex act. I felt it was selective prosecution. I appeared on her behalf and we lost at trial. The jury did not have any sympathy for her. However, the police changed their tactics and set up sting operations.

"After Pierce's trial the police would also arrest the 'johns'. I got to know her. She was what she was. Very honest, but she lived a pretty poor existence."

"Well, what is your thought on withdrawing from Jesse's case?" asked Tom.

"Who did Person hire, you or DeMarco?"

"He spoke to DeMarco first."

"Maybe he wants to go with DeMarco and you and Jenny can represent Jesse. That would cause the least disruption and we would not have to involve the court system. Person didn't confess to you, though?"

"No, Person did not say he killed Pierce or set fire to the motel."

"Have you looked at the witness statements Jenny has obtained in Jesse's case?"

"Yes, it looks like she could handle Jesse's case herself. Maybe we suggest she do just that."

"Jenny may be able to give the witness statements we obtained from Paddy and the manager of the Owl Motel to the police and maybe the State would drop the charge against Jesse."

"Why don't you work with Jenny and suggest she does that and we'll see where that goes," said Tom. "Meanwhile, Person may resolve the conflict if he decides to take the offer the State made in the kidnapping case."

***

Faircloth had prepared statements for the bartender at the Bell Bar, Eddie the pool shark, and the manager of the Owl Motel. The three men had signed the statements and the statements were notarized. The statements were delivered to the detective in charge of the homicide of Pricilla Bonnet.

The detective read the statements and went to his car and drove to the Bell Bar and re-interviewed the bartender and Eddie and then he went to the motel manager's new apartment and interviewed him. After confirming what the three witnesses said in their statements, the homicide detective went to the State Attorney and explained that they may have arrested and charged the wrong person in the case.

The State Attorney sent a sheriff deputy out to round up the three witnesses and the SA spoke to them personally, under oath. The State Attorney confirmed the testimony of the men that they had seen the man who was last seen with Pricilla Bonnet and that man was not Jesse Lee Rice.

The State Attorney filed a *Nol Pros* and attached the witness statements to the document dismissing the charge.

***

Jenny Barnes was invited out for a drink by the members of the firm. This was her first big win. She declined. She wondered who the man was who killed Pierce. There was nothing to celebrate. The killer was still on the loose.

***

On behalf of the firm, Tom Night wrote a three sentence letter to Mark Person. It stated as follows: "The conflict you complained of has been resolved. The State Attorney has dismissed the charges against Jesse Lee Rice. Please contact us in writing if you disagree that the matter is resolved."

The firm did not hear a reply from Person on the issue.

Chapter 26
The Innocent Client

Even after the State Attorney had filed the Nol Pros in the case against Jesse Lee Rice, Jenny was still interested in what the police had discovered in their investigation and she sat in her office and carefully paged through the police file. The file had been delivered to Jenny pursuant to the court's order as a result of the agreement between Tom and the Chief Judge when Tom was appointed to represent Jesse.

When Jenny reviewed the police file she had a chance to look carefully at the artist drawing of the suspect in the killings.

Jenny could see the resemblance that Jesse Lee Rice had to the drawing, but even more she noticed that Mark Person was similar in appearance to the person depicted in the drawing.

Jenny spoke to Tom about the resemblance.

Tom told her, "It's not our job to solve this or any crime."

***

Jenny wasn't one to leave a stone unturned. She wanted to prove who killed Pierce Bonnet. Jenny decided on her own to take a photo of Mark Person and show the photo to the witnesses at the Bell Bar and to the manager who saw the killer at the Owl Inn.

When she showed the photograph to the witnesses at the Bell Bar, they were unanimous that Mark Person "looked just like" the man who was last seen with Pierce. The manager of the Owl Inn said he was positive that the person in the photograph was the killer. Jenny did not identify Mark Person to be the man in the photograph to the witnesses.

Jenny was excited by what she discovered. She went to DeMarco's office and sat there until he was finished with what he was doing so he could concentrate totally on what she was saying ... that their client, Mark Person, had killed Pierce Bonnet. Jesse Lee Rice was innocent of the crime.

"Isn't that case over?" DeMarco was squinting at Jenny. He had been reading all day. "Didn't the State Attorney drop the charges against Jesse Lee?"

"Well, yes."

"Then why are you worried about who killed Pierce? Your job was to represent Jesse Lee."

"Don't you think I should tell someone? Like the police?"

"Absolutely not. You should not talk to the police," said James. "Did you talk to Tom?"

"Yes, he said it isn't our job to solve crimes."

"Tom is right. We defend people, we do not solve crimes. I think he was just trying to tell you to leave things alone."

"Why?"

"It looks like we represent two people and one of them may be the killer. At this point the State Attorney has filed the *Nol Pros* (dismissal) of the charge against Jesse Lee and Mark Person was never charged, so neither one is charged with the crime. We need to let this play out by itself. Let the State Attorney figure it out. That's the SA's job. Hopefully they will get it right."

DeMarco continued. "Has either one of the men admitted they killed Pierce?"

"Jesse Lee confessed to the police but told us the confession was coerced. Mark Person has not admitted to us he killed Pierce. Person told us he objected to our firm handling Jesse's case. Tom put two and two together."

"Well there you go. Jesse confessed. There must be some problem why these witnesses identified the picture of Mark Person. Did you conduct a line up?"

"No."

"Did you show the witness a color photo of Mr. Person?"

"No."

"Was the photo you showed the witness an original black and white photo or a copy."

"It was a copy." Jenny was not going to quit. "But DeMarco, there was only one reason Mark Person would object to our firm representing Jesse and that was if Person was the killer and he was afraid the firm would find out he was the killer and cause him to become a suspect."

"Jeez, Jenny, this is the biggest can of worms I have ever seen and it looks like it is getting worse. Tom thought we were out of the woods when the State Attorney *Nol prosed* the charges against Jesse."

"I didn't know that. I was trying to defend Jesse."

"Understood. We need to talk to Tom."

Jenny cringed.

***

DeMarco and Jenny walked over to Tom's office. He was with Darlene. DeMarco explained what Jenny had done and what she had discovered.

"What do you think? Will you have to tell Person?" asked DeMarco.

"Person never told us he killed Pierce." Darlene reached for a cigarette. "The question is, do we have to tell Jesse Lee?"

"I think we will have to," said DeMarco. "I don't know what Jesse will want us to do. If he tells us to pursue the matter further, we will have to withdraw in his case. We would have one client telling us to put another client in jeopardy."

"I think we should withdraw in both cases," said Darlene. "At this point we have done nothing to cause either client to be charged with a crime. If we do anything to try to defend either client from this point on, we will jeopardize the other client."

"Or, we could do nothing and see what happens," said Tom. "I don't know if Jenny's investigation, showing Person's picture to the witnesses, will necessarily cause the police to investigate Mr. Person. If the State Attorney takes no action against either client in the future there is no harm to either client. If, out of the blue, our firm makes a motion to withdraw on both cases someone is going to become suspicious. The judge will require us to state the reason the firm is withdrawing in open court. If we tell the court we have a conflict representing both Jesse and Person everyone in the courthouse will understand we think Person is guilty of the crime Jesse was charged with."

"That's true," added DeMarco. "And right now neither one of the men is charged with killing Pierce Bonnet. There is no reason to withdraw at this time. We may have to do something in the future if Jesse is charged again or if Person is charged."

Tom rubbed his chin. "What's the consensus on the question of whether we tell Jesse and Person about the identifications by the witnesses?"

"I think we have to tell them both," said Darlene.

"I say we don't tell either one of the men," said Tom. "Too many bad things could happen if Person is aware Jesse knows the witnesses identified Mark Person as the killer. Person may take it upon himself to eliminate Jesse or the witnesses."

Part VI

Making Sense of it All

Chapter 27
A Drive in the Country

Tom had Mark Person in his office on three occasions speaking to him about the plea bargain offered by State Attorney Charles Young. Person not only rejected the offers, he would not even make a counter-offer. DeMarco spoke to Person separately trying to make him understand that there was a high likelihood that if the case was tried he would be convicted of the kidnapping and if the State could assemble a modicum of evidence that he committed the homicide of one of the five girls, he would face the death penalty and, more likely than not, he would be executed.

No matter who talked to him, Person would go into his shell and there was no talking to him.

Tom even drove to his aunt's home in Archer and talked to her, trying to explain why it was better to work out a plea agreement then to try the case. Tom wanted her to speak to Person. The aunt understood and spoke to her nephew, trying to sway him, but to no avail. The aunt told Tom that Person told her he was doomed and so it did not matter if he lost at trial.

Tom tried one final time using his last argument. Person also expressed frequently to Tom that he was doomed. Tom rolled this thought over in his mind and came to the most cogent thought on the state of mankind. Tom reasoned that we were all doomed (we die) but it was the quality of life while we were alive that made the difference. Tom argued that even if Person was sentenced to 30 years for false imprisonment, the quality of his time in prison sentenced to 30 years would be better than if he lost at trial and was sentenced to life in prison for kidnapping. It would be particularly bad if the State was able to prove he killed one of the five girls and he was on death row in solitary confinement.

Person ignored that argument, saying the quality of life for the five years he spent as a youthful offender was unbearable and he couldn't do thirty years. Nor, for that matter, could he do 20 years after the 30 year term was reduced for gain time.

Tom was convinced that if Person was convicted in the kidnapping of Becky Sue Painter, the State would use evidence of that conviction as evidence that Person committed the murders of the five girls. The conviction for the kidnapping would be admissible as similar fact evidence. He would surely be sentenced to the death penalty if he was convicted in the death of any one of the five girls.

***

Finally, Tom gave up and he called State Attorney Young and conveyed that Person rejected the state's offer.

Tom asked if the police wanted Tom to bring Person to the station in Glade City so he could turn himself in. Prosecutor Young said he would discuss the pick-up with the sheriff.

State Attorney Young called Tom back and told him that the sheriff decided that the deputy at the Safari Beach Hotel would arrest Person and transfer him to Glade City, where he would be jailed pending and during the trial.

Tom was asked not to mention the arrangements with Person. Tom agreed. Tom did not know when the deputies would affect the arrest.

Tom did not talk to Person about the timing of the arrest, but Person knew that when Tom rejected the State's offer, his arrest was imminent.

Person was also talking to Deputy John Bose, who told him the exact day and time the police would enter his room. Bose's intent was to prepare Person so he would comply and no one would be injured.

***

The following morning at 4:30 a.m. the police entered Person's motel room with a room key provided by the manager. Deputy Bose had a two man backup team to help with the arrest. The backup officers consisted of the two largest, meanest, most athletic deputies employed by the Summer County Sheriff.

The police went in the front door. They had been able to enter Mark Person's room without making a sound. They could see Person in the bed sleeping. Deputy Bose touched Person's shoulder and said, "Mark ... wake up ... Mark."

"Who is it?" Mark pushed himself up onto one arm.

"Police," they said.

The three officers grabbed him and pushed him into the bed.

"You are under arrest for the kidnapping of Becky Sue Painter."

"I hear you. I need to get dressed."

"No need for that. We have a van. No one will see you," said John Bose.

"I have clothes in a suit case. I will need my clothes."

"Your lawyer can bring them to you when you need clothes for court."

"Can't I just get into a pair of shorts and a sweater? It's going to be cold outside." Person flexed his arm muscles and was able to move the deputy holding his arm on his right side. The deputies pushed back with force.

"You have to listen to me. We have authority to shoot you if you don't cooperate." The deputy put his knee in Person's forearm. "Do you understand?" said Deputy Bose.

"Yes."

"We are going to cuff you and get you out of bed." The deputy really did not want to shoot Person. He explained exactly what he was going to do before they did it so there would be no surprises. Deputy Bose did not expect any resistance from Person. He told him when the arrest was going to be affected so Mark Person would not be surprised and he would be compliant. Person continued to flex the muscles in his upper body but he did not pull away.

One officer concentrated on cuffing Person's arms behind his back. The sound of the ratcheting of the cuffs resounded in the room. The three officers pulled Person off the bed and onto his feet.

"Can I use the bathroom?"

"Not yet. Open your mouth," Bose ordered.

Person opened his mouth. The deputy turned on his flashlight and inspected the inside of Person's mouth, in particular the area between his cheeks and gums. Bose had been trained that prisoners hid weapons and contraband between their cheek and gums. The officer was wearing latex gloves. He inserted his plastic clad fingers into Person's mouth and carefully traced his fingers between Person's cheek and gum.

He found nothing in the mouth cavity. He looked in Person's nose. Nothing.

"Sit on the bed," the deputy ordered.

"I need to go to the bathroom."

"Sit down."

Person sat on the edge of the bed. The deputy inspected Person's hair, head, neck and ears. He felt under his arms. He looked at his feet and calves and under his knees. The deputy manipulated Person's penis and scrotum, inspecting that area of his body.

Nothing.

"Stand up. Turn around and face the bed. Bend over."

Person followed the commands.

The deputy spread the cheeks of Person's buttocks and penetrated the rectum with his index finger, probing the cavity.

When the deputy was satisfied he told Person to sit down. The deputy removed the gloves.

"Now I really need to go to the bathroom," said Person, trying to get the police to loosen up and see some humor in the situation.

"Get up and we will all go with you into the john," said Bose.

The four men went into the bathroom. Two deputies straddled Person, one deputy each, at his sides as the third deputy (Bose) watched Person who was seated on the toilet.

"I can't go if you watch," said Person and he broke up laughing.

The deputies smiled. They had him, they thought. They relaxed. Person could feel the tension ease.

Person's hands were still cuffed behind his back. He began to urinate. While he was urinating he used a small hand cuff key to loosen the cuffs on his right wrist.

Person had retrieved the handcuff key from the glass jar in his apartment some two months back when he was driven there by Faircloth. Person had had the key in his mouth between his cheeks and gums while he slept.

Person awoke when he heard the police open the door with the hotel key. When the police came in the room he took the key from his mouth and put the key in his right hand in his fist. When the deputy went to look in his right hand he moved his arm and distracted the deputies who pushed down on his arm and then quickly cuffed him. The police never completely inspected Person's right hand.

Now Person was on the toilet with men beside him and in front.

Person finished urinating.

"I need help getting up."

Deputy John Bose, who was standing in front, moved in close and grabbed Person under his arms and began to lift him from the toilet. Person popped the snap on the leather strap of the holster of the deputy's .38 Caliber Police Special. With the officer bent forward in the process of lifting Person off the toilet, the gun slid out of the holster into Person's right hand as the deputy bent over Person to pull him up.

All three officers looked surprised when the first shot exploded. Deputy Bose fell back. "Mark," he said. He was shot in the groin. The deputy to the right was shot next in the knee and the deputy on the left went down with a gunshot to the thigh.

Person stood up and quickly fired three kill shots, one bullet to the head of each deputy as they writhed in pain on the floor. Mark Person shot Bose last so he knew what had happened to his fellow officers.

Person sat back on the toilet and finished his morning constitutional. As he sat he studied his handiwork. The officers laid motionless; one officer moaned.

The cuffs still dangled from Person's hand. He could not find his handcuff key. He searched the men and found another key and took the cuff off his hand. While he was searching for the extra key, he also stole the cash he found in the officer's pockets.

Person dragged the three bodies out of the bathroom. He removed their holsters, guns and belts and piled them in a chair by the door. He pulled the men up on the bed. He took their trousers and pulled them down to their knees exposing their sexual organs. He posed the men as though they were having anal intercourse. Person laughed. He covered his artwork with a sheet and a spread.

Person was a slimy, bloody mess.

Person went in the bathroom and took a shower. He did not worry about prints. He laughed. He even considered signing his name on the mirror with a bar of soap. He dressed in warm clothes. He wore a brown sweater over a T-shirt and jeans. He would be headed north.

He left the door to the room wide open. He had the guns, holsters and ammunition belts in his arms.

He walked into the lobby to the front of the hotel. There was no one residing there now but him. Even Jasper, the manager, had left the premises. The building would be demolished next week.

The police had not lied. There was a dark blue unmarked panel van parked in front of the hotel. He stacked the guns and ammo on the seat. The keys were in the ignition. He started the vehicle and drove out of the parking lot and headed west on Central Avenue.

Person slowed the van to 25 mph as he passed the St. Petersburg Police Station. It was 5 a.m. At that time the dispatcher for the St. Petersburg police was receiving a call from Lieutenant Jim McBride, Summer County Sheriff's Department, asking for assistance. The dispatcher was busy and put the lieutenant on hold.

McBride waited five minutes, then hung up and called back. McBride told the dispatcher not to put him on hold and then identified himself and explained that he had an emergency. He needed to have SPPD send a patrol car to the Safari Beach Hotel and look for his deputies.

***

Person headed west on 5thAvenue North to US 19 then turned right (north). He drove through Pinellas Park, then Clearwater and Tarpon Springs. There was a bit of country and then he was at the Pinellas/Pasco County line. He stopped at the B-19 Liquor Store. The store was open all night. He bought a pint of Crotty's Bourbon and a six pack of Bud.

Person sat in the van. He took a swig of liquor and sipped a can of Bud. The alcohol burned his throat and warmed his stomach. He repeated the process, taking a swig of liquor and sipping the Bud, until the pint bottle was empty. The B-19 Liquor Store was 25 miles north of St. Petersburg.

***

Back in St. Petersburg, the alarm had been sounded. The young SPPD officer who entered the room in the Safari had pulled the

and spread off the bed in Mark Person's room and was
/onted with the three corpses. He ran out of the room and
к to his vehicle and radioed back a description of the bodies in
ле room and then he vomited.

Lieutenant McBride told the desk sergeant that his men had
driven to the hotel in a blue unmarked police van. A BOLO (Be on
the Look Out) was issued immediately for the van and Mark Luke
John Person.

***

It was 6 a.m. Person drove north through New Port Richey and
then Port Richey and turned right at State Road 54. He drove
casually like a workman on his way to his job. Then at US 301 he
turned left and drove north to State Road 50. He headed east
(right) intending to catch the interstate and head north again.

But instead, Person was stopped by a Florida Highway Patrol
Officer on Highway 50 before he could enter the interstate's on
ramp.

The patrol car that pulled the van over was responding to the
BOLO issued by the St. Petersburg Police Department for a white
male, 6' 2", and 210 pounds and driving a blue van, wanted for
homicide of three Summer County deputies.

The officer was cautious. He called in the stop and described
the vehicle. He was told not to approach the van on foot and to
wait for backup. The dispatcher asked the officer to describe the
man. The officer could only see the brown sweater.

Person waited for the deputy to come up behind him on foot
with a pistol in his hand. When the deputy did not exit his vehicle,
Person started the engine of the van and pulled out on the road
and drove away. Person drove onto the ramp of the interstate
heading north.

The patrol car followed at a respectable distance and the
deputy communicated with the dispatcher by radio. Headquarters communicated that the police intended to try to stop the blue
van at the Paynes Prairie exit.

Person was listening to the broadcast on the police radio in the unmarked blue van.

The highway patrol officer called for instructions and was told to continue to follow the van at a distance and call in the van's location as they drove through Hernando County.

Before long, there was a string of patrol cars following the van, which was not speeding and was still heading north on the interstate.

At the Webster exit, which is before Paynes Prairie, Person turned off the interstate and floored the accelerator. The two-lane, paved roads through the area were full of sharp left and right turns. Person was familiar with the area. He could drive it in his sleep. He had cleaned carpets in most of the farm houses and trailers in this area over the last seven years.

Even though the van was not as fast as the patrol cars, Person was pulling ahead because he knew his direction of travel. He had some hope of escape until he heard the helicopter and saw its searchlight shining on the road ahead of him. Sergeant Rainey from the Summer County Sheriff's Department had joined the search inside the copter. Rainey got on the loud speaker and ordered Person to pull to the side of the road and stop the vehicle. Person ignored the broadcast.

When Person got in the van he had stacked the three handguns and ammunition he took from the officers on the front seat of the van. He was looking for a house with a potential hostage. He had no intent of going easily. He knew he would be killed in the process of his capture. He was doomed, as he had said so often.

Person turned off a paved road onto a dirt lane. He turned off the dirt lane to a single lane driveway that led to an old farmhouse. He drove under a car shed and grabbed the three guns and ammo. He ran to the front door of the house. An old man came to the door of the porch trying to understand the commotion in his front yard. His dogs were barking but the dogs were old and did not interfere with Person or try to bite.

Person aimed and casually shot the old man in the right flank. Person pushed the man on the floor of the porch. Person then grabbed the old man's polo shirt at the collar and pulled and tugged at the old man and they entered the house. It was dark inside. The only light was from the police cars that were now surrounding the house and aiming their bright lights at their target.

"Who else is here with you?" said Person.

"No one. I live alone."

"Liar."

The old man tried to get on his feet but he couldn't. The wound to his side was oozing blood. The old man crawled farther into the living room and pulled himself up on the couch.

Person walked into the living room. There was an old woman in the corner in a wheelchair.

"Is there anyone else here besides your wife?"

"No, god damn it," said the old man.

"Do you have any weapons?"

"A rifle."

"Where?"

"In the closet behind you."

As Person walked to the closet the old lady turned on the light switch. The switch turned on every light in the room. When the lights went on in the living room there was a blaze of gunfire from outside into the living room.

All three occupants, the old man, the old lady and Person were shot multiple times and killed by the police.

***

Mark Luke John Person felt nothing. He never felt anguish or pain as he was in the grip of death. He lasted three minutes at most. He heard the yelling and cursing of the police. He heard no sound from the farmer and his wife. The three were doomed.

Mark Luke John Person never felt guilt, because he did not know guilt.

Chapter 28
Aftermath

The cab rolled up in the parking lot of the firm of Night, Adams and Street at 6:00 am. It was cool and blustery, with the wind coming off Tampa Bay to the east. It was clear and first light with no humidity. Tom exited the taxi and paid the driver. The driver drove away. Sunrise was at 6:35.

Tom looked to the east and saw the lights. The pier was fully illuminated. He didn't remember that all the lights at the pier were on this early. Jenny and DeMarco drove up into the lot in DeMarco's VW. They rolled down the windows and told Tom to get in the front seat. Jenny hopped in back.

"What's up?" asked Tom as he scrunched in the seat. "This vehicle was not made for a full-sized man," he complained.

"There's something going on near the municipal pier."

"I saw the lights," said Tom. "That's unusual."

DeMarco pulled out and headed around Crescent Lake and the courthouse and to the bay. They immediately saw all the police activity at the Safari Beach Hotel. The parking lot was overflowing with police cars, technician's vans, ambulances and fire trucks.

"Someone must be dead," said DeMarco as he tried to wind into the lot between the cars. The emergency lighting on all the cars was all lit. It looked like a midway at a carnival.

Tom rolled down the window. He saw an officer that he knew directing traffic.

"What's up?"

"Tom, you can't come in here."

"My client lives here. Mark Person. Is all this for him?" Tom spread his hands out indicating the scene before them.

"I don't know if it was him but there are three deputies from Summer County that are dead in one of the rooms. You can't go in there. You have to leave."

A patrolman was putting up yellow tape and the press was pulling up to the hotel. The officer who was talking to Tom went to chase the reporters off the property. The cameraman was setting up the Channel 8 News camera and he refused to leave or move.

"We're doing our job, god damn it." Lucy Hale pushed her way to the front of the camera and began to berate the policeman. He held his ground. "Lucy, you get back where I say." The cameraman caught the confrontation between Lucy and the cop. That scene, the argument between the press and the police, was all that was broadcast on Channel 8 that morning. The argument was the only evidence of the action in the parking lot of the hotel.

Tom told DeMarco to park and he got out and walked into the hotel and through the lobby into the hallway past the elevators while the cop argued with the press. No one was in the hall outside the rooms. Tom walked forward until he got to an open door. He stood and looked at the mound of naked bodies covered in blood, guts and shit. The colors in the pile, flesh, blood and fabric melted together. Tom became dizzy and began to sweat. He wretched and then swallowed hard.

"Who are you?" The technician was taking photographs.

"Is Mark Person in that mess on the bed?"

"No." The tech adjusted his lens. "You don't belong here. You have to leave."

Tom turned and retraced his steps back to the VW.

"We have to leave. Go back to our office." Tom was pale.

"Was Person there?"

"They said he wasn't. It's hard to tell. It's a real mess in there." Tom paused and thought a minute. He remembered that his old client Jasper Lee Smiley still managed the hotel. Tom told DeMarco to wait for him and he went to the office. There was a note on the door advising visitors that the hotel was closed and there was a telephone number for Mr. Smiley. Good, Jasper's not here, thought Tom, and he headed back for the VW and got in the car.

As DeMarco drove past the press, Lucy Hale yelled at Tom. He ignored her. DeMarco drove on and Jenny turned to watch Lucy shoot the "bird" with her finger at their car.

Intense, thought Jenny. She scrunched down in the seat hoping no one saw her.

It took only a few minutes to get back to the law office. When they walked in the door Darlene was on the phone with Lucy Hale. The two were friends since Tom was arrested and had his trouble with the Florida Bar. Darlene was repeating, "I don't know, Lucy" over and over.

Tom took the phone. "Lucy, you tell me what you know and I'll tell you what I know."

"Don't lie to me Tom."

"I won't."

Lucy then told Tom that the news department picked up chatter on a police scanner of a shooting at the Safari. There were three deputies from Summer County who came to St. Pete with the permission of the local authorities to arrest a man named Mark Person for a kidnapping in Summer County. The three deputies were shot and killed.

"Then we heard there was a slow motion car chase that had half the police cars from Hernando and Citrus and Summer County trailing a blue van on the interstate through Hernando

County. Then, there was a high speed chase up near Bushnell and there was a shootout at a farm house. Three people dead at the farm house," finished Lucy. "What do you know, Tom?"

"I have a client named Mark Person. His last address was at the Safari Beach Hotel. I saw the activity there at the hotel and went to see if he was involved and spoke to the police at the front. They said three deputies were killed. The cop told us to leave. I went inside the hotel and walked to my client's room. He was not there but the police were doing an investigation. As soon as I knew Mr. Person was not at the scene I left and returned to the office."

"Look at the TV," said Jenny. She pointed to a picture of Person on the screen. The announcer was telling the public to be on the look-out for the individual shown in the picture. "He is armed and danger-ous," said the announcer.

"Got to go," said Lucy.

"Keep us out of the newspapers if you can, Lucy." Tom hung up and looked at Jenny. "So what's your guess as to whether you are going to get a call from Patty or Eddie at the Bell Bar or the manager of the Owl Inn?"

"The odds are pretty high." Jenny went to her office.

Tom followed her into her office. "If they call you and ask you about the picture of Person, what are you going to say?"

"I'll tell them I was representing Jesse Lee Rice and I was trying to find out if the picture I showed them was the picture of the man who was last seen with Pierce Bonnet."

"That's good, but 'what else'?"

"What do you mean 'what else'?"

"You're also going to say, 'But we will never know if the man in the picture is Mark Person, Pierce's killer, because Person is now dead and we don't have to worry about it.' "

"I get it." Jenny asked Tom to turn off the light in her room.

Tom flipped the switch and closed Jenny's door.

Jenny rubbed her temples with her thumbs as she rested her elbows on her desk.

I really hate this job, she thought.

Chapter 29
Press Briefing

The Sheriff of Summer County was at home when he received the call from Lieutenant Jim McBride with the bad news. He drove to the office and told the lieutenant to find out as much as he could about the incident and to be prepared to explain how this escape could have happened.

The sheriff took the news of the death of the five innocents and the botched arrest of Mark Person badly. The loss of six persons to gun violence on the same day in Florida was unusual to say the least. The deaths of that many folks when it wasn't an accident, but was rather the result of an intentional act, required an explanation from some member of the political establishment. The Sheriff of Summer County realized he was in the spotlight and he realized he had to offer a lucid explanation for the tragic loss of life of three of his uniformed deputies and two elderly and respected residents of Summer County.

As a result of this tragedy, the sheriff's plans had been thwarted. The election was soon. The sheriff had expected the arrest of Mark Person, the animal preying on children of East Pasco, would have guaranteed his re-election. The sheriff had even considered a run for the US Congress. That was all impossible now. He would be lucky to be elected to any office.

The sheriff had proposed the strategy that if they arrested Person in the middle of the night while he was sleeping he would be caught off guard. The officers would have time to speak to him and obtain an inculpatory statement during the three hour drive from the hotel in St. Petersburg to the jail in Glade City.

Lieutenant McBride had advised it would be safer to have Person's attorney bring him to jail. The sheriff did not want to give the defense the ability to obtain television coverage of Person voluntarily surrendering to charges that Tom claimed were not based in fact. Tom would use the arrest to proclaim his client was innocent; that the suspect trusted the judicial system would produce a proper result, (a not guilty verdict) and that his client was volunteering to turn himself in.

Now the sheriff was searching for a scapegoat. Someone he could lay blame for the deaths of his men and the old folks.

***

Lucy Hale called the sheriff for a comment for The Noon News. She always had a spot on the Channel 8 TV News program covering the Criminal Courts.

Normally she got nothing but "no comment" from the sheriff, but today would be different she felt. The sheriff took her call and spoke to her without attribution, meaning she could not say she was given the information by the sheriff, but she could report that "a source high in the sheriff's administration" had provided the exclusive briefing.

During their conversation, the sheriff blamed the death of his officers and the escape of Person on Person's attorney, Tom Night. The sheriff claimed that the State Attorney had advised Attorney Night of the pending arrest and Night had warned his client and his client was prepared for the arrest, and because Person had that foreknowledge he was able to escape and now five people were dead.

***

Lucy Hale began to prepare her broadcast, but the more she thought about the allegation against Tom Night the more she felt she was being used as a shill by the sheriff.

Lucy Hale called Tom's office and he agreed to speak to her under the same conditions as earlier. Truth for truth. Hale had to tell him what she knew and then Tom would tell her what he knew. Hale agreed.

Lucy then told Tom what the sheriff had alleged.

Tom said nothing for a minute and then explained the arrangement Tom had made with the prosecutor, Charles Young. First, Mark Person agreed to live at the Safari Beach Hotel and he was under surveillance of a Summer County deputy at all times. Second, the defense and the prosecutor had entered into negotiations for a plea to a lesser charge and there was no indication the prosecution would charge Person with the murders of the five girls. Third, Person had rejected the prosecutor's offer and was preparing for trial. Fourth, Tom had offered to turn Person in at the jail if he was charged, and fifth, the prosecutor had told Tom that Person was to be arrested and he was asked not to tell his client. Tom did not tell Person, as he had agreed.

"Thanks," said Lucy Hale, "got to go."

Tom knew the cases an attorney took and the clients he represented would bolster or weaken his reputation. The jury was still out on whether Mark Luke John Person would drag Tom through the mud.

***

The sheriff watched The Noon News on TV. There was no mention of the information about Tom Night warning Person.

The sheriff decided to hold a news conference in Glade City. The conference was well advertised. There were leaks to the press advising that the sheriff would reveal the name of a third party, other than Mark Person, who was responsible for the deaths of his officers and the elderly couple in Summer County.

By the afternoon of the day of the conference, it had also been leaked to the press that Mark Person was the child killer who had killed five middle school students and kidnapped Becky Sue Painter. None of those crimes had been proven in a court of law and the only evidence linking Person to the crimes was DNA fingerprint evidence from bodily fluids found on Becky Sue's clothing.

The sheriff did not leak the fact that Florida had not as of that time allowed the use of DNA matches as evidence in criminal cases. It was also uncontroverted that the three deputies were killed during an attempt to arrest Mr. Person, and no one knew the circumstances of those deaths as the officers and Mr. Person were deceased. The sheriff certainly was not going to reveal the circumstances in which the bodies were found. And the sheriff would shy away from the fact that the two innocent persons killed in the farm house in Summer County were killed by law enforcement and not by Mr. Person.

The sheriff was determined to lay blame and the press convened at the County Auditorium and took a seat for the show. The local press from Tampa, St. Petersburg, Gainesville, Jacksonville and Tallahassee were there. Channel 2 News from Orlando and Channel 8 News from Tampa covered the briefing as did a number of radio news stations. The media normally deferred to the news print reporters for questions. Lucy Hale would ask questions for sure.

The sheriff lined up the principals in the matter. There was State Attorney Charles Young, Lieutenant Jim McBride, Sergeant Joseph Rainey, and Becky Sue's grandmother, Alma Lee.

The sheriff began by thanking each person on the stage with him for their help in solving these most heinous of crimes. "There is no doubt that Mark Person is an animal who needed to be brought to justice. It is sad that the price was the death of five innocent human beings."

"But there is something that needs to be aired by our community and that is the fact that the death of my men in St. Petersburg occurred because Mark Person's lawyers warned him that they were coming to arrest him."

"What evidence do you have of that, Sheriff?" yelled Lucy Hale from her seat in the front of the press corps.

"There is no way my men could be overpowered by one man unless he was warned they were coming."

"Why were your men there at 4:00 a.m.?"

"We were there to get the jump on him."

"Who knew they were going to be there at that time?"

"Only Lieutenant McBride."

"Did the lieutenant tell Person's lawyers the deputies were coming at 4:00 a.m.?" pressed Hale.

"Of course not," the sheriff spoke forcefully, "but the attorney knew the arrest was imminent."

"How did the attorney communicate this information regarding the imminent arrest to his client?"

"How would I know that?"

"If you don't know how the information was communicated or when it was communicated, how do you know the lawyers warned their client?"

"Because there is no way my deputies could have been caught off guard. Use your common sense. Person had to know they were coming. The only individuals who could have told him were his attorneys."

"Did Person's attorneys offer to surrender their client to you at the jail in Dade City?"

"I'm not aware of that."

"Mr. Young, would you please take a question?" asked Lucy Hale.

State Attorney Young stood up and moved forward.

"Mr. Young," said Lucy Hale. "I spoke to Tom Night before coming here. He said he spoke to you about surrendering his client. Is that true?"

"Yes."

"If Attorney Night had surrendered his client to the jail to face charges would these five deaths have occurred?"

The sheriff broke in. "That's pure speculation."

"Well, aren't you just speculating that Tom Night told his client he was going to be arrested?" Lucy pushed back.

"I'll stand by my assertion. Tom Night warned his client he was going to be arrested and Person lay in wait for my deputies and killed them. They were bushwhacked."

"Were your men shot?"

"Yes, all three were shot in the head."

"Whose weapon was used to shoot the men?"

"I don't know yet."

"Wasn't Person found with three weapons at the farm house in Summer County? And weren't those weapons the ones that belonged to your men; three .38 Caliber Police Specials?"

"Yes, but Person threw away his gun."

"Who said that?"

"One of the deputies following the van said he saw Person throw something out the window of the van."

"Wasn't it true that Person and his attorney agreed that Person would stay at the Safari Beach Hotel where your men were killed?"

"Yes."

"The reason he was at the hotel was so you would know where he was at all times, correct?"

"Yes."

"Didn't the State offer Person a plea deal?"

"Yes."

"Wasn't the plea deal one that did not involve the murders of the five girls from Summer County?"

"Yes."

"There was no evidence Person killed the five girls. Isn't that correct?"

The sheriff refused to answer and walked off the stage.

The sheriff is going to have a tough re-election campaign, thought Lucy Hale.

Part VII

Shake-Up

Chapter 30
Thompson Timber Fund Bankrupts

Thompson Timber Fund (TTF) was incorporated in the State of Delaware. When the corporation filed the petition for bankruptcy the case came to be heard by a Federal Bankruptcy Court judge in Wilmington. The case was filed under Chapter 7 of the Bankruptcy Code. The officers and directors of the company did not intend to reorganize the company and continue to operate. Rather, the intent was to sell its assets and pay off creditors and then, if there were any assets remaining, they would be paid to the shareholders, who were called "unit holders" or "unit investors". Then TTF would close the business.

There was a question whether a filing under Chapter 7 was appropriate because the petition listed substantially more assets than liabilities. The company appeared to be liquid although there was an allegation in the petition that the company was unable to pay its debts as they came due. The company appeared to have sufficient cash to continue operating and the petition claimed there were assets valued at 17 billion dollars and liabilities of only 10 billion dollars.

TNT's attorney presented the petition in the court. The company was controlled by a single individual, Thomas N. Thompson. TNT's attorney alleged that Thompson was incompetent and unable to communicate. The federal judge set a hearing so that he could speak to Mr. Thompson. Thompson did not appear at the subsequent hearing and Thompson's attorney was unable to say where he was or when he could be made available.

The judge issued an Order of Contempt and ordered Federal Marshalls in Savannah to enter the premises of his home and business and take Thompson into custody and bring him before the court forthwith. However, Mr. Thompson was nowhere to be found. In addition, it was discovered that his wife had divorced him and moved to Canada.

It had been over 18 months since TTF had purchased the 51% interest in Belize Resources and Barnes Lime Rock. TTF had taken control of the companies and Thompson had been appointed the Chief Officer of the two lime rock companies and he and his wife were the directors of the companies. The Barnes Family had been removed as directors and officers and they had no role in company operations. Bob Barnes did not work for the companies.

Thompson's lawyer from Savannah handled all legal matters and Frank, Bob and Bea were totally out of the loop. During those 18 months the flow of dividends to the Barnes Family from the companies went from a little to none at all.

The Barnes' had realized they would probably lose control of the companies when the 51% interest was sold to TTF and they realized they would probably not receive dividends, but they still owned 49% of the companies and they thought Thompson would communicate with them and not cut them off completely from the day to day operations of the businesses. But Thompson would not even take their calls. Frank was left to leaving messages or writing letters to Thompson, but Thompson would never communicate with him.

Bob Barnes had personally hired most of the managers of the operations of the lime rock businesses so he was able to call them as one would call a friend and obtain information from them about the companies. Bob found out that the businesses were struggling and there was word in the industry that company checks were being dishonored.

Frank Barnes finally got up the courage to speak to Tom about the problem shortly after Frank received the Notice to Creditors from the clerk of the bankruptcy court notifying him that

Thompson Timber Fund had filed bankruptcy. The petition alleged that Barnes Lime Rock and Belize Resources were assets of TTF and that Barnes Lime Rock and Belize Resources were to be liquidated to pay the debts of TTF. If the lime rock companies were liquidated the Barnes Family would receive nothing. They would suffer a total loss. However the family had been repaid most of the money they had invested in the lime rock mine when they sold the 51% interest in the lime rock companies to TTF.

Although Frank had been too embarrassed to speak to Tom, Jenny and Albert had kept Tom informed of the economic implosion that was occurring to the Barnes Family. Imminent financial ruin had begun with the theft of proprietary information from Plantation #7. Then, Homestead Creamery was managed poorly and the value of the stock dropped from $14 dollars a share to $2.50 per share and dividend payments were suspended. There were rumors the company would reorganize, which further eroded the value of the stock and the stock had junk status on Wall Street. Worse, now the assets in the lime rock operations were at risk to be sold to pay the debts of Thompson Timber Fund.

Eighteen months earlier, the Barnes Family felt they had dodged a big bullet. The infusion of cash through loans and the sale of the 51% interest had provided the lime rock companies with sufficient funds to repay all debt owed to Frank, Bea, Marla, and Bob, and the loan to JRD Corporation had been repaid. Treasury stock in the companies had been issued to TTF. The effect of the issue of the shares was to dilute the value of the shares held by the Barnes Family members. But the Family had been repaid their loans.

Now the lime rock businesses were to be liquidated in bankruptcy. The stock in those companies would be worthless. Further, the Barnes family faced lawsuits. The unit owners of Thompson Timber Fund were enraged once they discovered that Thompson had taken almost all of the cash from TTF and used it to purchase the controlling interests in the Barnes Lime Rock Company and Belize Resources. The unit holders in TTF threatened to bring suit against Frank, Bea, Bob and Marla to force them to repay the TTF funds that were used to pay back their loans.

Marla had only invested one million dollars of her savings with Barnes Lime Rock and she was a wise and prudent investor. Jenny had followed Marla's lead and she never invested in Barnes Lime Rock. So, Marla and Jenny were mostly unaffected by the TTF bankruptcy.

Frank, Bea and Bob were the individuals affected by the attempt of the TTF unit holders to claw back the re-payment of the loans made by Bob, Frank and Bea to the lime rock companies.

Albert's situation was different. When Bob and Albert incorporated Barnes Lime Rock, Bob had used all of Albert's funds for a loan to start up the lime rock operations in Florida. When Marla told Tom what Bob had done, taking advantage of Albert, Tom spoke to Frank. Albert was incompetent. Using Albert's funds was wrong. Frank agreed and he and Bea took their own funds and purchased Albert's interests in the lime rock business. The funds Frank and Bea repaid to Albert were placed in a trust fund for Albert's use. Albert owned no interest in the lime rock companies. His trust fund was handled by an independent corporate trust fund advisor which paid Albert's bills from conservative investments.

Frank, Bea and Bob needed a lawyer to defend against the lawsuit from the unit holders. Tom and Alphonse agreed to represent Frank, Bea and Bob. Marla hired separate counsel in Wilmington. All four shared a common defense and the attorneys worked together on the case.

***

Tom's apraxia disorder had become worse and he relied on Alphonse to present their oral arguments in court in civil matters. DeMarco and Jenny assisted in criminal cases. Darlene acted as intermediary for Tom as he was more prone to bouts of anger from frustration caused by his inability to perform his duties in court. Tom's neurologist was experimenting with drugs that would be helpful but no magic remedy had been discovered to date.

***

TTF's bankruptcy caused chaos in the country of Belize. Since Thompson Timber Fund obtained control of Belize Resources, receivables owed to Belize Resources were paid by the cement manufacturers to TTF in Savannah. TTF in Savannah was then supposed to fund the operations in Belize.

Once the bankruptcy was filed, TTF's offices in Savannah paid all funds it received for Belize Resources to a bank in Wilmington, Delaware pursuant to the order of the bankruptcy court. No receipts for gravel paid by the cement manufacturers were transferred to Belize. As a result, there were no funds to pay workers at the mine in Big Creek. The economy of the south of Belize depended on the payment of the miner's salaries. The clinic depended on the workers being paid. The stores and bars and restaurants, everything, depended on Belize Resources continuing to pay its bills and the salaries to its workers.

Further, the cement factories in Mexico and Florida depended on the gravel from Big Creek for their separate operations. The cement was used to construct roads. Without the supply of gravel, road construction would come to a halt.

Tom spoke by phone to Andrew Prince, Jr. Esq., his law partner in Belize. After the conversation he took the first plane south to meet with Herbert Johns, Esq., who was the Chairman of the Board of Directors of Belize Estate Ltd. The Belizean company still owed Belize Resources $500,000 from the sale of the land and capital assets of the company that had been purchased by Senator Barnes in the 1950's and sold by the Barnes Family in 1973. In addition, the Belize law firm held $100,000 in trust that was paid for mahogany timber, FOB.

Tom's idea was to use the $500,000 note as collateral to obtain a line of credit from Barclay's Bank or to sell the note at a discount and use the money from the sale of the note for operations at Big

Creek. Tom also intended to have the Belizean law firm of Night, Adams, Street and Prince bring suit in Belize against the unit holders and Thompson Timber Fund. The unit holders and TTF had no rights under the laws of Belize to liquidate the assets of a Belizean Company. Andrew Prince, Jr. Esq. agreed to argue that jurisdiction for a suit was in the courts in Belize or in the World Court and not in the bankruptcy court in Delaware.

Herbert Johns was sympathetic to the argument that the unit owners had no jurisdiction over Belize Resources in bankruptcy court in Wilmington, Delaware. He also knew the damage that was being caused by the action being taken in the USA to the economy of their small Caribbean country. Johns was a Member of Parliament and a cabinet minister. He was now the Solicitor General of Belize and when Andrew Prince, Jr. filed suit on behalf of Belize Resources, Mr. Johns filed an amicus brief agreeing that the court in the USA had no jurisdiction to enter any order or judgement affecting Belize Resources or its operations.

Further, Belize Estates Ltd, volunteered to make early payment of the $500,000 note and the funds were paid to a local bank in Monkey River Town so that the money was available to cash the checks of the miners and the shop owners in the south of the country.

***

Once Belize Resources had money to operate, it needed a manager. Tom spoke to Rosemary Ferlita, Albert's psychologist, asking whether Tom could send Albert back to run the mine at Big Creek. The psychologist thought it was a workable idea. The job would give him a feeling of self worth and he would have a mental challenge which was absent since he was hospitalized in Honduras. Albert was not taking any psychotropic medication. Ferlita had weaned him off the drugs. He would be at Big Creek and there was a doctor there. The clinic had international phone service as had most of the country, since communication satellites were ubiquitous throughout the third world. If Albert was acting up they could put him in touch with Ferlita and she could talk to him and the doctor at the clinic and make arrangements for his care.

If Albert acted as the mine operator, the mine would function 365 days a year subject to acts of God or man beyond Albert's control. And if Albert faced trials at work he would be the best person to try to outwit an adversary.

Albert moved back to his house on the beach near the harbor entrance. His clothes were still in the closet. He had a cook who also cleaned the small house and slept in a small bedroom. Albert had no worry except the operation of the mine. He enjoyed the workers and was often at their homes and he met with their wives and children.

Once Albert was back in Big Creek he was home and at ease. Any misgivings he had about returning to work evaporated as soon as he saw the mine in operation again.

***

Meanwhile, Thompson was discovered to be living in the old city of Antigua, Guatemala with a Conchita who he claimed was his wife.

The couple was living in a local home learning Spanish through the immersion method. The immersion method required that TNT was not to speak his native language (English), but to only communicate in Spanish during all his waking hours. That way he was immersed in Spanish and he would learn the language quickly.

Thompson had been in the local home for over a month. He and his girlfriend visited all the landmarks in the city. There were many Catholic churches that had been constructed in the Baroque style in the 1600's. Architecture students from throughout the world visited the city to study its churches.

The city was also in the highlands and there were three volcanoes in the surrounds. Guatemala lies on a tectonic fault and the area had suffered numerous earthquakes that were recorded since the Spanish arrived in the 1500's. Antigua was the third seat of the capital of the kingdom of Guatemala. The city had been the center of government of what is now the States of Guatemala, Belize, El Salvador, Honduras, Nicaragua, Costa Rica and Chapais, México. The city had a population of more than 60 thousand. However, the city was destroyed often by volcanoes and earthquakes before being rebuilt.

***

Thompson had entered the small gallery and was inspecting the tropical plants, orchids and bromeliads, that were growing in pots fastened to an interior wall. A child came over to him and he reached down and lifted the two year old.

The child giggled and Thompson and his girlfriend began to faun over the child and the Conchita told Thompson that they should have a child.

The remark was overheard and the owner of the shop came over and said: "No, no, you cannot have the child."

"You misunderstood. We were not trying to buy the child." Thompson attempted to say in Spanish, however what he actually said was, "How much would you charge for the child."

The gallery owner grabbed the child and went outside and called over a policeman and made a complaint. There was a fear among the locals that foreigners would steal their children.

Thompson tried to talk his way out of the situation in Spanish but it only got worse. He was arrested and taken to the station. He had false identification and ten $1,000 bills in his wallet. The police interviewed the Conchita, who was from Mexico City and had no allegiance to Thompson. She gave his correct identification and said she thought he was wanted in Belize for business fraud.

The Conchita was correct; the Court in Belize had issued a warrant for Thompson's arrest. The Belize Defense Force had also obtained his photograph and fingerprints from the State of Georgia. The fingerprints and likeness matched with the prisoner in Antigua, Guatemala, but Thompson insisted he was named John Smith and he was a Quaker.

A member of the Belize Defense Forces was sent to arrest Thompson. Thompson attempted to bribe the soldier, to no avail. Thompson was taken to the jail in Belize City. The jail was a large room with cots and a latrine. It was noisy, dirty and dangerous. Thompson took no action to bond out although Belize did allow release pending trial if the defendant posted bond.

Thompson claimed he had no money. He claimed that he had once been rich but that his money had been stolen by unscrupulous individuals who he refused to identify except to say they were hedge fund traders.

The federal authorities in Savannah had begun an investigation and it was discovered that Thompson had diverted funds from TTF operations and investment accounts to personal accounts and then to cash and then the money disappeared. It was noted during the investigation that TTF purchased airline tickets from Atlanta to the Netherland Antilles and the Caymans and to Panama. Each of those countries allowed banking cus-tomers to remain anonymous. The FBI suspected that the unit investor's funds were in accounts in those countries.

The idea that Thompson had a large amount of money that came in the door and he spent only a small amount of money and there was no money left over was not believable. It appeared that there was more than thirty million dollars that was unaccounted for, which was probably the reason he blamed the loss of his unit investor's money on the hedge fund operators. Thompson conceded the Federal authorities could add and subtract. It was obvious money was missing, so Thompson had to blame someone.

***

Tom Night and Alphonse Alesse filed a motion to dismiss the bankruptcy petition filed on behalf of Thompson Timber Fund. The TTF attorney had not appeared on behalf of TTF since the hearing on his motion to withdraw was granted after Thomas Thompson went missing.

Thompson was in jail and his wife returned from Canada and was a witness for the Federal authorities. When Tom and Alphonse argued that the petition was a sham, that it was filed to hide the theft of funds by Thompson, there was no one who argued against these allegations. Therefore the judge granted the motion.

Although the suit against the Barnes Family members was dismissed, it did not remedy the losses suffered by the Barnes Family or the unit investors. The only way they would recover their investment was if Thompson loosened his tongue and told everyone where the money he stole was located.

Chapter 31
Reynolds Returns to the Plantation

James M. Reynolds had retired as Chairman of the Board and CEO of JRD Corporation. As part of his retirement package he had been given cash, stock, the home and car and dog in Rochester, New York. The perk he knew he would miss the most was the Boeing 727, but he could not justify the expense of the plane. It was an asset that would quickly depreciate in value. It was better to take cash in his retirement package.

Reynolds' most important decision to be made at retirement was what to do with his wife, Marla.

Reynolds and Marla needed to decide together what to do with each other now that he had retired. Reynolds had learned when dealing with Marla that she was always a step ahead and unless he wanted the situation to become messy and public he would have to hear her out and make a decision about their future with her input. He planned to take his last flight in command of his favorite toy to meet Marla in Daytona Beach and then relinquish control of the Boeing 727 to the new CEO of JRD Corporation.

***

Marla Reynolds met her husband in the loading zone of the Daytona airport. Reynolds was carrying his own suitcase. That fact caused Marla to laugh. "I give advice to presidents of the United States," she mimicked her husband. As Reynolds approached the car, she went to the rear of the old Packard automobile and unlocked the trunk. She took the suitcase and manhandled it into the boot and gave her husband a big kiss.

"Why were you laughing?"

"Seeing you carrying your own case and walking without an entourage is unusual."

Reynolds crossed his arms. "I refuse to be the butt of jokes. My retirement depresses me."

"We'll take care of that. I thought we would spend some time on the beach. Drink a few cold beers. How does that sound?"

"Actually it sounds good. How are the waves?"

"It's been pretty calm. I'll take A1A and we'll see what the ocean looks like."

"Great. I want sunshine and salt air."

Marla drove east on US 92 from the airport straight to A1A and turned left (north). You could smell the salt mist in the air. There was a cooler on the back seat. She reached over the seat while they were stopped at a traffic light and removed the lid and there were rows of long neck Buds sitting in ice. She handed Reynolds a bottle of beer and told him to get the opener from the glove box. Reynolds found the church key and popped the cap and took a long drink of the beer.

He burped and they both laughed.

"Where are we going?"

"To the beach near the Plantation," said Marla.

When they arrived at the right of way off A1A at the beach north of Ormond, Marla parked and looked both ways on the highway. There were no cars. She slipped out of her dress and wiggled into her one piece suit that she had in a grocery bag in the back seat. She removed a pair of swim trunks from the same bag for Reynolds. He changed his clothes in the car. They both wore flip-flops.

Marla told him to leave the cooler. She had a surprise for him. The beach was hidden by a forest of miniature oak trees. The pair wound through the path in the scrub oak down the sand dune to the beach.

There on the beach was a blanket and an umbrella, another cooler, and two surf boards.

"This one is yours." It was a large surf board, 10' 2" long. It had a laminated wooden skeg (rudder). The brand name on both of the handmade boards said "Wardy". Reynolds lifted the larger board. It was stout. The wind caught it and he had to push back to keep from being knocked over.

Marla picked up the other board. It was smaller, (9' 6"). She ran into the ocean carrying the board and Reynolds followed. They pushed the boards into the surf and lay on top and paddled past the small breakers. They sat up straddling the board with their legs submerged from the knees down. The water was frothy and blue/green. There was seaweed floating in the waves. The sea weed was from the Sargasso Sea. The weed was a gold color with yellow berries. The plant material floated in every fall, driven to the shore of Florida by late summer storms.

During past trips to the beach, Reynolds had watched the surfers from the dunes at the beach and he knew that they paddled with their knees on the board. He tried to get on his knees, slipped off the board and fell into the water. He held on to the board. He tried to touch bottom but couldn't reach. Marla saw panic in his eyes. She went over beside him, reached into the water and grabbed the waistband of his swim trunks and pulled upward as he hefted himself back on top of the board.

They both tried to catch waves unsuccessfully and realized surfing was harder than it looked. They were exhausted after half an hour.

"Enough for today?" asked Marla.

"Yes," said Reynolds and they paddled back to the shore. They stacked the boards in the sand.

Marla had made potted ham sandwiches with romaine lettuce and mayonnaise on white bread. She had trimmed off the crusts. She also prepared potato salad and coleslaw. She was a good cook and Reynolds appreciated the trouble she had taken to prepare the food herself.

After they ate, it became dark quickly. Marla had gathered drift wood early before she went to the airport and she set Reynolds to the job of lighting a fire while she collected the dishes from the meal. There was a brisk breeze from the south. Marla used the large beach umbrella to block the wind and they sat and enjoyed the warmth of the fire shielded from the cool air.

Marla knew better than to try to discuss their future together now.

Reynolds was enjoying himself talking about business deals. His past exploits were like war stories told by a soldier to his comrades. Reynolds became more animated with each beer he drank. Before long he had cut a trench walking across the sand and over the dunes through the sea oats to relieve himself.

Marla lay on the blanket and made a spot for Reynolds. She held his head in her arms and they watched the planets and stars. Occasionally a satellite would pass high in the atmosphere blinking uniformly as it flew above. Reynolds nodded off. He was asleep, then awake. He was at ease. He had forgotten how relaxed he became on this little stretch of sand. He had no family left on this earth. His mother, father and two sisters were deceased. Like Marla, he was childless. He hated Rochester. It was too cold. New York City was empty and heartless and full of anxious memories. He needed a new destiny. He had forgotten how much he loved the Plantation in Ormond Beach, Florida.

It was late. Reynolds was intoxicated. Out of the blue he asked: "Do you think Frank would want to sell the Plantation and the operations?"

As they walked back up the dune to the Packard, Marla replied, "I could ask."

***

Two weeks earlier, before Reynolds asked Marla if Frank and Bea would sell Plantation #7, Marla had opened the front door to her house early in the morning and Frank and Bea were sitting on the porch in a swing rocking quietly.

"Did you knock?" asked Marla. "I didn't hear you."

"We didn't want to disturb you."

"Do you want to talk?" Marla was confused.

"We wondered if you and Reynolds would want to buy the rest of the plantation, the operations and the grove and the sales division, or what's left of it," said Frank. "I don't think we can afford to keep operating the company."

Marla knew the business was suffering and she had worked without pay trying to revive it to profitability, but it was like a huge ship. Once momentum was against you the mass of the vessel was difficult to turn.

"I would love to own it, but I would feel bad to make a purchase when you are down and on the ropes. I think the business will come back if you are patient."

"We just got the bill from the attorney. We can't afford to pay it. We realized the expenses of the business will eat into our savings."

"You know Tom will wait to be paid. He's never pressured you for payment of his bill."

"We are too old to be running up big debts. This business isn't our only problem. We have some cash and the 860 acre Homestead and that's it. Anything we get for Plantation #7 would help." Really, Frank and Bea were not hurting. They were multi-millionaires, but they were not as flush as they had been. They were still being sued and could lose their savings to the other unit owners of TTF. Bea was right when she anticipated they would be taken down a notch.

"I'll talk to Reynolds about the purchase. He'll be back here in a couple of weeks. Meanwhile, you come up with a price and we'll see if it's feasible."

"Good, good," said Frank and Bea together.

Marla invited the couple inside and they sat in the kitchen and had coffee and crescent rolls with butter and guava jelly. Bea and Frank commented on the freshness of the preserves.

After a bit, Frank stepped outside and looked at his dad's grave. "I forgot the senator's grave was so close to the house. Have you ever thought of moving him to a graveyard?"

"No, The senator being here in the back yard doesn't bother me. This is where the senator wanted to be. It's actually not a bad idea. I thought I might plant myself right next to him."

"Maybe there's room for all of us," said Frank.

***

The morning after Reynolds arrived from Rochester; Marla told Reynolds that Frank and Bea were interested in selling Plantation #7. She explained they said they needed the money, but also explained they had understated their financial situation. They were far from poverty. Reynolds wanted to drive over to the Homestead and make an offer immediately, to strike while the iron was hot. Marla explained that Frank and Bea were in the process of deciding the value they would place on the asset. Marla wanted to let them come to her with an asking price.

"Besides, what do you want to do about the two of us? Are we to be single, a pair, a couple, or a marital unit?" asked Marla. "I thought we would talk about us first before we jump into business together."

Reynolds had a hard time talking about their relationship. He knew Marla had made quarter for him. She had accommodated his business interests when his work cost them their relationship. He had abandoned her in New York and when she returned to Florida he did not come to her to bring her back home. He had let her go. When she re-established her old relationship with Bob, he ignored it so long as she pretended to be the perfect loving wife. She had played that role very well. She was a good corporate wife, not allowing her emotions to disrupt the flow of commerce. Reynolds owed her for that but he never acknowledged that fact.

"Are you and Bob still seeing one another?"

"No, not for a while. He's working, running a sawmill."

"Can you put up with me?" asked Reynolds. "I mean permanently, in the future."

"Yes I can. But you will have to stay at home. I think this business is perfect for us. It will keep us in the game but not so much that it's not fun."

***

Frank and Bea asked for one million dollars net for their interest in the business called Plantation #7, including the grove, the jelly factory and the good will. Reynolds and Marla did not quibble. Jenny drew up the papers and the sale closed in a week.

Chapter 32
Palatka – Bob Barnes Starts Over

It was a dark evening in Palatka, Florida, a city whose primary industry was a large paper mill and sawmill on the St. Johns River (the River May). The paper mill produced smoke, containing the permeating odor of sulfur, that infested the air. The odor infused into your clothes and hair. It was awful, but eventually you got used to the smell, much like rotten eggs.

The evening newspaper was delivered to Bob Barnes' residence at the sawmill. Bob began to read as he hefted the Thursday news. Behind him the chip-n-saw mill that he managed was roaring to life. The sound of the blades ripping wood and seething steam shocked the air. Bob looked around and all was well in the world. He was surrounded by the sound of industry.

Back to the news ... the headline said: "Another Senseless Murder."

The story related an incident from early the preceding morning. Three men had bushwhacked another man at his truck in a parking lot next to an apartment house in town. The driver of the truck had been able to retrieve his handgun from the seat of his vehicle. He shot back, concentrating fire at one of his assailants, then reloaded as he jumped behind the wheel and sped away, firing random shots as he drove from the apartment complex.

After the battle there were only two men alive at the apartment house. They called the police. The police found the third assailant dead at the corner of the building with a bullet hole in his right eye. He was a teenager. He was found with a .22 caliber squirrel rifle at his side. The two men claimed the man who left in the truck was a murderer. "He started it," they said. The police were conflicted based on the evidence that they found at the scene.

The man in the truck went to a lawyer in Palatka and argued he was the victim and not a murderer. The lawyer wanted $10,000 before he would give any advice or talk to the police on behalf of the potential client. The man left the law office, not knowing what to do. The only thing he knew for sure was that he did not have $10,000.

The police could not tell who did what and consequently no arrest was made.

The funeral for the deceased was on the first Saturday after the incident. All four men had been friends and worked at the sawmill and the three survivors attended the funeral, although they sat apart on different sides of the church, surrounded by their respective families.

The pastor was worried gunfire might erupt in the church during the funeral service. Most of the parishioners at the service carried guns everywhere, even to church. You could never dismiss the possibility of gun violence.

The pastor was a practical man. "Everyone lost in this deal. We should all put it behind us." That idea was the theme of the pastor's sermon. He expressed the idea every way he could.

The congregation responded to each variant of the theme and repeated "Amen."

Finally, the pastor asked for a song.

The congregation wailed "Amazing Grace."

Everyone wept and all felt they were forgiven by God.

***

The three survivors had been subpoenaed to the State Attorney's office to testify as to the events that resulted in the death of the seventeen year old. When the men arrived at the courthouse they were confronted by a technician who was there to administer a lie detector test. They all refused to take the test, and when asked questions about the incident they refused to answer, asserting their rights against self-incrimination under the Fifth Amendment to the US Constitution.

All three men were concerned they would be arrested, and they wanted legal advice. The three men went to talk to Bob Barnes, their boss at the mill. Bob called Tom Night and Tom said he would speak to the two men who had been firing weapons from the apartment building.

The conference was short. Tom asked if the State knew of any witnesses to the shootout other than the participants. To their knowledge, the two men believed there were no other witnesses. No one had come forward and they doubted there would be anyone who would get involved in the controversy.

Tom advised the two men that the State Attorney could not prosecute the case without a witness or a confession. Tom explained the lie detector test was a ruse. It could not be used in court. The test would get the men talking and if they talked they would provide the State with the witness they needed to prosecute.

"So long as every one of the three of you keep your mouths shut, there won't be an arrest or a trial."

The two men thanked Tom and left him with a copy of the newspaper with the screaming headline about a senseless murder.

The men went to the parking lot and spoke to the third man who survived the shooting. The third man had followed the two men to the appointment in St. Petersburg. They talked for a while outside their trucks. Tom watched them from his upstairs office as they spoke. After an hour the men got in their trucks and drove back to their jobs at the sawmill.

Tom put the newspaper in the file and wrote the words "Close the file."

The State Attorney in Palatka wrote those same words "Close the File" on his file. No one talked and no one would be prosecuted for the death of the seventeen-year-old.

***

Bob Barnes had moved out of the Homestead after the family lost their interest in the lime rock mines. Since Reynolds was now living at the Plantation with Marla, it would be inappropriate for Bob to move back there.

Bob knew the lumber business and was a good manager who could work men effectively. He approached his old company, CCC Corporation, for a job and he was hired to run the sawmill in Palatka. The mill wasn't far from his parent's home and he could visit them on weekends.

This wasn't the way Bob had seen his life playing out, but he accepted it the same way he accepted the fact that he was over 40 years old and he was going bald.

The manager of the sawmill was provided a house on the property. A facility like the mill had men on site 24/7. There was always the possibility of an emergency and there were deliveries of logs to be cut and processed during the two shifts when the mill operated from 7:00am to 11:00 p.m. The manager was always being called to the site, so it made sense for the manager to live at the mill.

The manager had to be prepared to handle any problems, and finding a criminal lawyer to give some legal advice to one of his workers was par for the course.

It was also expected the manager would be single and not have a woman or his children living on site. Bob was allowed to have female companionship in his company house so long as the girlfriend did not move in with him. Local girls knew the rules. They knew they could stay over but they should not bring a suitcase.

Bob came to like beer and line dancing. He hung out at a club/ roadhouse on Highway 100. He was an able dancer and the girls thought he was a lot of fun. Bob had a date most every night and he tried to wear out as much local Cooter as he could.

***

Three months after he was hired, CCC moved Bob from Palatka to manage the pine sawmill in Jacksonville on I-10. This was CCC's biggest facility. The mill had a merchandizer and it could handle every size pine log cut from the woods. From pulp to pole logs, the mill produced every type lumber product there was to produce, except tooth picks.

Bob accepted each promotion as they came and he was good for the company. Soon he was regional manager for the Southeast US. He was in a plane most days. It reminded him of his work for his family except for the fact that now he got a regular pay check and he wasn't being sued constantly. All he had to do now was keep the machinery running producing lumber.

The upper echelon of CCC came to see Bob's value to the company and they asked if he would move to the Northwest US and run the operations that were headquartered in Seattle, Washington. There were different issues in the West. There was tension between the environmentalists and the timber companies. The main distinction was that in the west most of the timber that CCC was harvesting came from public lands. In the southeast the timber companies owned the land and the timber. People in the South believed you should be able to do what you wanted with your property once it was bought and paid for.

Bob had grown up and been taught in university and by his father Frank that you had to be a good land steward or you would lose your investment. The Barnes Family had thinned their land for pulp and then replanted timber seedlings in plantation as they clear cut timber for their mills. In the West CCC clear cut the timber but CCC did not replant the public lands. Timber companies out west relied on natural regeneration of the land.

Bob said he would take the job in the Northwest but he warned his bosses that he would do things differently. Nothing was working for CCC in the West. CCC had become a pariah ... a public relations disaster. The company was spending more time in court defending their rights than in the woods. The officers of CCC were willing to see what Bob could do.

Sight unseen, Bob hired a young timber surveyor who had not worked for the company for very long. Bob required the surveyor be certified in Graphic Information Systems (GIS). Bob wanted to know what land CCC owned and leased but he wanted the surveyor to be apolitical. The employee turned out to be a woman named Smiley, AKA Smiling Waters Brown. She was a single mom and had one male child named Robert Brown, Jr. Bob had expected he would be working with a man, but Smiley had the qualifications he was looking for.

***

Bob had Smiley search for the most environmentally sensitive parcel of timberland owned by CCC. It needed to be a large piece of land that had gone through the appellate process. It had to be legal for CCC to cut the timber.

Smiley found a 13,000 acre tract with old growth timber that was said to be ripe with endangered spotted owls and salamanders. Regardless of how sensitive this land was, CCC had every right to cut the land. Once Bob had a survey (map) of the property completed by Smiley, Bob and Smiley made an appointment with the local environmental council (LEC).

The LEC meeting was well attended in a school cafeteria. The local environmentalists tended to be yellers, shouting their position. Bob spoke in a quiet voice which caused everyone in the room to remain silent so he could be heard.

"I have been given authority by CCC to try to work with the environmental council (LEC) to negotiate a settlement of our logging dispute."

Bob had a large map showing northern California.

"We are familiar with the map," said the Chairman of the LEC. "What do you propose?"

"The LEC is trying to block every logging operation in the entire north of the State regardless of whether the timber is old growth or second growth and whether CCC owns the land, or has a lease from the government for public land, or it is land owned by a private citizen who is trying to lease CCC his timber rights."

"Correct," said the chairman. "And CCC has insisted on cutting on public lands that are home to endangered species."

"It doesn't make for good neighbors, does it?" asked Bob.

"What do you propose?" the chairman repeated.

"Starting with this 13,000 acre environmentally sensitive tract that LEC prizes, we will trade off acre for acre, the lands you desire to save for environmental reasons for timber lands that CCC owns or leases that we need to harvest to keep our mills operating. This will also keep jobs for the small towns in the north of the State. CCC will cut privately owned lands with no endangered species."

Bob unfurled a map of the 13,000 acre tract that the LEC had been trying to save. "We will try to meet you more than half way, beginning with this tract of land."

"You have that authority?"

Bob nodded. "Yes, I do."

The LEC Board closed the meeting and went into private session. Bob and Smiley sat outside the hall and waited.

"You think they will agree?" asked Smiley.

"Of course they will. They have no choice. They lost the appeal on this 13,000 acres. We could be out there now cutting timber."

"What if they did what they threatened and put activists in the trees? Or they drove metal spikes in the trees? Or they put their bodies in front of our machines so we could not harvest the trees?"

"There are way more trees than there are activists," said Bob. "They cannot save all the trees in the forest."

***

Bob's success with the environmentalists made news at CCC's headquarters in New York City.

Bob's personnel file was passed around among the officers and directors of CCC. The history of his family being in the timber and dairy industry since 1843 was important. Bob was seen as a potential political counterweight to the environmentalists. The timber and mining industry felt the environmentalists controlled the staff at the Department of the Interior.

The CEO of CCC asked if anyone knew Bob Barnes political affiliation. Like Senator Barnes, Bob was a Republican.

"Perfect. The US President is looking for a new Secretary for the Department of the Interior. I'll suggest Bob Barnes for the post at lunch."

The CEO of CCC met with Bob after he met with the US President at lunch. The President was interested in having Bob vetted for the position of Secretary of the Department of the Interior. Bob really had no interest in politics. Bob reminded the CEO of CCC that his family had been embroiled in litigation involving the Thompson Timber Fund and that would have a negative impact on his application. The CEO of CCC said that wouldn't matter. There would be a fight no matter who the President proposed for the vacancy in the post.

Bob promised himself that he would disclose the controversy involving Thompson Timber Fund before he was appointed and went before the Senate to be questioned by the committee.

Chapter 33
A Short History of Smiley's son Robert Brown, Jr.

Robert Brown, Jr., the son of "Smiley" Brown, was born on December 30th 1985. He took the last name (Brown) from his mother, Smiling Waters "Smiley" Brown. Smiley was the only parent identified on his birth certificate. His mother's mother was named Helen Bad Heart Bull. She was 100% Oglala Sioux and a direct descendant of Amos Bad Heart Bull (b. 1869) who was a great Native American artist and historian. The name Robert was the first name of his grandfather, Robert Brown, who was 100% Scot/Caucasian and a businessman in the town of Wall, South Dakota.

Mr. Brown owned and operated a saloon just outside the boundary of the Sioux reservation near The Badlands in South Dakota. Robert Brown sold whiskey to the Indians and the tourists.

Robert Brown married Helen Bad Heart Bull and she gave birth to Smiley. Then, when Smiley was six years old, Helen was spirited away by a rich dentist, who met her in Robert Brown's bar. The dentist was riding a motorcycle through the Pine Ridge to Sturgis for the annual motorcycle rally. The dentist and Helen fell in love and Helen left Smiling Waters to live and grow up at the bar with her father. Helen and the dentist rode his Harley-Davidson to Minneapolis, Minnesota, where the dentist maintained his practice pulling teeth and applying braces to the teeth of rich white children of the Lutheran faith.

Helen Bad Heart Bull completely abandoned her child and filed for divorce, citing irreconcilable differences between her and her oft drunk husband Robert. Robert agreed to the divorce so long as Helen gave up all rights to his child, Smiley, and to any equitable interest Helen gained in the saloon which had been named "Smileys" in his daughter's honor. Smiley said she did not want to see her mother ever again.

Smiley attended school on the reservation and worked at the saloon wiping down the tables and the bar and sweeping the floor after school, preparing the business for the night trade in legal whiskey and the sale of illegal contraband – guns and dope (hemp weed, and homemade methamphetamine). The dope and weapons were stored in the trunks of cars parked in the saloon's dusty parking lot.

Robert Brown did not allow his daughter to enter the saloon when it was in operation. She stayed in their home, a concrete block house built to the rear of the property, and learned her lessons from school on the reservation and also took college courses on the Internet offered by Arizona State University. (ASU) Smiley completed all the work the university required to obtain an Associate in Arts degree in Native American Studies. The term papers she submitted were so impressive that a teaching assistant at ASU brought her work to the attention of the Dean of the Department of Native American Studies.

A university representative visited Smiley at her home in Wall and saw the saloon and her living conditions and spoke to Robert Brown. The representative convinced him that his daughter could do much better living and taking classes on campus in the university at Tempe, Arizona. Robert Brown was concerned that his daughter at age 13 was too young to be away from home. The school's representative said she was mature for her age and she had essentially completed high school and the first two years of college on her own. Robert Brown had to admit the saloon was no place to raise his child and he agreed Smiley could go with the representative back to Tempe.

***

Tempe is a suburb of Phoenix, Arizona, in Maricopa County. The original inhabitants, the Hohokam people, lived in the area and built canals from the Salt River for irrigation for farming. No one knows why, but the Hohokam abandoned the area in the 1400's. Eventually there was a fort constructed in the area by the US Army and then a railhead, and then the residents re-established the irrigation canals originally constructed by the Hohokam near present day Phoenix and grew alfalfa, wheat, barley, oats and cotton.

Arizona State University was established in 1885 as a "territorial normal school". One hundred years later, the city of Tempe had a permanent population of over 150,000 when Smiley took up residence in a dorm on the West Campus. The total student population at the university was almost 70,000 students and it was the largest university by population in the United States. The sister city of Phoenix had a population of over one million souls.

It took only a short time before Smiley was lost in this crowd of humanity. By comparison, her hometown of Wall had less than 300 residents. She was overwhelmed by the size of the classes in the lecture halls, sometimes attended by 500 or more students. Attendance at football games was over 50,000 fans.

Once she was lost, Smiley tried to re-root herself and took a job at a saloon on the outskirts of the campus. She did not attend her classes. When she was not working at the saloon she stayed in her dorm room and studied on the Internet. She had no transportation and she walked to and from work.

One night at 2:00 am the representative who had convinced her father to allow her to attend school in Tempe was driving home and he saw Smiley walking to the dorm. The representative stopped and picked her up and he drove her home. It was then that she was found out. Robert Brown was summoned for a conference. The decision was made that Smiley was too immature to handle college classes in Tempe and she was brought back home to Wall.

The university agreed that she could continue her classes online from home in Wall. It was a win/ win.

***

After her return home, Smiley resumed her work for her father cleaning the saloon and she kept up with the chores around the house.

Some days, as she went to enter the business at 10:00 am, there would be men loitering outside in the parking lot. They had nothing to do but wait for the bar to open. In the meantime they sipped on pint bottles of liquor which they hid in their coat pockets.

Smiley had to run the gauntlet of the men, who called her, "squaw". This word, squaw, was meant to disparage. The word was vile. It was an epitaph. The men did not refer to Smiley as a wife or mother, but they used the word as a reference to female genitalia. They were referring to Smiley as a "cunt". They were disrespecting her. They were calling her out as if she was a disease.

When confronted by these drunken men, Smiley would put her head down, cover her face with her shawl and forge ahead as though she was bending into a gale force wind full of heavy wet snow. The leering men put Smiley in fear and she told her father about her encounters in the parking lot. The young Indian braves had not been so bold before she went away to university. Robert Brown explained that things had changed. Some of the men were taking drugs that made them brazen—cocaine and PCP.

Smiley's father gave her a gun for her protection. She held tight to the center of the .45 Caliber Colt with her fingers grasping the cylinder of the weapon. When her father gave her the weapon he instructed her to use it if she was attacked, but to do nothing but ignore the men if they did not touch her. She was afraid to place her finger on the trigger for fear the gun would fire accidently. She held the weapon under her shawl like a club.

The men often spoke about Smiley as they sat drinking. They imagined what she was like sexually. She was 15 years old and to the best they knew, she was chaste. These men had not known a woman like her. They only knew barflies. Smiley kept them awake at night thinking about the pleasure she could give them.

***

When the spring came, one man, Yellow Dog, could no longer stand the unfulfilled desire he harbored for Smiley. His dreams were insufficient.

Yellow Dog was working in the oil shale fields in the north. The oil find had just been discovered. He was a roustabout, a member of a crew drilling for oil from the Bakken Shale Formation. He made thousands of dollars working double shifts, and sleeping rent free in employee trailers out in the oil field. In his first month he had earned $15,000, but he could not think of anything to spend the money on in the boom town besides booze and nasty women.

After working the first month straight through, Yellow Dog filled his old Dodge Charger with gas and drove to his mother's home near Wall. On the way home he thought about nothing but Smiley, the squaw. It was a lonely drive through the prairie and over the Black Hills of the Dakotas. He determined that he would go to the saloon before he went to see his mother.

When he arrived at the saloon it was 11:00 pm. Yellow Dog parked behind the saloon and in front of Robert Brown and Smiley's home. He entered the bar and with a flourish, he threw ten twenty dollar bills on the counter and offered drinks to everyone. Then Yellow Dog drank his fill. He said his farewell after a few hours and claimed he was heading home to his mamma's house.

Instead, Yellow Dog crawled in the window of Smiley's dark bedroom. He snuck up on Smiley, who was deep asleep in bed in the cold unheated room. She was warmed by a buffalo skin blanket.

Yellow Dog put a knife to Smiley's throat and the cold steel woke her.

Yellow Dog said nothing for fear Smiley would recognize his voice. In the past, she had heard him call to her as she crossed the parking lot to go in to clean the saloon and she would know his voice. When she felt the steel she awoke immediately and fear gripped her every muscle and nerve ending. She was also trying to know who this was who was violating her in her own bed.

As Yellow Dog entered her, Smiley felt under the covers until she could grasp the cylinder of the old Colt .45 caliber pistol.

Yellow dog was oblivious and in ecstasy as she lifted the weapon to his head, drew back the hammer and pulled the trigger and the gun fired. The bullet caught Yellow Dog in the left temple and lifted the seams of his skull apart. His eyes rolled in his head and a wisp of smoke slithered from his nostrils. Yellow Dog was very surprised by the outcome of the affair, or so it seemed from the look on his face.

Smiley rolled him off of her and inspected her body. She had his blood on her face and Yellow Dog had ejaculated. She went in the bathroom and tried to rinse herself at the sink but the damage was done. Her hymen was broken and a ribbon of blood coursed down her inner thigh. She had to tell her father, so she wrapped herself in the buffalo skin and walked barefoot to the saloon and went in the front door. The men ignored her as she walked to the bar and leaned over and whispered to her dad. He took her to the restroom and looked her over for any wound.

Robert Brown closed the business, locking the door, and took his girl back to their house. He entered the bedroom and inspected the remains of Yellow Dog. He called the police and the tribal authorities.

The police officer and the tribal elder called the family of the deceased. There was little the authorities could do. Yellow Dog's mother wanted Smiley prosecuted for murder. No one thought Smiley was guilty of any crime except being desirable to a horny drunk who crawled into her bedroom while she was asleep and raped her. They refused to arrest her.

Robert Brown took Smiley to the hospital in Rapid City. The doctor confirmed Smiley could be pregnant. They asked what she wanted to do. She said there was little that could be done but to wait and see.

***

Nine months later on December 30, 1985, Smiley gave birth to Robert Brown, Jr. at her home with the aid of a mid-wife. Robert's birth was uneventful and it gave Smiley and her father great joy; however, the joy was short lived.

Yellow Dog's mother insisted the child be raised in her house under her custody and control. Robert Brown was her grandchild. Smiley refused to surrender her child. Further, she would not live with Yellow Dog's mother.

In addition to claiming custody of her grandson, Yellow Dog's mother filed a wrongful death action against Robert Brown and his business. She claimed he had allowed Yellow Dog to become so intoxicated in his saloon to the point that he lost all inhibition and sexually attacked Smiley, who shot and killed him.

On the custody claim, the tribal council sided with Yellow Dog's mother. The child was to live with his grandmother. As soon as she knew of the decision, Smiley took her son and placed him in her father's truck and drove away. She told no one, not even her father, where she was going. When she left, even Smiley did not know where she was going to end up. Smiley knew from her studies of the Native American legal system that custody of the child could be determined by the council. She removed Robert from the Oglala jurisdiction in the Dakotas to Arizona, and she hid among the Mexican immigrants who had entered the United States illegally. She had no trouble finding work in a McDonald's Restaurant. She had computer skills that were highly prized by the owner of the franchise and he was willing to ignore her fugitive status as he ignored the fact that most of his employees did not have a green card.

***

After six months, Smiley contacted her father to be updated on the news from Wall. Yellow Dog's mother was ill. She had been suffering from diabetes in the past and now she lost her left leg to the disease. She no longer intended to pursue custody of her grandson. She felt the child was bad luck and had caused her illness. Further, Robert Brown spoke to his insurance agent and the company was willing to pay $5,000 to settle the death claim Yellow Dog's mother was asserting against the saloon and Smiley for shooting and killing Yellow Dog.

When she was paid the $5,000, Yellow Dog's mother had her revenge for the loss of her son and she was satisfied. She dropped the lawsuit and signed a release of all claims. She also withdrew her petition for custody of the child. Robert Brown, Jr. was now in the legal care, custody and control of Smiling Waters Brown.

***

Smiley and her son Robert continued to live in Maricopa County, Arizona. She was still reticent to return to the Dakotas where she and her son would come under the jurisdiction of the Sioux Nation. Robert's father Yellow Dog was 100% Sioux and Smiley was 50% Sioux. Robert and Smiley would be subject to the rulings of the Tribal Council.

Smiley worked for the McDonald's from home online so she could care for Robert by herself. She did not train him in Indian ways. The child did not hunt or camp. He was suckled at his mother's breast. When he was old enough, he ate Happy Meals.

Smiley was still enrolled in college at Arizona State and she continued to take classes. Within three years she had her degree, a Bachelor of Arts in Native American Studies. Unfortunately the degree was useless in helping her find employment. She tried to transfer the courses she had taken into a career. Except for teaching school, no career path was available. She spoke to the representative of the university who had first enlisted her into the program and he suggested she obtain a GIS certificate.

A Geographic Information System (GIS) is designed to capture, store, and manipulate geographical data so that the data can be analyzed. The data can be used in engineering, planning, management, logistics and businesses. The first operational geographic system was developed by the Canadian government to analyze information collected for the Canada Land Inventory. The GIS mapped the soils, recreation, agriculture, wildlife, forestry and uses of Canada's lands. Once Canada's GIS of its land was made other governments and businesses followed suit and used GIS to develop policy. GIS was a new tool to collect and then analyze data spatially, such as on a map, so it could be easily studied.

Once Smiley had the certification, which was awarded by Arizona State in their Geography department, she found a job in the oil industry working for Halliburton. That company provided multiple services for the oil drillers. Halliburton offered to collect data and apply the data to a GIS for companies such as Exxon to use to manage their vast land holdings. Halliburton's offices were in Lafayette, Louisiana, which was about two hours from Houston and two hours from New Orleans. Smiley didn't care where she was living, she wanted a good job so she could care for her son. Time was passing, she was twenty years old, and Robert was four years old. The year was 1990.

***

Robert entered a public pre-school. The school was poor. Without the tutoring the boy received from his mother he would not have learned his colors, to count to one hundred, and to memorize the simple books Smiley read to him repeatedly after his bath and before he was fast asleep.

Smiley did not date, although there was some interest shown by her co-workers. She was not afraid to date; she was more interested in her son than in an adult relationship.

***

On January 17, 1991 Smiley was in the commissary at work, grabbing an apple and coffee for breakfast. There was a television in the corner and just after 8:00 am Central Time (2:00 am in Iraq) there was a report that a massive air invasion employing jet aircraft and stealth bombers, cruise missiles and smart bombs had hit Iraq's air force, communications, weapon plants and strategic infrastructure.

The event was anticipated. The Iraqi leader Saddam Hussein had been warned by the UN and most nations in the region on numerous occasions that he was required to withdraw all his forces from Kuwait, but he had refused and the attack was justified by Resolution of the United Nations.

There was a crowd that gathered around the TV and they did not leave. There was a loop of video that was replayed showing the collision of allied bombs into Saddam's government buildings and there were explanations given by generals who were using pointers to show the audience throughout the world of the destruction being caused by US aircraft which was bombing the enemy with pinpoint accuracy and allegedly with little collateral damage. The US President let the generals do the explaining and let them garner the glory. Since the Viet Nam war there was little praise that came their way.

Depiction of war to US citizens was not new. The audience had seen film of the Viet Nam war play out on TV before their eyes as they ate dinner. But this was war in real time ... it seemed so real. The audience still did not experience the smell, the dust, or feel the impact or noise. The air was not electric; there was no blinding flash of light. But the television viewer knew we were in a war. It was self-evident. People were dying before their eyes. The enemy could not survive the concussions that leveled large buildings.

When Smiley saw the first building collapse and watched the soot and ash cloud she believed she had to take action to save her child. She left Halliburton's commissary and went to her secondhand car and drove to the pre-school and retrieved her son, Robert Brown, Jr. They left everything in Lafayette and drove back to her father's house in Wall, South Dakota.

***

In Wall, life did not skip a beat. People had to eat, people had to drink. The bar opened on time.

Smiley no longer wanted to work in Lafayette for Halliburton. She wanted to stay close to her home and her father.

Meanwhile, Halliburton was going in a new direction. One of its subsidiaries obtained government contracts to provide ancillary services such as logistics and commissary to the US military and the State Department and they were downsizing the GIS department to support the subsidiary.

Halliburton and Smiley parted ways amicably and Smiley moved permanently into her father's house behind the saloon. She found work for the Tribal Council as an administrative assistant and liaison for the Council to the Bureau of Indian Affairs, which was a department of the Interior Department of the Executive Branch of the US Government.

The Kuwait War ended in weeks. The Allies were victorious. The Iraqis were driven from Kuwait. But Saddam remained in power and the air war continued. There was a no fly zone that was implemented by the US and its allies. If there was death, it effected the enemy and the poor minority residents of Iraq—the Kurds and the Shiites. America tamped down the enemy and ignored the problem, waiting to see if there was a next shoe to drop, but nothing seemed to happen except a group of Saudi men tried to blow up one of the Twin Towers in New York City. The terrorists caused death and destruction. However they were so incompetent they were arrested almost immediately.

Smiley gained more confidence and began to apply for work away from Wall. She felt her son needed more than what Wall offered. She saw the boys from the reservation loitering around the small food stores and the men waiting for the saloon to open. There was too much temptation. She had taken her son on a train ride west and they visited the Pacific coast with an open ticket, which allowed them to stop and spend time in a city before moving on. There were stops in Seattle, Portland, San Francisco and Los Angeles and then they looped back to the east and then north to Chicago and then on to Rapid City and back to Wall.

Seeing what was out in the world convinced Smiley that it was best for her son if they moved on. Smiley thought there would be opportunities for both of them on the west coast. They spoke about it and of the cities he had seen. Robert thought Seattle was his favorite. So Seattle it was.

Smiley sent out applications for employment to all of the large corporate entities in Seattle, including CCC Corporation.

Chapter 34

Bob Barnes' Perspective of Robert Brown, Jr. and his Mother

Bob Barnes had matriculated to Seattle as he advanced through his work for CCC Corporation. Bob's father Frank, and his grandfather, the Senator, had originally incorporated CCC, which was first known as Commercial Cartage Corporation. Tom Night was the attorney and registered agent for the corporation.

CCC grew by buying numerous timberland tracts and sawmills and a trucking arm to deliver two-by-fours and other lumber CCC produced to the Northeast for home construction. CCC grew on credit. CCC borrowed every dime it could.

Then, after CCC grew to 500,000 acres of land, CCC sold about half of its assets to Withlacoochee Lumber Corporation (WLC) to prepare for an anticipated recession. Frank and the Senator kept operating under the name CCC. The recession came and went and then there was a second recession. By this time the Senator had passed and CCC was now managed by Marla James. By buying and trading land, CCC again became the largest private timber owner in the Southeast US. At that time, Marla negotiated the sale of CCC to JRD Corporation. Bob Barnes and Marla had fallen in and out of love. Marla was married to James Reynolds after the sale of CCC to JRD.

After CCC was sold, Bob and his brother Albert were out of work. They started Florida Lime Rock and then its subsidiary, Belize Lime Rock, but they could not make a go of it. Running the lime rock mines was like throwing money into a pit. Fifty-one percent (thus control) of the lime rock companies was sold to Thompson Timber Fund, a corporation owned by Thomas N.

Thompson. Thompson was a crook who took investor's money and sold them a bill of goods. Ultimately, Thompson took a wad of cash and ran away. The investors blamed Frank, Bob, and Marla for their losses. The investors sued them, along with the lime rock companies.

Bob Barnes started work for CCC in Palatka, Florida, managing a small specialty sawmill that cut large trees into boards. He lived at the plant and was expected to learn all operations of the facility, even fixing the toilet. Bob was glad to have a job.

Then CCC moved Bob on to a chip-n-saw plant in South Georgia on the Flint River. In a chip-n-saw plant, small logs are skinned of their bark. The bark is burned in a boiler producing steam for electricity to power the mill. The skinned log is cut into two-by-four boards. The waste wood is chipped up to be used to make manufactured strand boards (MSB) at another facility. MSB is produced by gluing chips and pieces of wood together under pressure and heat to produce a laminated structural board, or Aspen board (like a sheet of plywood formed from wood chips).

The Flint River mill was one of the first computerized sawmills in the Southeast and Bob was sent there to learn the future of milling timber. He was there for only six months.

Once Bob proved he could run the computerized mill he was promoted to superintendent of the largest pine processing mill in the Southeast. The mill was located on Interstate 10 (I-10) in Duval County (Jacksonville), Florida. For the last 100 years Duval County had grown a huge monoculture of pine trees. From the air you could see more than 2,000,000 acres of pine timber in various stages of development. There were fields that were recently prepared and planted with seedlings. There were 1,000 acre tracts of one-year-old trees and thousands of acres of three-year-old trees and thousands of acres of five-year-old trees. There were also pulp-size trees for paper and MSB, and sawmill trees (chip-n-saw and large saw), and there were thousands of acres of pole timber and even taller and thicker timber that could be used in the construction of docks and piers for harbors.

Bob was in Duval County for just over a year. After that he was put in charge of all of CCC's operations in the Southeast. This was a position at CCC's headquarters in Atlanta, Georgia. It was purely an executive position. Bob developed policy for the company as it related to pine timber operations in the Southeast. For Bob, the work caused him no strain. CCC was well funded by JRD. Bob had no budget deficit. Home office for JRD had to make all the internal hypothecations of funds necessary for the next down-turn. Timber is a commodity and its value follows economic cycles. Home office for JRD in New York City had to make the call on the timing of the next recession. Bob was not responsible for anything except providing a supply of logs to the mills and keeping the mills running and the technology up to date. He held the position as executive head of SE CCC for two years.

Then he was given a challenge. Bob's company made a purchase of 600,000 acres in the Northwest. The seller of the acreage was a family that had collected the contiguous acreage over five generations. They had given up fighting with the conservationists over owls and salamanders. The family members just wanted to retire to a place where it was sunny and warm and there were no wars.

When Bob moved to CCC's headquarters in the Northwest in Seattle he was in his middle fifties, healthy and nearly bald.

***

Through work, Bob became aware of Smiling Waters "Smiley" Brown. Bob wanted an assistant who understood and could CAD (Computer Aided Design) a GIS (Geographic Information System) of the company's new holdings. Smiley held those certifications. Because Smiley applied to be an employee, Bob became aware Smiley had a child named Robert Brown and that she was a single parent. Her child's father, who was identified as Yellow Dog, was deceased. Her personnel record was muddled. There was no easy answer as to the circumstances surrounding how Robert Brown's father had died. The record said there was a domestic disturbance and that Smiley had acted in self- defense and shot her son's father, who was intoxicated. Unfortunately the man died.

Bob put down Smiley's employment application and looked out the window. The human resources (HR) officer who was shepherding Smiley Brown's application through the process noted in the margin that HR would obtain the police reports if needed, but pointed out that Smiley was only 15 years old when the incident happened, and so, as a juvenile, the records would be sealed and they could only be obtained with Smiley's permission, or after a court proceeding and with a court order.

Bob had enough of the courthouse. He had just recently received the final order from the court in Delaware on the suit to claw back the money TNT had paid him for his interest in the lime rock operations. Bob owed a million dollars. His father and mother were loaning him the money so the matter could be settled. Bob's parents were also paying a portion of the legal fees. The fees were nearly two million dollars. The amount was ridiculous, but the case was over for the Barnes family. Marla had also been sued, but she was found to be acting in her capacity as a corporate officer and she was determined to have no personal liability. Thomas N. Thompson bore the brunt of the penalties. He was sentenced to jail for fraud and theft and violation of the rules and regulations of the Security and Exchange Commission. Mr. Thompson was sentenced to 50 years in jail, fined $5,000,000 by the SEC. Civil consent judgments in the amount of $40,000,000 were also assessed against Thompson Timber Fund.

Bob Barnes did not need the police reports explaining how and why Smiley killed the father of her child. He was not interested in the facts contained in the reports, only the result of the investigation. Smiley had not been charged with a crime and two police agencies found that she had acted in self- defense. Further, there was no indication that there had been any repetition of any violent act since the unfortunate event, which was ten years ago.

Otherwise, the company's investigation showed that Smiley had a good understanding of bureaucracies, having worked for the Tribal Council and for Halliburton, a publicly traded corporation. She had also worked with the Department of the Interior and the Bureau of Indian Affairs. There were positive recommendations from everyone she had had contact with, from school through employment. She had impressed the HR officer, who hoped Bob would hire Smiley as his administrative assistant. HR had had difficulty meeting Bob's requirements for an assistant. Bob required the applicant to have a GIS certification. It was rare to find someone with that knowledge, but Bob felt he would need to compile a spatial system or map of all the CCC Corporation property in the Northwest USA and Canada, and so the GIS certificate was a necessity.

Smiley had the credentials. Bob looked closely at the 8½ by 11 inch portrait photo on the last page of the application. Smiley was exotically beautiful. She had long straight black hair and black eyes and high cheek bones. She was a Native American princess. She had a nice smile. This could be a problem, thought Bob. She's beautiful.

The background report showed that most of Smiley's out-of-work activities involved her son. She was a classroom mom and donated time at lunch and after school to help the teachers with children who were falling behind. She read to students and helped them with basic math. She had her son in a charter school. Most of the children were Caucasian and not Native American, African American or Hispanic.

Her son was involved in the Boy Scouts. He had advanced from Tiger Cubs to Cub Scouts to the Boy Scouts, and he was ranked a First Class Scout.

There was possible negative information in the report involving the son. The investigator found that the boy had no close friends and that he was a computer nerd. He had run away from school on one occasion. The boy told the sheriff who found him playing hooky in the tourist trap in Wall, South Dakota, that he felt discriminated against. He felt that he was different than the other children. The deputy noted that Robert was seen in the town panhandling, and the business manager at a drug store called to report him to the sheriff. The deputy found Robert with a sign in his hand that said he was an orphan Indian boy. He was begging for donations. The deputy reported that when he returned Robert to his mother, that she did not scold him but spoke to him quietly and that the boy was crying and then sobbing. The deputy did not take any further action, but noted in the report that the boy may need psychiatric intervention. No action was taken. South Dakota did not have tax money to spend on psychiatric intervention for an Indian boy.

***

Bob had the company fly Smiley and her son, Robert, from Rapid City, South Dakota, to Seattle for an interview.

Smiley was relaxed and her answers to Bob's questions were reassuring.

Bob wondered about her son. He knew that if the boy would give his mother trouble, she would have no family safety net in the area to watch over and take care of her son and Bob would lose his employee. She would quit or she would be an ineffective employee.

Bob met with Smiley and Robert at 11:00 am at his office. He asked Robert to wait in the reception room while he interviewed Smiley.

At noon Bob asked Smiley if they wanted lunch.

"Sure, Robert is always hungry." said Smiley. "Our stomachs are on Mountain time so it's really 1:00 pm to us."

"Does your son like baseball?"

"Yes, he listens to the teams on the west coast on the radio."

"Great."

Bob took them to a ball game. The Mariners were playing San Francisco. CCC Corporation had a box at the stadium. The Mariners won the game and Bob was impressed with Robert. He was as smart as his mother and he was engaged in life. Bob thought he would not cause his mother any difficulty at work.

"Would you and your mother like to go to the games, if the tickets are available?"

"Sure," said Robert.

Bob noticed that Robert kept looking at Bob's head. Maybe he has never seen a bald person before, thought Bob. Bob was 55 years old. He was starting to show some wear and tear on the edges. He tried to keep himself up. He ran a couple of miles daily for exercise. He shaved his head every morning in the shower.

Bob wondered.

"Would you excuse me for a minute?" asked Bob.

Bob went to the restroom and looked at his ears. They were full of shaving cream. He took a wad of paper towel and cleaned out his ears. On his way back to his seat he bought three bags of peanuts.

"Why didn't you tell me I had soap in my ears?"

Smiley and Robert just laughed. Bob joined in.

***

Bob Barnes was a nose-to-the-grindstone type. He may not have been the smartest, but he learned what his job was and he ground it out. It may not have been pretty but it was completed on time. Bob worked his entire life. When he was six years old his job was to wake up at night when his adopted brother Jimmy awoke and needed to have his diaper changed, and he had to awaken every two hours to roll Jimmy in bed to prevent bed sores. He always woke up because Jimmy's life depended on it. Bob learned that if Jimmy got a bed sore he could get an infection, and if he got an infection, he was too weak to fight it off and he could die.

Bob could remember his natural parents and he remembered that they relied on him for chores, and he watched his siblings,

Albert and Jenny, when they were young; particularly after the three of them were adopted by Frank and Bea Barnes after their mother was hospitalized with schizophrenia and she was put on the drug Thorazine. Finally, his natural mother was taken up North to live with her sister because she could no longer care for herself.

Then, there was work for the Barnes family businesses. Bob did not have a choice, there was work to be done and he was available and he was expected to help. Now, the family business was no more. It was sold and everyone should have been clipping coupons. But no, Bob and Albert spent all their money on investments in lime rock. First it was lime rock to build roads in Florida, then it was a lime rock agate mine in Big Creek, Belize. The lime rock agate from Belize was mixed with fly ash and sand and lime to produce cement for the highway systems in the southeastern United States and in Mexico. Bob had lost his investment. Bob walked away from the mine and from Marla. Marla was still a friend and Marla found Bob a job. He was hired by CCC Corporation, the company his adoptive father and grandfather founded. He was 50 years old and he was hired to run the sawmill in Palatka. He had started over ...

***

Bob hired Smiley as his administrative assistant. Together they worked to solve CCC's biggest problem, which involved procuring the necessary timber to keep his mills running. CCC owned timberland but mostly relied on public lands for its inventory of logs. Bob wanted an administrative assistant who understood CAD and GIS so he could simplify his argument as to CCC's rights to timber on lands it owned or leased. The conservationists claimed that all of CCC's lands were ancient, "Old Growth" timberlands, or they supported the habitat of protected species, owls or salamanders. By making these claims, the conservationists tried to starve CCC's need for logs in its mills. The conservationists were very resourceful in their arguments in court, and if they lost, they had been known to take illegal action, such as living in trees or driving steel spikes in tree trunks so they could not be run through a saw in a sawmill. They even burned down homes that were built with lumber con-structed from trees from old growth forests.

The first thing Bob did was meet with CCC's litigation counsel. CCC had been in court for over 15 years fighting their legal battles. The cases ran the gamut. First, CCC would be subject to a preliminary injunction because there were alleged sightings of protected species on their property. Then there would be a trial. Then there would be an appeal in state court. Then there would be an appeal in Federal Court, and then there would be litigation over trespass to lands and sit-ins.

As a result, CCC had to shutter some mills. Local citizens who worked in the mills lost their jobs and there was pay back by the locals against the conservationists. It was a war and Bob had to settle the matter or CCC would close operations.

Bob met with CCC's attorney. Bob wanted the attorney to identify one large parcel of land that would be prized by the conservationists. Bob wanted to identify a tract of trees that if the trees on that land were cut the opposition would feel the loss in their heart and soul.

The attorney knew just the piece of land. There was old growth timber on the parcel but not so much that the court felt there would be irreversible consequences if the forest were lost. There had been sightings of owls in the past but none had been seen recently.

In the past, if there was no expert to testify, a lay witness would offer testimony under oath that was a lie. No attorney for the environmentalists would call the witness or question the witness because they knew the witness was offering perjured testimony.

It was Bob's intention to file a suit against the perjurer for the cost of defending against the injunction and the cost of delay in taking the timber from the forest for use in the mill. The name of a suit against the lying witness is a "slap suit". They are effective because a witness who loses such a suit can be rendered bankrupt.

Bob authorized the attorney to file the slap suit if warranted. It had never been done in the past and the very threat of the slap suit caught the opposition off guard.

Bob also had Smiley produce a GIS that identified all of the CCC land that was particularly desirable to the conservationists and which were sensitive to degradation by clear cut logging.

Bob sent a copy of the CAD of the GIS to the citizen's group that had put up the vigorous fight that had stopped all logging in the Northwest for years. Bob requested a meeting with the group and proposed that CCC would trade off environmentally sensitive land that it owned and leased for the right to cut and log lands that were not old growth forest or known and agreed to be the forest habitat of protected species.

Bob knew based on the work Smiley had done that at least 400,000 acres of CCC's 600,000 acres could be logged without damage to the lands the conservationists wanted to protect. CCC would have sufficient timber to harvest for its operations in the future. There would be no necessity to file a slap suit. The parties could each claim victory and go home a winner. There was an agreement and a settlement document signed by all the parties and the governmental entities. The conservationists really had no choice. The newspapers were supportive of the settlement. It was basically fair.

This was unprecedented. Bob Barnes had finally found success. But success came with great cost and emotional pain.

***

During this time when he was starting over, back when he was in Palatka, Bob Barnes thought he was going crazy. His brother Albert was schizophrenic, as was his mother. His father was an alcoholic. Bob had bad mental genes, he felt, and he went to a psychiatrist.

"What is your first remembrance as a child?" asked the doctor.

"Do you mean a feeling, a memory of an event, or what?" asked Bob.

"An incident, probably ... something that is real in your mind ... a fully formed memory. Something that is fully fleshed out."

"Why is that important?"

"It's the way I work," said the doctor. "I need a starting point."

"All right ... fair enough. We were living in a very small house that my natural father built with used materials that were salvaged from the Army barracks that were built during WWII. We were living next to a big house called The Homestead. I wanted to live in the Homestead and I tried to make friends with the owners. The owners later adopted me and my brother and my sister ..." Bob's voice trailed off and he was silent.

"Is that what you remember? Is that your first memory that is vivid?" The doctor prodded Bob to continue his memory.

"There was a collision between a semi-truck hauling timber and a train. I was awakened from a deep sleep. There was a man sitting on the front porch. He was the truck driver. He was missing a part of his leg."

"What was he saying?"

"He was telling us what happened. He didn't see the train coming. It wasn't his fault he said."

"What do you remember?"

"He was bleeding badly and my mother was trying to stop the bleeding, but she couldn't and the man died on our porch. He bled to death."

"How did you feel?"

"Me? I wanted to get out of the little house my Dad had built."

"What do you mean?"

Bob didn't say anything more. He smiled at the doctor and left the room.

Bob Barnes thought the doctor was crazy. He never went back to the doctor. But he now remembered the incident with the truck driver vividly. He remembered that he was near the intersection of Flomish Road and the railroad tracks when the collision occurred. He was sitting in the front seat of his dad's Studebaker Coupe. The Studebaker was stopped, waiting for the train to pass. The train always came through going way too fast heading north to St. Augustine. The truck didn't stop at the intersection. It drove onto the tracks. The engine of the train hit the trailer of the semi-truck broadside just behind the cab. The cab of the truck bent around the front of the engine of the train and the driver of the truck was expelled from the front window of the cab like he was shot from a canon.

Bob's dad, Big Al, ran to the man, who was lying on the road. The man had propped himself up. He was just sitting there like nothing happened. Other human beings came to the scene. From where they came, Bob knew not where, and they all gawked and gave advice. The man was missing part of his right leg and he was pumping blood into the road. Bob just stared and he did not do anything. Why didn't he do something? It was like a dream. Bob was watching from afar. Finally, a lady wrapped the stump of the driver's leg. Big Al volunteered to take the man to his house. His wife would help.

Bob's mom helped as best she could, but she had no medical training.

The man died on Bob's front porch. The semi-truck driver never said anything except he did not see the train coming down the tracks. It wasn't his fault.

Bob knew the driver was mistaken. Bob saw the train. The train came by every night. The train sped by, trying to make time before it got to the rail head and switch yard in St. Augustine, Florida.

***

The settlement with the conservationists and the government assured CCC that in the Northwest it would have an inventory of logs for the foreseeable future. Bob received congratulations from all quarters—family, peers at work, and even Marla and Reynolds called with best wishes. Reynolds also spoke to the new CEO of

JRD, who had replaced him. That call put Bob on the political trail to the Department of the Interior.

This was really the first time that Bob had prevailed and he was a success.

Bob decided to take a victory lap and he asked Smiley if she and Robert would like to take a road trip.

"What did you have in mind?"

"Camping somewhere."

"Robert would love that. Have you been to Yellowstone, Jackson Hole and to the Badlands? That's where we should go," said Smiley.

***

Smiley had worked for CCC for a year and a half. Bob was right. Smiley's beauty would be a problem. Bob was struck by Smiley from the first time he saw her and now he was in love. Smiley appreciated Bob's maturity. The pair fell into bed late one evening and so enjoyed each other's company that they became lovers. Bob fell for Smiley the way he fell for Marla, except the roles were reversed. Marla was 10 years older than Bob and Bob was 20 years older than Smiley. Besides his relationship with Marla, Bob had never had a true loving relationship. He had women like the hangers' on in Palatka, who could not bring a suitcase to his house for fear they might move in. Bob wished Smiley would move in and he wanted her to marry him, but she wanted to give her son Robert a chance to become settled with the relationship. Robert thought the reason Bob spent time with him was because they were friends. They were friends but they were even more. Robert just was not aware.

Bob rented a separate apartment for privacy for trysts with Smiley. Otherwise, Bob and Smiley seemed to the public to be like the work mates that they were. As a trio, the three did appear in public together. The activities were benign. They went to ball games and museums. Bob spent time with Robert at Boy Scouts and helped him with the badges he needed that involved the outdoors. Robert slowly advanced to the Eagle Rank. If they went camping, he should be able to complete the work for his badges in cooking, outdoors, first aid, hiking and personal fitness.

Smiley would also take time while Bob and Robert were working on scouting to visit her father, Robert Brown, in Rapid City. She visited her father two times a year. She would fly to Rapid City on a Friday after work and be back at work on the following Monday. She would coordinate her trips with Robert's activities with Bob.

Her father was in a nursing home. He sold his home and the bar in Wall. He had never taken care of himself. His body was breaking down but he continued to coax the inevitability of death and disease along. He still drank and smoked and his eating habits were poor. Smiley waited for the call from the head nurse at the facility telling her that her father was gone. He was Smiley's only family. She had no memory of her mother. The time she spent with her father was empty. She did not know what to talk with him about. He had no memory of his grandson and had never met Bob Barnes. She was embarrassed by her father and was anxious when Bob or Robert mentioned her father. Smiley wanted to close that part of her life off from her other world and her work and life in Seattle.

Bob Barnes let Smiley be. He was happy to work for CCC and spend his off hours with Smiley and Robert.

Chapter 35
Boy Scouts

Adolescent males are a mess. They are trying to understand their body and their mind. They need 14 hours sleep a night but they do not get it and because of that fact they are generally thought to be lazy. Boys need structure and discipline. It's hard for a woman to deal with a boy. Foremost, the male child is too embarrassed to talk to a woman about the issues he's facing as he matures.

Smiley and Robert had become involved in the Boy Scouts when they were still in Wall living with her father. Single mothers were able to drop their sons off at meetings and there were men who would volunteer to work with the boys. When Smiley and Robert moved to Seattle they applied for Scout membership in a Catholic Church down the block from their apartment. Neither was Catholic but that did not seem to matter. They attended Mass on Sunday and Robert used the recreation facilities at the church after school while he waited for his mother to return home from work. On Monday evenings Robert Brown attended scout meetings. After a while Bob Barnes was at church for Mass (he was raised Catholic after the senator's death) and the Boy Scout meeting.

Bob told the scoutmaster of his plan to take Robert Brown camping in Wyoming and the Dakotas and received approval to use the trip for scouting advancement. (merit badges)

Although Bob spent a lot of time with Robert he could not get the boy to open up to him. Bob had a difficult childhood, being exposed to insanity and alcoholism, and he related to Robert, who had not known his father. Smiley took forever to reveal to Bob the fact that she had shot and killed Yellow Dog and that she had gone into hiding with her infant to deny the grandmother custody of the child. Bob had not told Smiley that he was aware of the circumstances of Yellow Dog's death; that he had been given that information when he received Smiley's employment application from Human Resources at CCC. Bob also realized that when Smiley explained the absence of Robert's father from his life she explained his death as being accidental and not an act of self-defense.

Bob had to wait many weeks before Smiley admitted to Bob that she had told Robert Brown a lie about his father. She had told him that Yellow Dog was a great warrior who was killed when he fell from his horse while corralling wild stallions and broke his neck. Smiley had been able to protect Robert from the truth by staying by his side as he grew up and continuing to perpetuate the lie throughout his life at school, at church, in the tribe, and even among the whites in Wall, where the truth that Smiley had shot Yellow Dog in the head was well known. The tribal council was embarrassed by Yellow Dog and was just as happy to have him remembered as a hero than as a rapist who could not hold his liquor. No one in Wall had any reason to tell Robert the truth about his father.

Bob told Smiley he thought she was making a mistake not telling Robert the truth. Bob received silence from Smiley in return for his advice and so he said no more on that matter. Bob thought that Robert knew something was not right about his father. Robert was an intelligent teen and he probably heard something about his father's demise that was hidden deep in his brain and psyche. There was a reason Robert had no friends; that he spent so much time on the Internet and he had to be dragged outside for play. Robert watched public television and listened to public radio if the content of the shows involved Native Americans. The shows, if they presented the truth, stated that Native Americans were not treated fairly. Their country was stolen from them. They dropped out of school. They used illegal drugs and were alcoholics.

Bob watched the documentaries with Robert and tried to engage him on the topics presented. Bob Barnes questioned him with the truth but without emotion. He tried to get a reaction. Robert Brown just absorbed the information about his race and refused to discuss it. Bob decided to retreat and wait for Robert to speak to him.

***

Smiley scheduled her trip to visit her father. The plane flew from Seattle to San Francisco and then the connection to Rapid City. The journey was tolerable.

Bob and Robert dropped Smiley at the airport and then they drove on to Wyoming in Smiley's old Subaru. The car, an old hatchback, had logged 150,000 miles. Bob said she should buy a new car.

"The Subaru is just broken in," insisted Smiley. "No need to spend good money."

Bob and Robert took it slow in the old car. Every time they stopped for fuel, Bob checked the oil and the water and the brake fluid. Bob did not want to get stuck somewhere in the middle of nowhere.

While Bob drove and fussed with the car, Robert read the handbooks for the achievement awards he was trying to earn for Boy Scouts. By the time the pair had arrived at Jackson Hole, Wyoming, they had spent one night in a campground. It had electricity, a shower and television, but they did sleep in a tent on the ground. Robert had completed and read almost all of the handbooks. Robert had also made notes in the margins of the books with facts that interested him and that he thought he should know.

Bob figured they would have three more nights to camp. Robert objected to them staying at any more campgrounds. They were not really camping. It was like staying out in your back yard. Robert was 12 years old. He did not think it was necessary to explain. He just gave Bob the look that children can give an adult that assures the adult that he doesn't know what he is talking about.

Bob understood. He began to look for an opportunity for the primitive outdoors. He took a side road off the highway that led into a forest and then they were in the hills and turning left and right and Bob was lost.

Robert was no help. He had not kept an eye on the road, he was finishing his books. He looked up. Bob had stopped the car in a small glen. There was a small pond. The sun was starting to dip below the trees.

"Where are we?"

"I don't know."

"Do you think you can back track?"

"I could try, but it's late. I say we camp here on the side of the road."

They pulled the gear from the back. When Bob suggested they light a fire Robert just looked at him, saying with his look, "You got us lost and now you want to start a forest fire."

"You're right." Bob began to replace the ax.

"We may need the ax," said Robert. "Put it by the car."

"Do you want me to chop wood for a fire?"

"We might need the ax for protection."

"Right." Bob had not thought of that, but then realized they were in the middle of nowhere and they were vulnerable.

"Here." Bob handed Robert a spare key to the ignition switch to the car. "You may need to drive."

Robert understood. Smiley had taken him to a large parking lot on his 12th birthday and let him drive her car to his heart's content. When she felt he knew how to operate the vehicle in an emergency, she took over and drove home. Every so often, Smiley repeated the exercise and added tasks. She had her son put water in the radiator, put air in the tires, and even change the tire.

Robert explained to Bob that his mother had taught him to drive and it was a good idea now that they both had a key.

It was chilly, in the 50's, and the sky was clear, blue and big. Because there were no clouds at night the temperature would drop quickly, probably into the 30's. The camping badge was enhanced if the scout slept outdoors in sub-freezing weather for three consecutive nights. Smiley's car had a thermometer and Robert checked it periodically, waiting for it to dip below 32 degrees F.

"What's the reading?"

"29 degrees."

Bob dug around in his knapsack. He had a gallon of water and crackers, hard sausage, and cheese and two apples. They ate all the food, used the facilities, buried their refuse and talked a bit. Which means there was little said.

"Cover up and let's get to sleep. No telling what we will see tomorrow."

Robert rolled onto his back and admired the stars. There was no light pollution, no clouds or humidity. He heard Bob begin to snore. Robert wiggled out of the bed roll. He had a sheep wool lined jacket that he put on and zipped tightly to his neck. He was wearing Levis and wool socks and hiking boots. He added gloves and a wool cap. There was a half moon and there was sufficient light to allow Robert to follow the road and he began to walk briskly.

***

Robert figured he had walked about a mile and he stopped as a small thin cloud interfered with the light of the moon. When he stopped he heard a footfall. Robert felt a cold finger on his shoulder at his neck. Robert swung about and attacked.

"Whoa," said Bob. "You'll kill an old man."

"What are you doing sneaking up on me?"

"I wanted to see where you were going."

"I wanted to get to the top of the hill and see what's over there to the northeast. I thought I saw a light in the sky over in that direction."

"Fair enough," said Bob and they continued another mile around a big bend in the dirt roar. As they proceeded the road improved and there was gravel laid on top of the road base. There definitely was a light ahead and to the right. They continued a few hundred yards and they looked across a plateau and could see a strange mountain.

"Devil's Tower," said Robert.

"Then we are not lost."

"No. My grandfather, Mr. Brown, took me here once ... looks like we must have driven up the back way." said the boy. "This isn't the way the tourists come to visit."

"Can we stay there tomorrow at the tower?"

Robert rubbed his chin. "It's still pretty cold at night. We should be able to camp. We won't need reservations. There won't be too many visitors this time of year."

"Let's get back to the car and get some sleep. We can drive in in the morning."

***

Bob found a pay phone and called the nursing home in Rapid City. He left a message that they were in the camp at Devil Tower and would be there for two nights and use the camp as a base and from there they would travel to Mt. Rushmore and the Badlands. They might go to Wall. They would check for messages at the Ranger's office a couple times a day.

"Everything is fine," Bob added.

***

When you see someone daily you don't really know them. You have to study a person to know them. Bob had a chance to study Robert. He was going to be tall and slender. He was almost Bob's height, six foot tall. He had a little fat at his belt line. He was sinewy, with long arms and fingers, legs and feet. He had a well-developed chest and would have good upper body strength. He was built to run long distances.

Robert had high cheek bones, shallow cheeks, a slender nose, ears close to his head and full lips. His coloring was reddish tan. His hair was black and straight and pulled into a pony tail in the rear.

Robert was correct. There were very few people in the camp. They had snow, a late wet snow. When Bob checked in with the Ranger and explained that Robert was trying to collect outdoor badges, the Ranger advised they had a primitive campground that would be perfect for their needs. Robert could cook their meals; they could hike. There would be no one to bother them, particularly since it snowed and was expected to keep snowing for the next two nights and the temperature was expected to drop below zero degrees.

"Great," said Robert.

***

Within two days Robert had finished all the requirements for his badges. They had not heard from Smiley and Bob left another message asking her to call the Ranger and tell him where she was.

Bob had driven Robert through the Black Hills and The Badlands. The Badlands was a government park of unique hills and pinnacles and valleys and cliffs and buttes that were formed by the process of erosion by the wind and water over millennia. The land features were made more unusual because there were concentrations of minerals in the landscape that were colored in hues of beige and pink and mauve and olive.

Native Americans, Robert's ancestors, Oglala, Lakota, and Sioux, inhabited this land. They hunted bison and antelope and elk and deer.

The first bull buffalo they encountered was wandering free through the hills. It brought a smile to Robert's lips and admiration for the animal's size as it stood looking in their general direction. The bull was at least six foot tall at his shoulders and his head was four foot in width. The pair felt threatened though they were inside the Subaru. The car did not seem to be big enough to deflect an attack or fast enough to elude the animal if he attacked.

Driving through The Badlands Robert and Bob saw antelope, wild sheep and deer but no elk. They were amused by the prairie dog colony. They drove for a bit, but then they wanted a snack and Bob drove up onto the interstate for a convenience store.

The town of Robert's birth, Wall, South Dakota, was an exit along the interstate. Robert shrugged his shoulders when Bob asked if he wanted a snack. They pulled off, parked, went in the drug store and bought an ice cream.

When they returned to the car and Bob started driving back to the interstate, Robert said, "Turn left up here."

"Where are we going?"

"You want to see what's up here, don't you?"

The car was aimed for two dilapidated buildings. The building in front had a sign that said, "Smileys". There was no signage on the building in the rear.

"This where you were born?" asked Bob.

"Conceived and born and where my father was killed by my mother."

"I did not know you knew," said Bob.

"Robert Brown, my grandfather, told me. He said it was best I knew so it wouldn't be a shock later in my life. He told me to learn everything I could about my ancestors."

"Does your mother know your grandfather told you?"

"I don't know. We have never talked about it, at least the part where my mother killed my father and the fact he raped her."

"That's a cruel word ... rape."

"Yes it is, but that is the truth. My father was not a great warrior."

"Few children have an exceptional father. That's just the truth of the matter."

"Why does my mother say it though? Why does she say Yellow Dog was a great warrior?" Robert laughed. "What a name. How can someone with the name 'Yellow Dog' be great? Whoever named him hated him if they called him a dog."

Bob Barnes did not reply right away. "The person in your life who is exceptional is your mother."

"I realize that."

"Have you told her?"

"I guess I should." Robert leaned back in his seat and was quiet. Bob told him to get some sleep as he pulled the Subaru back onto Interstate 90 and headed for Rapid City. The snow over the last two days had melted in the warm afternoon. The springtime thaw had begun in earnest and the rivulets and streams that fed the West River were full and swift and overflowing their banks. Bob could hear Robert breathing monotonously and deeply; snoring.

***

Bob drove to the nursing home and when he entered the reception room he saw Smiley.

"Where have you been?"

"We were camping near Devil's Tower. I left you a message."

"No one told me. I called the sheriff. They wouldn't take a missing person's report until you were gone three days. I was going to call this afternoon."

"How is Mr. Brown?"

"He's the same. They keep saying six months and he lives another six months."

"Can we see him?"

They walked toward the room past the smells in the hall and past the unpleasant ambient noises. Bob wondered where his natural mother and father were now. If they were alive they would be in their late seventies. Most men who drank and caroused had chronic physical problems, HBP, HC, diabetes, or all of the above. No telling. Bob had considered searching for Mary and Al but he always found an excuse to avoid that confrontation with his past.

Mr. Brown was sitting up. His room had a window. He was looking out onto the Black Hills. There was little to see and he turned when Robert called. "Hi, Grandpa." But when he looked at his grandson he could not recognize him and mistook him for an aide. There were a number of Native Americans who worked in the rest home, CNAs LPNs and a few RNs. So Mr. Brown may have mistaken Robert for a member of the staff. But even when Robert made an effort to have his grandfather search in the recesses of his mind for the memory of his prodigy, he could not recognize his grandson.

The three visitors stayed only a short time.

"He looks about the same, don't you think?" Smiley grabbed her son's hand.

Robert had seen him about a year back and Robert thought he had made a huge step backward, mentally and physically. Mr. Brown had recognized him the last time he saw him. Robert did not want to say his grandfather looked like he was at death's door and upset his mother, who still had some hope that her father would rally.

"I agree," said Robert. "He looks about the same."

***

The trio had retreated to the Rapid City Diner to reconnoiter and plan their trip back to Seattle.

Bob Barnes had in mind that they loop south, head for Reno, Nevada, and then go west across the Sierra Nevada Mountains and visit the Yosemite National Park, and head from there north to San Francisco (spend the night), and then north and to the home base in Seattle.

Bob laid out his plan of travel. The plan was accepted with little enthusiasm. Bob continued ignoring the dour mood caused by the visit with Mr. Brown. Smiley excused herself and went to the restroom. Bob reached in his pocket and removed an engagement ring. "I was going to ask your mother to marry me. She will ask your opinion and permission. I thought I would ask you first."

"You ask her and we will see what she has to say."

"I could crash and burn."

"Yes, you could." Robert relished the possibilities.

When Smiley returned, there was 15 minutes of small talk before Bob found an opportunity between bites of sourdough toast to propose.

Smiley turned to Robert. "Did you know he was going to ask me this question?"

"Yes, he told me."

"Do you give me your permission?"

"If you will be honest with me about my father I will."

"Do you know the truth?"

"My father was a rapist."

"Yes, that is the truth."

"We will not talk about him again. We will not say he was a brave warrior. If we have to talk about him we will tell the truth. Can you live with that?"

"Yes."

"Can we all tell the truth?" Robert looked at Bob Barnes.

"What do you want to know."

"Who are your parents?"

"Honestly?"

"Yes."

Bob Barnes explained how he came into the custody and control of Bea and Frank Barnes and how he took care of their boy, Jimmy, and that the Barnes family then adopted Bob, Albert and Jenny, and that a few short years later Jimmy had died.

Robert and Smiley did not know the story of how Bob was adopted. They had not met Bea or Frank at that time.

There were many questions about Bob's natural and adopted family. The trio ordered lunch and kept talking until the three had told each other every secret they hid from each other. By 1:00 pm they were exhausted but exhilarated and Robert gave permission for the marriage and Smiley accepted the ring.

They were married in the Chapel of the Stars in Reno, Nevada. Robert was one of the witnesses at the civil ceremony. The other witness was the Elvis impersonator.

Chapter 36
Frank Jr. Passes

Upon their return, Bob and Smiley duly reported their marriage to HR. The boss married his administrative assistant and this news flew through the offices that occupied the top two floors of the Columbia Center Building in downtown Seattle. There were a few snickers, but Bob and Smiley were well-liked and the news was accepted quickly, with little actual disapproval. Smiley showed off her ring. It had a large, proud stone.

Bob Barnes did not have time to talk about the matter. He had been out of the office for a week and the boss of his boss was coming in for his annual review. The appointment was perfunctory. It was more a chance for the CEO of JDC, Inc. to meet face to face with one of his top managers and "kick the tires".

The CEO first mentioned how excited the home office in NYC was that Bob had resolved the dispute with the environmentalists. Now there was an agreement that had been signed by all the parties and the federal and state government. Because the company had a written agreement it could book the asset and a banker could value the asset and JDC, Inc. could borrow against the asset. The piece of paper was worth billions of dollars.

While they ate lunch in Bob's office, the CEO surprised Bob with the news that he had spoken to the US President a few days earlier. The President was looking for a name to fill the cabinet post for Secretary of the Interior. Bob explained that he wasn't interested.

"I'm married. I want to settle down here in Seattle."

"If you were appointed, it would be good for our company. It's good for business if we have a voice in the government."

"I do not like politics."

"No one likes politics."

"I'm not a politician."

"That's an asset, not a liability."

"You know, I had that litigation involving TNT hanging over my head."

"The matter is settled. You can put it behind you. We are not taking "No" as your answer on this. You would be good for the company and good for the country and good for business."

"I don't know."

"Talk to your wife," said the CEO. "She will be proud."

***

Before Bob spoke to Smiley about the new job, he called the Barnes family attorney, Tom Night. Tom had a call from Bea Barnes earlier about Bob's marriage to Smiley and had to listen to the xenophobic questions from Bea about Bob marrying an Indian.

Tom advised Bea that as far as Tom knew, marrying a Native American was not a violation of the law and Bea should withhold judgment until she met the lady. An hour later, the advice Tom rendered was communicated with one simple question. "Bea, do you want to cause a scene and lose the chance to be loved by Bob and Smiley's children?"

Bea loved her grandchildren and Bob was sure to have a few. Bea promised Tom that she would hold her tongue.

***

"Hello, Bob," Tom said into the receiver.

"Tom. My boss came in and told me he had proposed my name to the US President for the office of Secretary of the Department of the Interior."

Paul Casper Scherer

Bob then went on to explain his misgivings and they isolated on two issues. The first was the claw-back action by the shareholders who lost money investing with Thomas N. Thompson in what turned out to be a Ponzi scheme.

Tom had been representing the Barnes' on that issue.

"The case is settled. My CEO said JRD, Inc. will fund the settlement. Dad also said he would pay the judgment."

"Well then that problem is solved." said Tom. "What else do you have?"

Bob then went on to explain how Smiley's child Robert Brown had been conceived.

So you are worried about what? How old is Robert Brown."

"Thirteen."

"Does he know the circumstances of his father's death?"

"Yes."

"So you are worried about what? Is this about your feelings or your wife's feelings or Robert's feelings?"

There was silence, and then Tom continued, "It seems to me all the hard work has been done here. I assume the police investigated the death of Robert's biological father, Yellow Dog, and the police determined he was killed by Smiley, who was acting in self-defense."

"True."

"Well, I don't believe the matter will be brought up and if it is you and Smiley and Robert should tell the Senate or the investigator for the president's chief of staff the truth."

"Are you sure?"

"Absolutely. All the investigators will want to do is verify the facts in the police report and they will let the matter alone. If you or Robert or Smiley lie to the investigators or try to camouflage the truth you will be slaughtered with the fact that you lied. But the truth sets you free. Just tell the truth and you will do just fine."

"Ok."

"By the way, do you need the firm to represent you on this appointment?"

"I guess. But Tom, I don't have any money to pay you."

"Whatever." Tom didn't care. He wanted to be on C-span sitting next to his client, who would be the next Secretary of the Interior. "Bob, one other thing. You need to visit your mother."

"I saw Bea last week."

"No, I mean your natural mother." said Tom, "Mary, your mother is still alive. She lives in upstate New York."

***

Bob explained to Smiley and Robert that there may be a quick change in their lives. They may be moving to Washington, D.C., and he may be working for the government and the President of the United States.

Smiley and Robert were good with that.

That night, Smiley had news. Bea Barnes would be proud. Smiley was pregnant.

Bob also had news. "If we are going to accept the nomination, Tom says I need to visit my natural mother.

Smiley asked if Bob wanted company. Bob said, "Yes."

Although Bob was unaware of the fact, Tom regularly heard from Mary's sister, who asked Tom for money for Mary's upkeep, room and board. Bea had been funding the cost of Mary's care since she had given up her children. Bea gave money to Tom, who deposited it in his escrow account and Karen, Tom's assistant, would write a check each month and mail it to Knoxville, New York.

Tom would make arrangements for the visit.

***

One bitterly cold day in the middle of winter, with snow flurries and 100 foot visibility, Bob and Smiley were in a taxi that had driven them from the airport in Albany to Mary's sister's house in Knoxville. The house was on the outskirts of town about a mile from the interstate. There was nothing in the farm town. In 1900 there were 2,000 residents and by the time WW II and the Depression ended, the population was as low as 700 residents. It had built back up to 1,500 souls or so but the town had no industry.

Mary knew who Bob was. He was her son. But she only knew that fact because her sister told her. She did not recognize Bob and did not remember her other children, Albert or Jenny.

Mary was confused by Smiley. "Who was she again?" asked Mary.

Mary said she was well fed and cared for. The house was pleasant and clean and warm. Just Mary and her sister lived in the house and they did not use the upstairs. Bob was invited to see their quarters. Mary had a small bedroom with a chair and a table and lamp. There was a dresser and drawers. On the furniture were photographs of Bob's brother and sister and one of Bob. There was also a photo of Albert, Sr. He was in his sergeant's uniform. He was standing at attention.

The three shared lunch in the large kitchen – tomato soup and grilled cheese sandwiches. Mary said very little. She seemed more confused as the visit wore on. Bob did not want to upset the routine of the household and so after a couple of hours they called the taxi.

Bob didn't think his mother shared any recognition or memory of him until Bob hugged her as he left and when he said "Goodbye, Mom," Bob gave his mother a stick of gum and Mary broke down and cried.

***

The Chief of Staff was reviewing the files of the potential candidates for Interior with his investigators. Every aide was assigned a particular candidate and they had compiled a fact sheet on their man (all the candidates were men). The President had been having trouble with appointments to his cabinet. The

Democrats controlled the Senate and the Interior Committee and they had announced they intended to block all appointments unless the President agreed to suspend all leases of grass land, timber and oil, gas and minerals.

"I'm not going to agree to that," said the President to the Chief of Staff. "I will put up a nominee and let the Senate committee meet on the nomination. If they fail to give consent we will propose another name until they are sick of asking questions."

And so began a battle of wills between the executive and legislative branches of government. The public hated this political gamesmanship. It was destructive to the President, the Senate and the individual nominees.

A year and a half into the President's term in office he had only been able to obtain approval of three members of his cabinet—the Secretaries of State and Defense, and the Attorney General. The other offices were filled with temporary "recess" appointments (the President made the appointment when the Senate was not in session). The President was also able to obtain approval of the HUD Secretary, but only because he had appointed a Democrat.

The President told his Chief of Staff that if he couldn't break the logjam that he was going to be out of a job and looking for work.

"I have reviewed this Bob Barnes file. He has a compelling story. He was adopted. He helped build the Barnes Family Companies. He is married to a Native American. He adopted her Native American child. They have a child of their own, a girl who is a year and a half old now. He has good political connections through JRD, Inc. and CCC Corporation through his employment; otherwise he has no political enemies. He is a good Republican. He is known as a compromiser. He settled the impasse involving the old growth timber and protected species in the Northwest. No one was able to accomplish that for the last 25 years. His wife worked with him on the project. She had a tough life but no one will hold that against her. What do you think? Should we take a chance?"

The aides agreed to recommend the President propose Bob Barnes as his nominee to Interior.

***

Bob, Smiley, and Robert presented themselves to the Senate Committee's investigators. These civil servants were employed to ask the embarrassing questions and then cut to the chase and provide their bosses, the senators, with zinger questions to embarrass the Republican appointee. The examiners had problems with Bob and Smiley and Robert. They were honest to a fault. They could not be embarrassed. They told the truth and when you boiled it all down, nothing in their life's story proved them to be a bad actor. Rather, they were the victim, not the perp. The worst the civil servants could say was that Bob was a Republican.

Bob, Smiley and Robert met with each member of the Interior Committee. Each member of the Senate was impressed with their plain speaking and honest demeanor. Bob even offered that he would agree to resign after a year on the job if he had, in the Senate's opinion, not acted in the best interest of the public.

When the day of decision came, the senators each asked questions before a gallery that was filled with interested parties – ranchers, loggers, farmers, American Indians, lobbyists. The questions were all low intensity pitches. There were no hardballs. The Chief of Staff had personally prepared Bob for the meeting and the likely questions. Tom had also taken time to make Bob aware of the importance of the meeting. Bob had good instructors.

There were opening remarks by the Chairman of the committee. Then each senator made a short speech and explained how he intended to vote. Tom kept score, marking the back of an envelope with the Yeas and Nays. In the end it wasn't close. The chairman suggested the committee make its vote unanimous. All members agreed.

This was the apex of Bob Barnes' political career.

***

Bob loved being Secretary of the Interior. The politics involved meeting with the nation's citizens and relating to them. He had no problem with that. Bob had lived the all-American life. He had been stung early with disappointment. But he had also enjoyed success. He had been indebted and he had been flush with wealth. He could talk to anyone he met on their level. He was honest if he could be honest or he said nothing. But if he was asked directly and if forced to answer he told the truth.

The president ran for re-election and won. Bob kept his job. Smiley and Robert and Mary loved Washington, D.C. Bob hoped that at the end of this presidential term, if he retained his appointment as secretary, he could find work on K Street as a lobbyist. He would be secure and wealthy. Anticipating this career path, Bob and Smiley bought a house across the river in Alexandria, Virginia, but they maintained their domicile at The Homestead in Holly Hill, Florida with Bea and Frank. Smiley and Bea became good friends. Jenny and her three children visited often. Whenever Bob was in Florida for his work he paid from his own pocket to bring the family along.

Robert and Frank Barnes shared a love of Florida's nature and history. Frank had converted a large room on the ground floor of The Homestead into a library and he began collecting books about Florida's birds and animals and its pre-Columbian people. Frank and Robert searched the acreage of The Homestead for arrowheads and other blades and points. There was an outcropping of Chert rock near the spring that fed the stream that ran north across the property. Frank believed the Native Americans used the site to collect rock to manufacture into weapons and they traded the Chert for shells and other valuables from Middle America.

Frank and Robert also enjoyed fishing and dipping for shrimp. One year Frank got Bob and Smiley to agree Robert could stay for a month in the winter. Frank had rented a license from the state of Florida to take clams and oysters from a water bottom site in the Matanzas Inlet near old Ft. Matanzas. The Spanish had built the fort to guard their rear against an attack on St. Augustine from the south.

Bea objected to the trip. To get to the site, Frank and Robert would have to take a small boat and operate an outboard motor. They would be wet and the air in the winter on the inlet was cold. Frank would be eighty-five years old. He had had a heart attack. Frank said he wanted to do it. Bea relented.

Frank did not really feel well when they went out and when they arrived at the leased submerged land it was low tide and they had to slosh through the mud, which tugged at their hip high boots. It was a lot of effort and when they finished, Frank asked Robert to collect the buckets of clams and oysters and the heavy rakes. Frank sat in the small boat near the front and Robert filled the boat with their equipment and then he started the engine with three strong pulls of the rope on the motor. Robert had to pull the motor up from the transom so the propeller blade would be out of the mud.

The boat made slow progress. Frank turned to face the wind and Robert covered his face with a cloth and looked ahead and at his grandfather's back. The wind was brisk, cold and wet. They said nothing.

When they arrived at the public boat slip just off Granada Avenue in Ormond, Robert revved the engine and guided the boat onto the shore. Robert debarked and secured the boat. When he looked at his grandfather he could see he was slumped forward with his head on his chest. Robert felt his neck and could find no pulse. There was a pay phone. He called 911. The fire station was located just up the street and the emergency truck was there in a minute or less. Robert had tried CPR but Frank was cold. The firemen said he had been dead for at least an hour.

An hour back ... Robert remembered Frank was settled in the boat. Frank had said how good it was that the two of them had spent the day together. They shook hands. Man to man.

When the fireman confirmed to Robert that his grandfather was dead, Robert began to cry and he could not stop until Bea came to the boat ramp and held him and consoled him.

***

Frank was buried in the back yard under the centuries old live oak tree behind the old house on Number 7 Plantation next to his father, the Senator. Marla and James Reynolds were gracious to let the interments occur in their back yard. They had offered the parcel of land for their friends and they had cordoned off an area with a wrought iron garden fence for the purpose.

Robert gave the private Eulogy at the old house and Tom spoke for Frank at St. Mary's Catholic Church during the celebration of life ceremony.

Robert stayed at The Homestead with Bea until she settled down and accepted the fact that Frank had died.

Robert spent hours in Frank's library exploring his books on Florida and its Native Americans and the European explorers. Bea recognized that Frank had collected the books for Robert to allow him to search the history of his race in the Americas, at least from the European prospective. Frank had written a short note to Robert saying he had intended the books to be his on his death. Bea honored the gift.

Part VIII

Confusion to the Enemy

Chapter 37
Confusion to the Enemy

Jenny Barnes was determined to resign her employment with Night, Adams and Street. She had always looked to Tom for advice and thought he would be the one to talk to. She didn't want anyone to talk her out of quitting. She wanted someone to tell her it was acceptable.

Tom, however, discouraged her from quitting. "If anyone is going to quit it should be Darlene and I."

Tom called an office meeting. Everyone; secretaries, clerks, investigators and attorneys, stuffed into the large conference room/library.

Tom ordered the phones to be put on hold.

Tom brought the bottle of Johnny Walker Scotch from the top drawer of his desk along with a stack of paper cups and he gave the bottle to Alphonse Alesse and told him to open the bottle and pour a drink for each person in the room. There were 28 ounces in the bottle so everyone would receive a cup containing about one and a half ounces of alcohol. That is, if Alphonse could open the bottle. Tom had gone to the top drawer of his desk many times, having decided to fall off the wagon, but he was unable to remove the top from the bottle and he always gave up on the thought of reviving the habit and drinking again.

Alphonse was unable to muscle the cap from the bottle and he retreated to the kitchen and used a wine opener to put a hole in the cap. He inverted the bottle over a water pitcher and the liquid dribbled out. It took a few minutes to empty the bottle, but the method was effective. Everyone had their cup. Alphonse poured each an equal share ... egalitarianism.

Tom raised his cup. "To all, we survived another day."

Everyone replied in unison, "Confusion to the enemy."

"What is the topic of this meeting?" Karen raised her hand containing a pencil. She intended to take notes.

"We want no record of this meeting. No notes," ordered Tom.

Without thinking, Tom put the cup of Scotch to his lips and there was a silence over the room. Tom stopped in mid motion and set the paper cup in front of him on the top of the huge piece of Mahogany from the Mennonites' sawmill in Belize. Tom had lowered his drink from his lips to the table without taking a drink.

"This stuff could be habit forming," said Tom.

There was a collective titter in the room, then laughter.

As per the rules of the firm, every person had the right to ask any question they wanted and say anything that would not cause a fist fight.

Karen stood up. "Me first." She turned to James DeMarco. "When are you going to ask Jenny to marry you?"

DeMarco looked across the table to Jenny and said, "Jenny Barnes, will you marry me and have my children and love me every day until the end of time?"

"Are you being serious?"

"Of course I am serious."

"I will marry you," said Jenny, "but no strings attached."

The room erupted in applause.

"Meeting adjourned," said Tom and everyone filed out. Faircloth proposed that everyone who could should meet at the Bell Bar and they would continue the celebration. It appeared no one had court or an appointment that afternoon because everyone but Karen, Tom and Darlene left the building.

Karen looked at Tom. She asked him why he told her to ask DeMarco when he intended to ask Jenny to marry him. "How did you know he would say yes?"

"He wanted to ask her," said Tom." It was just a question of him being given a little shove."

"Well, it worked."

"You did an admirable job, Karen. Now go join your work mates." Karen hugged Tom, grabbed her purse and she was out the door.

"What are we going to do now?" asked Darlene. No one was in the office and she lit a cigarette and passed the pack to Tom.

"I guess we need to hire a couple of attorneys. My guess is that Jenny and DeMarco will move over to the East Coast. Bea is not going to let her grandbabies grow up in St. Petersburg. She will want them over there with them at the Homestead. Marla will want them over that way too, she looks at Jenny like she's her child."

Tom took a deep drag on his cigarette. He coughed.

"Would you like to take a vacation?"

"Where to?"

"The beach sounds good. I have a hankering for the Caribbean Sea. How does the ocean in Tulum sound to you?"

"Why do you want to go there?"

"I want to see if H. Patel ever got his bar built near the Mayan ruins."

Afterword

The Trap is Sprung

Afterword
The Trap is Sprung

Tom had great confidence in the legal skill and ability of his partner Alphonse Alesse regarding the practice of civil law. Civil law is best distinguished from criminal law by the fact that the remedy sought in civil law is compensation for monetary loss. In criminal law the remedy is loss of liberty – jail. There are many other distinctions between criminal and civil law. The most important difference at trial is that the burden of proof to obtain a judgment in civil injury law was merely proof by the preponderance of evidence, unlike proof beyond a reasonable doubt that is required in a criminal case.

Two days earlier, before Bob's confirmation hearing, Tom had received a letter from an attorney named Richard Sumpter. The letter was very nasty demanding that the firm of Night, Adams, Street, DeMarco, Alessie and Barnes return the sum of $400,000 to him on behalf of his client, the aunt of Mark Luke John Person.

Attorney Sumpter alleged that the aunt had paid the money to the law firm under false pretenses. The lawyer alleged that James DeMarco had told the aunt that she was responsible to pay her nephew's legal fees when in fact she had not entered into a written agreement to pay the fees; she had no obligation to pay for the nephew's defense, and that her nephew had not gone to trial on the kidnapping or child murder charges so the fees were not earned.

Tom had taken the letter from Mr. Sumpter in to Alphonse. Alphonse asked if a grievance had also been filed with the Florida Bar.

"No. I haven't received a grievance."

"That's normally the way Sumpter works his scam."

"Are you saying Attorney Sumpter will file a grievance against the law firm?" asked Tom. "That is illegal, isn't it? It would be extortion."

"Sumpter does not file the grievance with the Florida Bar. His client will file the paperwork and then she will leak the allegations to the press. Do you remember how badly the firm was hurt when you were found guilty of contempt? How long it took to restore your reputation?"

"Yes, I remember."

"Do you also remember telling me the story about the bulldogs in Belize that were used to hunt wild pigs and boar?" asked Alphonse.

"Yes, I remember."

"Do you remember how you described that some of the dogs would grab the ear of a black, razorback boar and hold on and never let go?"

"There is a moral here," said Tom. "I can hear it coming."

"Richard Sumpter is just like one of those bulldogs that clamps down on an ear and never let's go."

"That bad?"

"Worse. He will manipulate his client, Person's aunt, into believing that you worked against the best interests of Mark Person and that you caused his death. He will only take this case if he has received a substantial fee from the aunt. So he will be well paid regardless of the outcome."

"How will he attack our firm? We have timesheets recording the amount of time we spent working for her nephew. We sent her copies of all the bills and all the records for the expenses paid."

"Do not expect Attorney Sumpter to fight fair. He will tell his client to file a grievance against every member of the law firm who represented her nephew claiming the representation was incompetent; that there were misrepresentations made by the attorneys; that there were missed opportunities to enter into plea bargains, that the nephew was incompetent and that there should have been incompetency reviews and exams conducted, that her nephew was a fragile individual who was obviously guilty of these crimes and that her money was wasted on a defense when there was no possibility that the nephew would prevail at trial."

"What do you suggest we do?"

"Did Mr. Sumpter make a settlement demand in his letter?"

"Yes. He said his client would provide the firm and its individual members a release and agree to keep the agreement confidential if $200,000 of the $400,000 retainer is repaid within 20 days of the date of his letter. If we do not pay, suit will be filed."

"Well, you know your choice. If we fight we will be in the bloodiest mess you will ever see."

"Has Sumpter had success with these type of tactics in the past?"

"I understand he has had great success with proceedings such as these and that he files cases against attorneys across the state. I have heard he is a very wealthy man."

"What are you going to do?" asked Alphonse.

"I need to speak to Darlene," said Tom. "You need to keep this conversation between the two of us confidential. Could you do that please?"

"No problem."

***

Tom went to Darlene's office and asked her, "Got a minute?"

"Sure."

"When did you last have a cigarette?"

"I don't want to incriminate myself."

"Truth or Dare."

"I don't do that. It's a bad game for old folk."

"Do you have a cigarette?"

"Yes. I always keep a pack."

"I need a cigarette."

Darlene went in her purse and dug around for a minute. She had a three pack. There were three Winston cigarettes in a thin box that was wrapped in cellophane. Darlene pulled the tab and the plastic wrap came loose. She opened the top of the box and pulled the foil that covered the filters of the cigarettes and then she removed two of the cigarettes and handed one to Tom. They lit the cigarettes using a lighter Tom carried in his pocket. The lighter had belonged to his father.

They both inhaled the smoke deep in their lungs and they both coughed. Then they laughed.

Tom never showed Darlene the letter he received from Mr. Sumpter until they were sued.

End of Book IV

Preview of Book 5: Chattahoochee

Chapter 1
Florida Hospital for the Criminally Insane

Tom Night had been recently diagnosed with Parkinson's disease. Early on he had primarily struggled with his Apraxia of Speech due to a lesion on the left hemisphere of his brain. Then he began having difficulty with his balance in addition to his ability to speak. The year was 1988 when he had a bad fall and broke his right femur in three places.

When Tom had to leave his home after he broke his leg and it healed, he could maneuver short distances with a walker or a cane but he hit a plateau in his rehab and he could not go out of the condo apartment without the assistance of an aide to help him with the wheelchair if he needed to go shopping or to the office. He also needed someone to express his wants and desires if he needed to make a purchase. The doctor had promised that with time he should be up and out of the wheelchair and more mobile, and with more practice he should speak better.

Tom became depressed. He spent much of his time in an overstuffed chair by the large picture window in the condo he shared with his wife that overlooked Tampa Bay. He watched the pleasure craft and the freighters pass in the distance below him, maneuvering through the channel heading for the docks.

Tom's wife, Darlene Street, was semi-retired. She still handled pro bono appeals. These were cases no one wanted involving civil rights issues and death penalty appeals. Pro bono clients were "for free" – non-paying. Tom still maintained a limited practice for old clients. He expected payment for his work.

Tom also followed one old case carefully. That was the case against Clemenso Me Bondi (aka "Clem Bondi") for the murder of Tom's investigator, Anthony Stewart, back in 1970.

Tom blamed himself for Anthony's death. Tom had assigned Anthony to surveille Clem's house alone late at night. Anthony should have had assistance. Anthony was shot dead by Bondi's criminal conspirator, Detective Richard Cook, a St. Petersburg police officer now deceased. The shooting of Anthony Stewart was performed on the order of a notorious killer named Clem Bondi.

Clem was the primary suspect in five homicides, however, he had never been convicted of the crimes. The number of killings would have reached six were it not for the fact that his last intended victim, Regina Cameron, was able to outrun Clem and he was severely injured in the chase.

Because of injuries Bondi sustained when he was chasing Regina when he rammed his head into the trunk of a mangrove tree, Bondi did not appear to understand the nature of the legal process and he was declared mentally incompetent and unfit to proceed to trial on any of the five homicide cases.

Two medical experts examined Clem every six months. In order for a court to find a defendant incompetent to stand trial it meant the State psychiatrist found, continuously, that the prisoner did not understand the charges, the possible penalties, the adversarial nature of the legal process; could not communicate with his attorney; could not act appropriately in court, or testify relevantly. Therefore, because he was determined to be incompetent to stand trial, Clem had never been to trial on the homicide charges and he had remained hospitalized in the Florida Hospital in Chattahoochee, Florida.

Tom followed Clem's case through the system. Tom wrote to the State Attorney at least once a month looking for an update; however, his letters to the State Attorney were late being answered, if they were answered at all. Tom's information about Clem was delayed coming from the State Attorney and normally a response arrived two months after Tom's inquiry.

While convalescing for his impairments, Tom rarely went to the office though he had a secretary (Karen) assigned to handle his court filings and correspondence. Darlene had purchased a set of computers, one for Tom and one for Tom's assistant, Karen, and the machines were connected through the phone so Tom could communicate with the office by email or use of a phone. Tom was embarrassed using the phone because of his speech defect, and the computer and e-mail were god-sent. The Internet also allowed Tom to communicate from home with Alphonse Alesse, who handled all civil cases in the office, and James DeMarco and Jenny Barnes, who handled all criminal cases.

A few years back the law office had been renamed, "Night, Adams, Street, Alesse, DeMarco and Barnes, Attorneys at Law." Although the firm had been re-structured, Alesse, DeMarco and Barnes still looked to Tom for advice. Tom would spend time reviewing case files that had been scanned onto discs and delivered to the condo for his review. Then Tom and Darlene would respond to questions from the attorneys who were partners in the firm. Tom and Darlene were listed on the firm letterhead as being "of counsel" to the firm, meaning they held a special relationship with the firm as senior counsels to the firm and its clients.

Tom and Darlene appeared to be well off, safe and secure. Tom's bank, Century Bank in Tampa, always covered the law firm's checks. The firm had a line of credit. The firm deposited their earnings with the bank and the bank paid the firm's checks as they were presented. Tom's health issues were unfortunate, but they could cope and Tom's condition was expected to improve.

Chapter 2
The History of Forensic Patient Clemenso Me Bondi

Clem was awakening from a dream that he was running on a kickoff intending to tackle an opponent. But then he awoke and realized that he was trapped in bed and that fact caused Clem Bondi the most agonizing depression a human could experience. Clem was not on a football field, he was in the medical ward at the Florida Hospital for the Insane.

The ward was in a building first erected as a military arsenal by the US Army during the Seminole Wars early in the 1800's. Then the arsenal was captured by the Confederate forces in the Civil War. The brick building was constructed near the river in the small North Florida town of Chattahoochee. The facility was converted from an arsenal into a medical hospital and then later into a mental hospital for the insane in the 1870's. The hospital derived the derisive name "Chattahoochee" from the name of the river nearby. In Florida if you were sent to "Chattahoochee" you were dubbed insane.

The ward that housed Clem had large windows with screen mesh embedded in the glass. The steel mesh strengthened the glass to prevent breakouts by the inmates/patients. The patients in Clem's ward were not considered likely to escape as the patients were all bedridden because of infirmity or paralysis. They could not walk. Clem was the worst. He was paralyzed from the neck down and could not or refused to speak or communicate. The doctors thought the inability to communicate was probably due to a psychological overlay due to his paralysis because there did not appear to be any physical impediment to speech.

When he awoke each day, Clem saw the windows and realized where he was and tears welled up in his eyes. This was purgatory on earth. It was St. Vitus's Dance of the brain. It was horror and hot, inflamed. He tried to wish himself dead. He prayed to God for a friend like the one he was for Detective Richard Cook; someone who would turn off the respirator, someone who would end it, someone who would kill him like he killed Detective Cook—a mercy killing.

It was rare that anyone spoke to Inmate Bondi. He was a forensic patient being held by order of a trial court pending a trial on the homicide charge for the death of Anthony Stewart. Because he was a forensic inmate, at least once every six months two medical doctors visited him to conduct an examination to determine whether his mental status had improved and he was mentally competent to proceed to trial.

This examination was required by Florida Statute 916.12 titled: Mental Competence to Proceed. Another statute (916.145) stated the charges should be dismissed without prejudice if Clem was found to be continuously incompetent to proceed to trial for a period of five years. It was rare that an inmate would remain continuously incompetent and unable to stand trial for five years, but anything can and will happen.

The specific reason that Clem had been determined to be incompetent to aid his attorney in his defense was because he could not communicate (verbally or in any way) with his counsel. The doctors were of the opinion that he was not malingering or faking a mental illness. He was either suffering a defect of the brain due to the impact of his head with the tree trunk or he suffered a psychological overlay from the physical injury and paralysis. In either case he could not communicate and was incompetent to proceed to trial. The doctors also relied on nuclear testing for their opinion. Regular CT Scans showed there was an infarct or bruise to the brain stem in the area of the stem cell barrier, and he also had severe degeneration and herniations of the spine of the discs at C-2/3 in his neck. These defects of the spine could cause paralysis and therefore there was objective evidence for the paralysis. The paralysis was real.

The doctors were required to treat Clem with psychotropic medication ("any drug or compound used to treat mental or emotional disorders affecting the mind, behavior, intellectual function, perception, mood, or emotion and include any anti-psychotic, antidepressant, animatic, and antianxiety drugs." (FS Section 916.12.5). The hope was that some drug would cure his mental disease or defect and he could stand trial for murder, be sentenced to death and executed.

Tom thought it was ironic that this extreme effort was expended by the state to cure Clem's incompetence and then kill him. However, the law required that Clem understand why he was being executed and therefore he had to be cured so he could be killed if he was convicted and sentenced to the death penalty.

The doctors used every modern modality to treat Bondi's brain and even reached back to the psychiatric Stone Age employing shock therapy. The doctors even suggested a lobotomy. Clem's attorney objected and the judge agreed the operation using a metal probe to scramble the frontal lobe of Clem's brain was not medically reasonable. A member of the Board of the American Psychiatric Association objected, arguing that any psychiatrist who performed the lobotomy would violate the Hippocratic Oath which states the physician treating a patient was first to do no harm. A lobotomy would more likely do harm the expert testified, and no good.

Of the two primary treating doctors, psychiatrist Adolph Frierman M.D. was the most liberal in suggesting treatment that could somehow jar Clem out of his psychotic state. He argued vigorously for the lobotomy procedure. The other psychiatrist thought the only appropriate treatment was palliative care. The idea was to make the patient comfortable and ease his mania and depression using the newest and most effective drugs available.

Nature would run its course and Clem would arise mentally or die of sepsis from his bed sores. A slow death from infection was horrible enough. Certainly, Dr. Gene Chorloff argued, it was at least as horrible as death in the oak arms of "Old Sparky" (death in Florida's electric chair in Raiford Prison).

Dr. Chorloff also pointed out that Clemenso Me Bondi was presumed innocent and had never been convicted of a crime. Florida Statute 916 provided procedures for individuals like Bondi and he was to be released after five years to a facility where more likely than not he would die of natural causes.

***

Then, just before the five year statutory period had expired, serendipity intervened. Bondi was dropped by two orderly's, who were transferring him by stretcher to the baths at the facility for treatment of his decubitus ulcers. When he fell he hit his skull on the tile floor. He bled profusely but remained silent, expressing no alarm or concern.

Clem was transferred from Chattahoochee to Shands Hospital in Gainesville, Florida for examination and medical treatment. The emergency room doctor was accustomed to treatment of inmates and prisoners and patients in Florida's correction facilities and mental wards. Normally the injuries were from inmates on inmates. Attacks, rapes, etc. This case was much more interesting. The history showed the patient to be paralyzed from the neck down and uncommunicative. However, the ER physician was able to elicit movement in Clem's toes and his fingers. He also was able to elicit a response (a grunt) when he asked Clem his name. The doctor noticed a glint in Clem's dark murky eyes.

Clem was transferred from the ER to the orthopedic ward with orders for surgery to the neck to relieve the pressure on the spinal column and nerves at the level of the disc at C 2-3 and for intensive physical therapy and deep tissue massage to coax life back into his nervous system.

Later, the Board of Inquiry at the hospital would ask why the ER room would transfer an inmate who came from the hospital for the insane, who was the suspect in five homicides, to the orthopedic department for surgery and treatment without contacting the mental hospital to obtain permission. The ER department said they were not told Clem could be dangerous. The orderlies who delivered Clem from the hospital for the insane to Shands were told to drop off the patient for treatment and they were to return to their duties at the hospital in Chattahoochee. The orderlies did as they were told and signed Clem in for an examination and treatment. The finding at the inquiry was that the treatment Bondi received at Shands was ordered by the mental hospital and that the ER doctor had violated no procedures.

While Bondi was in Shands, the balance of the five year period of Florida Statute 916 expired and an efficient clerk presented the court with an order dismissing all five homicide charges. The judge who signed the order did so without reading the text of the form order and without speaking to Drs. Frierman or Chartoff. The judge had been presented with a stack of orders to sign and he did not take the time to read each one. With the order signed, Bondi was a free man.

The short story was that Clemenso Me Bondi received exceptional treatment at Shands in the orthopedic department from the best surgeons, therapists and physicians in the Southeast USA, and he was released from care wearing a pair of pants, a shirt and a dark wool overcoat. He was rehabilitated and let go – walking and talking – onto the streets of Gainesville, Florida.

It took two months for the various hospitals, agencies and bureaucrats to understand that Clem was gone. By that time, the trail was pretty cold. Investigators from State Attorney Young's office were able to determine that Clem was first on the streets of Gainesville, then Jacksonville, and then Atlanta and Savannah, living with the homeless. After Savannah, Clem became a ghost.